Ragna lift
hear fully."

Shrugging,
speak your words."

Again, the woman remained silent. Rorik pinched the bridge of his nose in frustration.

"Do you not deem it best to put on your tunic?" she suggested, stepping closer and brushing the garment against his arm.

Slowly, Rorik lifted his head to look at her. Even her words sounded different. They were almost a plea, not filled with terse venom. A rosy stain had blossomed on her ivory cheeks, and her breathing appeared labored. He pondered two things—either his naked form disgusted her or perchance appealed to her. *Surely, she despises me, nothing more.*

The barb he wanted to fling out at her became trapped on his tongue. He guzzled deeply from the aleskin. Wiping his mouth with the back of his hand, he dropped the empty skin next to his sword and swiftly got off the boulder.

Ragna gasped and clutched his tunic to her breasts. Yet she did not avert her eyes.

He dared to move toward her.

Her eyes widened, and she stumbled back, dropping his tunic.

Rorik reached out and grabbed her hand, preventing her from falling. The contact of her skin against his sent a tremor of warmth up his arm. This time, his breathing became labored while he stared into her gray eyes. He found no hatred there—only beauty within their depths. His gaze traveled down to her full red lips, partially open and begging to be kissed.

Praise for Mary Morgan

"I highly recommend this book not only for the romance, but for so many other reasons that are too long to list."

~Long and Short Reviews

~*~

"If readers have not yet read a book by Mary Morgan, jumping in with "Magnar" is like plunging into a raging river of pure writing force."

~InD'tale Magazine, November 2020 Issue

~*~

"Morgan's pen is powered with magic of days gone by! I hope you join me in reading this series and if you haven't read her others, please do!"

~Booktalk with Eileen

~*~

"The minute I received this book to review I put everything else aside and readied myself for an exciting historical romantic adventure just like all the previous by Ms. Morgan I have read. I sat glued from page one till the end enjoying every minute of Magnar and Elspeth's story."

~ Linda Tonis, Paranormal Romance Guild

Rorik

by

Mary Morgan

The Wolves of Clan Sutherland,
Book 2

This is a work of fiction. Names, characters, places, and incidents are either the product of the author's imagination or are used fictitiously, and any resemblance to actual persons living or dead, business establishments, events, or locales, is entirely coincidental.

Rorik

Contact Information: info@thewildrosepress.com

Cover Art by *Abigail Owen*

The Wild Rose Press, Inc.
PO Box 708
Adams Basin, NY 14410-0708
Visit us at www.thewildrosepress.com

Publishing History
First Edition, 2021
Trade Paperback ISBN 978-1-5092-3743-2
Digital ISBN 978-1-5092-3744-9

The Wolves of Clan Sutherland, Book 2
Published in the United States of America

Dedication

To the group of lovely lasses on the Morgan Warriors Street Team! You are each unique and a treasure. Thank you with love!

Glossary of Old Norse Terms

Āsgarthr – Home of the Norse Gods
Hamnavoe – Current day town of Stromness, Orkney
Hnefatafl – Viking chess
Kærr – dear, close, beloved
Kirkjuvágr – Kirkwall
Njörd – God of the Winds and Sea
Orkneyjar – Orkney
Skald – Norse bard/poet
Skinnleikr – Viking skin throwing game
Völva – Wise woman

The Nine Noble Virtues of Wolf Lore

* Learn to control the beast within. If not, the man will cease to exist.

* First lesson for the wolf—the man is always Alpha.

* Scotland is our home. *Orkneyjar* calls to our soul.

* When conflicted, follow the path of the stars. Odin will shine his light upon you.

* Keep your weapon as strong as Thor's hammer.

* Discipline your beast to honor the code of the Brotherhood.

* Honor the Gods. Do not beg at their feet for mercy.

* When All Father calls you to His table, storm proudly across the void.

* Remember your ancestors and honor their wisdom.

Prologue

What began as a magical, whispered, thought deep within a dark forest between a druid, a raven, and Norse Seer, eventually took shape within the minds of seers and druids who belonged to five ancient clans that carried blood from both the Norse people, as well as the Picts.

While feuding clans and marauders continued to ravage the Scottish realm, the blood of their victims seeped into the land, and the people wept as they cried out for vengeance. Despite the pleas for war from their people, the chieftains, after seeking counsel from their druids and seers, sought another plan to ease the conflict tormenting the clans.

These chieftains called for an order of guards to protect their current king and those who would follow to reign over Scotland. Though these ancient clans had ties to two different countries—Norway *and* Scotland, they deemed the strongest king should rule over both.

After much debate, they came to a settlement. If the King of Scotland were to govern over both countries, he would require strong men to protect, serve, and even spy on his behalf. Men whose bloodline would be filled with the magic of the Norse God Odin and the Pict God Dagda—a bridge linking all the people's beliefs.

The runes were cast on a stormy night, and the men

were chosen. 'Twas on a Moon Day within the Black Frost month on *Orkneyjar* that the blood of a wolf and an eagle were mixed with a powerful magic.

Each selected man from these ancient tribes entered the stone chamber—to be one with the bones of the wolves. What emerged was dominant and commanding—feared by those who witnessed the pairing of each man with his wolf.

And as the centuries bled into the next, within the boundaries of Scotland, the wolves became more of a myth—one told by bards on a cold winter's night.

Especially for the one they call the Dark Seducer.

His smooth charm and power of persuasion have enticed many women to his bedchamber. Pleasure is his motto as he obtains secrets for his king. Love is simply a weakness. His heart is as frozen as the silver that graces the fur on his wolf.

Yet one unfulfilled conquest has plagued both man and beast. He must either submit to the darkness or confront his greatest fear.

Rorik from the house of *Aodh O'Neil*—descended from the ancient *Uí Néill* dynasty of High Kings of Ireland.

This is his story.

The MacNeil Wolf Saga.

Chapter One

Castle Steinn - Early October 1206

A cold draft brushed across his skin, stirring Rorik from a deep slumber fraught with another nightmare. He lifted his head and inhaled the sharp scent of the approaching storm. Opening his eyes, a shaft of gray light pierced through the open window, and thunder rolled in the far-off distance.

He blew out a curse and tossed aside the fur covering. Sitting on the edge of the bed, he scrubbed a hand vigorously over his face. Pain shot through his left shoulder, but he ignored the burning agony.

"Must you leave so soon?" purred the soft female voice from behind him.

Rorik grimaced. He had forgotten about the woman. His intention last evening was to give Lilias pleasure, obtain the information regarding lands her father wished to seize, and quickly leave soon thereafter. He despised spending an entire night within the bed of *any* female. They were simple pawns for information and bedding.

What possessed him to linger this one time? The truth glared at him. *You yearned for a night of rest but found none.*

Still his mind and body continued to be plagued with endless weariness and his dreams troubled with battles from the past—ones that haunted him often during his daily duties.

He glanced over his shoulder at the woman. "I must leave now. A fierce storm is coming across the lands."

She rose from the pillows on the bed.

Rorik ignored the naked vision she presented him and stood. Her body tempted him to slake his pleasure one last time before departing, but he scowled in contempt—more at himself than the beauty behind him. He would waste valuable time by remaining here, and he grew weary of the game of seduction with this woman.

You must finish what you have started and leave her sated. Give her another plan to rid her of wanting you.

Turning around to face her, he cupped her chin and placed a light kiss on her pouting lips. "If I recall, Robert returns today to claim you."

The woman's eyes flashed with fury. "I will not be wed to a man old enough for death's grip."

Dropping his hand, Rorik shook his head. "The agreement has been arranged and signed by your father *and* Magnar."

Her lips thinned in protest. She eased up further. "What if I tell my father you have taken me to your bed?"

He tugged on a curl trailing over her breast, and then let it slip from his fingers. He pinched her hard nipple. Lilias raked her fingers along his thigh, and his cock swelled.

Her lips parted in invitation, and Rorik lowered his head and teased her lower lip with his tongue. "Then I shall inform your father I was *not* the one who stole your maidenhead. It was another, aye?"

Lilias smacked his hand away. "You would not dare?"

He arched a brow and slid his hand lower to her nest of curls. "And I ken who the man is, as well. Is he not your father's enemy? And an enemy to King William?"

The woman swallowed but made no attempt to free his hand from his pleasurable assault. "How…*how* do you ken?"

Rorik stroked her sensitive nub. "Do you wish to hear the truth, or shall I finish giving you pleasure?"

Lilias' breathing came out in gasps. "I can…cannot think when you are touching me."

With ease, he stroked the passion inside her, using first one finger and then another. A great sob escaped from her lips. He lowered himself onto the bed. "You have not answered me, Lilias?"

"Aye…tell me," she begged.

Her soft whimpers surrounded Rorik. After he stroked her to a powerful release, he wiped his fingers off on the furs and stood. Reaching for his tunic at the end of the bed, Rorik tossed it over his head. "The man likes to boast after several cups of ale."

Her face paled, and she drew the covering to her breasts. "He was my first. He promised to make me his *wife*."

Rorik cursed inwardly. Sitting beside her on the bed, he took her hand into his. "The Cameron is ruthless—in his lands and the women he beds. Your father has mentioned this many times. You should have heeded your father's words and stayed away from the man."

"And you are nae better," she snapped, yanking her hand away. She lowered her head.

Blowing out a frustrated sigh, Rorik conceded, "Aye, yet I made you nae promises. Did I not speak the truth last evening, Lilias?"

Sliding a glance at him, she nodded. "You made my body burn with passion. Is one night of pleasure all I can take from you?"

Rorik gave her his best smile. "Aye, 'tis only the one night. I can offer this knowledge to you. Give Robert a son, and he will grant you anything thereafter for the rest of his days. None of his other wives gave him any heirs before death took them."

Lilias frowned in obvious concentration. "I had not considered this possibility. If I take him to my bed the once—" She gasped and clutched a hand over her stomach. Her eyes lit with fear. "What if I am already carrying a bairn?"

Someone please remind me to be more cautious with my next conquest.

Rorik shook his head and picked up his discarded trews on the floor. "Let me assure you, my seed did not take root within your body."

"How do you ken?" she whispered.

Because only when I profess my love to another can the magic be undone. Therefore, making it possible for the woman I claim to carry my child.

After lacing up his trews, Rorik fisted his hands on his hips. "Trust me."

She nodded, giving him a small smile.

"Be happy in your marriage, Lilias," offered Rorik, grateful their encounter had ended.

As he strode toward the door, her words made him pause.

"Will *you* ever find love?" she asked within the cold chamber.

A knot formed in his gut. *The marriage bed and love are not in my plans.*

"Nae," he confessed. Retrieving his boots, he left the chamber without glancing back at the woman.

****

Lands near Castle Vargr, Scotland

"Foul tempest!" Rorik clenched his jaw fighting the burning pain throbbing within his shoulder. He spat out another curse to the storm lashing across his path. His cloak whipped around his body, and he gave no regard as the rain pounded him with its brittle sting against his face. He pushed his horse onward across the muddy landscape.

Thunder crashed above him, and he narrowed his eyes in preparation for the oncoming onslaught. When lightning flashed with a forceful menace along his route, he barely had time to swerve out of its path.

"'Tis not my day to die!" he bellowed. Rorik raised a fist into the air, challenging the elements to defy his order.

Another flash of lightning seared the darkened sky and grazed his arm. His wolf lunged within Rorik's body, absorbing the powerful shock. Nevertheless, the pain clouded his vision, and he let out a guttural cry. Bile rose from his gut, and he fought its bitter release. In an effort to regain his sight, he blinked several times, doing his utmost to squash the torment within him.

Rorik would not be deterred from his path and

surged forward through the pounding storm.

By the hounds! Had he angered Odin? Thor? The storm had attacked Rorik with vengeance the moment he departed the safety of Steinn Castle. He had important messages to deliver to the king and refused to shift into his wolf for the duration of the journey to Vargr.

Was this a storm brought about by Loki? Did the God dare attack the beast loyal to Odin?

His wolf let out a low growl, displeased with where his thoughts were leading.

Rorik ignored his beast.

His only hope would be to make it to Vargr before night descended. Otherwise, he'd be forced to find shelter within the trees. And it appeared the storm refused to abate anytime soon.

Even the sound of the nearby falls presented as barely a whisper compared to the fierce storm raging all around him. Rorik grimaced when another arc of lightning dared to cross too near his path and split a tree in half. He missed the impact of the tree's heavy limbs, though several smaller branches left their mark across his face.

This time he allowed his wolf to howl his protest.

Rorik bent his head and leaned closer to his horse, ignoring the animal's flying spittle. "Keep steady, Bran. You can guide us swiftly home."

As he approached the last hill before Vargr, he eased up on the reins. With steady movements, he steered Bran's ascent across rocks, mud, and through dense trees. Arriving at the top, Rorik brought them to a halt and scanned the castle below.

He inhaled sharply. Rain mixed with the salty brine

of the sea filled his senses. Though he could not see the vast ocean nearby, he felt the lure of another home.

Orkneyjar.

Weeks ago, he had left the isles in a haze of fury and bitterness. Only one woman made him seethe with anger on that day. *Ragna.* She stirred his fury each time she stepped along his path. How could he forget the look of contempt across her features when they met weeks ago? The woman despised everything about him.

"Have you spouted this cursed storm to delay me, witch?" Rorik snarled, furious he would even dwell on her now.

He rubbed a fist over his left shoulder. Blinding pain shot across his neck and down his back. Wiping a hand across his brow, he let out a frustrated breath, trying to ease the torment. The injury to his shoulder from a battle fought weeks ago continued to afflict him. He thought time would heal the burning agony, but it only grew worse.

His wolf snapped.

"Aye. I ken you can heal me. Given time, I would welcome the shift to let you tend to the wounds. Yet there is none. The deep sleep will hinder my plans."

Again, the words of Ragna entered his mind.

"You are stubborn to not let your wolf aid in your healing. I noticed your shoulder plagues you."

"Damnable woman," he bit out. Rorik slammed the door on his wolf and his annoying thoughts over the Seer.

Despite the intensity of the storm, Vargr and King William awaited him. Giving a nudge to his horse, Rorik swiftly descended the hill.

By the time he reached the gates of Vargr, the

storm appeared to have lessened, and a shaft of sunlight pierced the gray, dreary sky. Quickly crossing through the portcullis, Rorik brought his horse into the bailey. The young lad, Arnulf, dashed out from the direction of the stables with mud and muck covering most of his body.

Smiling, Rorik dismounted and held the reins outward for the lad.

"'Tis a fierce storm, aye? Thor's hammer split the sky many times. The horses feared for their lives." Arnulf stole a glance at the sky and then returned his attention to him.

Rorik tried to hide his mirth while he removed his satchel from across the back of his horse. The lad's devotion was to only one—the horses in his care. He slept, ate, and tended to their needs all inside the stables. From the moment Arnulf could walk, the lad was often found within the stalls babbling to the animals.

Rorik lifted his palm upward, intent on not adding his own misery over the tempest. "'Tis nothing but a fine mist."

Arnulf snorted in disgust and placed a gentle hand on Bran's side. "You have journeyed hard, my friend." Ignoring Rorik, the lad gently led the animal away while continuing to speak softly.

Raking a hand through his hair, Rorik charged across the bailey and entered the keep. The torches hissed within their holders, a warm welcome on this bitter day. Making his way into the great hall, he regarded two other men from the elite guards—Bjorn and Gunnar who were engaged in a game of *hnefatafl*.

"God's blood!" Gunnar's eyes widened. "You are

bleeding. Have you done battle with another foe or the raging storm?"

"Tree limbs," he muttered in disdain.

"Your Gods and mine kept you from harm. The king is in Sutherland's solar."

Rorik dropped his satchel by the large table near the blazing hearth and removed his cloak. He held his hands outward, relishing the warmth. "I swear I thought I had angered the Gods," he spat out, wiping a hand over the scratches on his face. "It took me *five* days to make it through the storm. Yet when I drew near Vargr, the tempest ceased."

His friend laughed bitterly. "I always deemed the sharper the north's winds blast, the sooner one shall notice Thor's hammer streaking across the thunder clouds. I barely missed being singed by lightning on several occasions."

Gunnar's hand hovered over a game piece on the board. "Nevertheless, you have arrived safely. Praise God."

Rorik nodded. "Aye, *aye*." He had no desire to discuss any Gods, including the one of the new religion Gunnar followed.

"Drink a cup of mead before you leave the hall," suggested Gunnar. "It will banish the bite of the cold."

"I would prefer *uisge beatha*," argued Rorik, stepping toward the table. After filling a cup with mead, he drank deeply.

Bjorn lifted his head. "It has been many moons since I have sampled a cup of *uisge beatha*. Was it not at the feasting after we assisted the Earl of Moray?"

Gunnar laughed. "You are correct. A fine drink, but I prefer the sweet mead we had on *Kirkjuvágr*."

Wiping his mouth with the back of his hand, Rorik smiled. “Steinn recently found a barrel hidden in their cellars.”

Bjorn smacked the table with his fist. Games pieces toppled everywhere, and Gunnar let out a sharp hiss. “I knew we should have traveled to Steinn after the wedding,” remarked the man.

Gunnar leaned back in his chair. “So how is the married leader of the wolves?”

Rorik placed the cup on the table and reached for his satchel. “Magnar appears happy and contented.” Though he would never admit to the others that his bond with their leader had become strained over the past several weeks, and he’d spent many a night avoiding Magnar. How could he explain his own unease with another when he had no answers?

“Next time you return to Steinn bring back some of that liquid amber,” stated Bjorn, rising from his chair.

Rorik shook his head while retreating from the great hall. “I have nae plans on returning until spring. You can make the journey and replace another guard from the brotherhood. I ken Steinar is yearning to return to the seas.”

The tension in his shoulders eased as Rorik made his way along the corridor and up the stairs. He was grateful to have some distance between himself and Magnar. What he required were missions from the king that would take him farther south into Scotland and away from the leader of the wolves. The man continued to study his every misstep, often pointing out the misdeeds.

One of the king’s guards approached from the side. He pounded the oak door twice and then opened the door.

Rorik gave the guard a curt nod and stepped inside.

"It appears as if the storm took its anger out on you, MacNeil," observed William, moving away from the arched window and to his table.

Rorik chuckled softly. "Aye, but my Gods favor me."

The king grimaced. He gestured to one of the chairs by the hearth. "What news have you brought?"

Withdrawing the messages, Rorik then handed them to the king. "Magnar sent Steinar south to the MacKay clan near Urquhart. Apparently, the MacKays have seized messages meant for King John."

"Continue," stated William.

Settling down in the chair, he watched as the king broke the seal on several folded parchments. "Magnar received news from Stephen MacKay that there were several skirmishes around Urquhart—"

"Until all the MacKay brothers are united, I fear their lands will face many battles," interjected William. "How did Magnar come upon this knowledge?"

"Stephen sent a messenger. He and his brother, Duncan, did not trust anyone to travel with the letters." Rorik leaned forward, trying to ease the strain from the last several days.

"Wise decision." William rubbed a hand through his beard. "Though I am certain they both broke the seals to read the messages and then resealed them." Pointing to the jug, he ordered, "Pour yourself a cup of ale."

Heaving a sigh, Rorik complied.

"Have you eaten anything on your journey?" asked William while reading the messages.

Pinching the bridge of his nose, he replied, "Dried fish and bread." In truth, the fish soured his gut on the first night, and the little bread he had was gone in two days. Rorik guzzled the ale in one gulp.

William grunted a curse. "Michael!" His bellow echoed within the solar, and the king's wolfhound lifted his head from his place by the fire.

The guard opened the door.

"Fetch some hot food, if any, for MacNeil."

Michael nodded and left, silently closing the door behind him.

"And what about Malcolm?" demanded William. "Does he pursue more lands east of his? Will he battle against me? What have you learned?"

"Nae. His loyalty remains steadfast to you. He sought to strengthen his clan by marrying off his daughter, Lilias."

"Do not be fooled. Malcolm's keen interest is as sharp as a hawk. I shall send a message to Magnar to keep a watch on his movements. For now, I have other urgent matters that concern *England*."

Rorik watched the flames snap within the hearth as the king resumed reading the letters. Moments drifted by in quiet solitude. He brushed a hand over several days' growth of beard, allowing the warmth of the chamber and ale to ease the tension from his weary body.

Rising from his chair, William went to the hearth. Rorik watched as he tossed the letters into the fire—the edges of the parchment curling into ash with each lick of the flames.

"As always with John, he attempts to thwart my power in the lands within England that are *mine*. He continues to disregard my requests for the return of these lands and castles." William braced a hand on the stone above the hearth.

"Is he plotting with another against you?" asked Rorik, stretching out his legs.

William smacked the stone with his hand and returned to his desk. "John courts favor with any who will listen to him. If they disagree, their lands are forfeit. He shall always seek to gather another spy to his table." Picking up another letter, he held it outward. "I have a quest for you."

Rorik straightened in his chair. Hope soared within him. Would it be south? Edinburgh? He would only require a night's rest before taking up this new task.

Michael returned with a trencher. Placing it on the table, he then resumed his post outside the door.

William motioned him over. "Eat while I discuss my plans."

Rising, Rorik dragged the chair across the room to the table—one littered with maps, more messages, and spilled ale. The scent of venison stew slammed into him, and his stomach growled in protest of going without food for so long. He tore a piece of bread off and dug into his meal with fervor.

"Apparently, one of the Mormaers of Caithness—David Maddadsson is traveling to Steinn. He wishes to meet the new young chieftain and discuss this endeavor of Steinn becoming a secondary stronghold for my elite guard, which I favor. He talks of his brother, Jon, making the journey later in the year. For now, Jon will remain in Thurso."

Rorik frowned, and his jaw clenched. The mere mention of Ragna's brothers settled uneasily within his gut. "Do you suspect an argument from them?"

He dismissed the idea with a wave of his hand. "Nae. Their loyalty not only extends to the King of Norway but to me. David has recently returned from *Orkneyjar* with a certain traveling companion. Her name is Hallgerd Eklund. She is also betrothed to David. What I require is a delicate approach."

Rorik's hand stilled over his food. *For the love of Odin, do not send me back to Steinn.*

William dropped the parchment onto the table. "Magnar has written that he recalls David having dealings with Hallgerd's brother, Jorund, who is currently in York. I need to find out his purpose there."

Pushing aside the trencher, Rorik reached for the jug and refilled his cup. "Your concerns?"

The king braced his hands on the table. "I fear Jorund seeks to claim my lands. The house of Eklund has sought lands—*my lands* for years."

Rorik studied the king over the rim of his cup. "You wish me to gather knowledge from the sister?"

William arched a brow. "Do they not call you the *charmer* of the wolves? Entice her with words or whatever you so wish. Yet I require the information."

"The lass is betrothed. This may be a problem."

"For you?" The king laughed. "Do not tell me your certain skills will keep you from charming even those soon to be married."

William knew him well. The thought sobered Rorik, and bitterness clawed inside him. He'd thought to garner a quest far away from Steinn. Now he must return and seduce a woman to be married to one of the jarls of *Orkneyjar*.

His hand curled into a fist. For a moment, Rorik

longed to deny his king this task. He banished the thought. It would serve no good. After finishing his ale, he placed the cup onto the table. "When are they arriving at Steinn?"

William sighed heavily and sat down. Pushing aside the strewn messages, he reached for the jug and poured more ale into both cups. "Considering when Magnar received the news and how long it took you to bring it to me…" William paused and shrugged. "They may already be at Steinn."

Rorik abandoned his ale and pushed to his feet. "Grant me a night's rest?"

William smiled slowly. "Nae, MacNeil. Take two nights. I do not want you returning to Steinn too weary for this task."

Rorik nodded his head in humor. Picking up his satchel, he glanced at the king over his shoulder. "Even with my body battered, any quest involving a *woman* would not in any way hinder me. I can assure you I will gather the necessary information."

William's roar of laughter followed him along the corridor. Instead of seeking rest, Rorik yearned for the soft moans of a willing lass or two to ease the aches within his body.

His footsteps started for the path to the kitchens, and then he halted. Pain speared once again along his neck and shoulder. He let out a sharp hiss. Leaning against the cold stone wall, he gazed at the shadows flickering from the lit torches and waited for the burning agony to lessen.

"Two nights. Use them wisely, and then you can seek the pleasures of another," he muttered.

Rorik let out a frustrated sigh. Giving a passing

glance toward the kitchens, he then went in the opposite direction toward his chamber.

Alone.

Chapter Two

Northwest coast of Caithness, Scotland

"Blessed Freyja, thank you for keeping the storms away," whispered Ragna, walking forward on shaky limbs across the shore.

Never had a Seer from the isles traveled to this land. Ragna would be the first. The Goddess had demanded it from her, or so she believed. Uncertainty had tormented her since that first hesitant step on board the ship, continuing throughout her journey across the sea and when she came upon Scottish soil.

Words from long ago seeped into Ragna's mind, and she halted her steps.

"Do not let your foresight rule you, Ragna," rasped her mother. Great spasms wracked her body. When the woman settled, she raised a gnarled finger at her. "Feelings have nae place within the sight. Banish them as you would a foul gnat."

Clasping her hands tightly, Ragna argued, "'Tis an overwhelming urge I cannot discard so easily."

Her mother coughed, and blood trickled from her cracked lips. "Then you are nae good as a Seer and unable to give counsel to those who seek your wisdom."

Ragna's shoulders sagged in resignation. "With your help, I will abide by your bidding and knowledge."

"Good. Foresight can serve only one. You. Do not become its thrall."

Ragna clutched the amber pendant within the folds of her cloak. "Thank the Goddess you are long dead to not witness this recent folly of mine, Mother."

Her body trembled. How Ragna loathed traveling across the wide-open water. She glanced to her left at the towering cliffs of dark stone. The waves crashed behind her, and she resumed her progress slowly.

Bending down, she dug two fingers deep within the gritty shore. Coldness seeped into her skin as she tried to get a sense of this country. Others whispered to her from the land—ancient and unfamiliar. Wild and strange this Scotland. Never had Ragna considered leaving the *Orkneyjar Isles*.

Until recently.

Even now, the vision clawed at her with its images of blood, pain, and death—claiming its victim. Beads of sweat broke out along her brow at the memory as she stood slowly. When it appeared to her in a waking moment weeks ago, torment consumed Ragna. Never had her feelings of a vision entered her body. Her strength as a Seer made it possible to be simply a witness to a likely future occurrence. Yet this one so powerful, she struggled to breathe and collapsed onto the ground. After Ragna recovered, she knew that a message from another person to warn of the impending danger would have gone unheeded by the man.

There was only one course of action she believed necessary. Ragna must travel across the sea and deliver the foreboding of danger herself. If the Goddess had shown her this powerful vision, then surely she could quash her fear and make the journey.

She placed her fist against her racing heart, trying to force her own emotions deep within her. They would serve no good by tormenting her with doubts and indecisions. Soon, her breathing returned to its normal rhythm.

"You are quiet," observed Hallgerd, shoving back the hood of her cloak as she approached Ragna's side.

Ragna gave her a sharp glance. The woman's blonde hair glimmered in the bright sunlight. "I was giving thanks to the Goddess for our safe passage across the sea." She returned her attention inland.

"As did I before we left," stated the woman.

Hallgerd's lack of respect had become as thorny as a nettle's sting. Ragna remained calm.

"Your *brother* has told me you are unmarried."

Ragna refused to discuss her lack of a husband. She countered, "Half-brother. We share different mothers."

The woman tilted her head to the side. "Blood is blood."

"Scotland is a rugged landscape," declared Ragna, intent on discussing another subject.

Hallgerd's smile came slowly. "Like their men."

Ragna disagreed. She believed the men whose bloodline came from both—*Orkneyjar Isles* and Scotland were far more rugged and wild. But she was not about to debate the qualities of men with Hallgerd. "You mentioned you have made the journey many times with your brother. Did you favor this country over your own?"

The woman closed her eyes as if in thought. After several moments, she opened them and pulled the hood of her cloak back over her head. "It was a journey that has procured a husband."

Ragna studied her. "Will you be content living here? You have left all that you ken behind on the isles."

She waved her hand outward. "There is vast wealth in this land. When I marry, I can help David unite the two countries."

"I believe the king of Scotland is doing all in his power already," Ragna countered dryly. Did the woman not understand the jarls' authority was limited in the north of Scotland? That their loyalty tied to both kings—Norway *and* Scotland?

Shrugging, Hallgerd turned toward her. "Is King William doing all in his power?"

Stunned by her remark, Ragna kept silent.

The woman pursed her lips. "But then I would not expect a *Seer* to understand."

How wrong you are, Hallgerd. You had best keep your tongue silent.

Ragna smiled fully and glanced over the woman's shoulder. "I see David has returned with the horses. I am eager to see Steinn Castle and renew my friendship with the new chieftain." Returning her gaze to the woman, she added, "I believe my brother forgot to mention I am also a *völva* for all of *Orkneyjar*."

Hallgerd's eyes grew wide. "He did not mention this to me."

Ragna's smiled faded. "He only recently came upon this knowledge that I have become the wise woman for the isles. David and I have not spoken for many moons. I sought him out when I learned he was in *Kirkjuvágr*, so that I may take advantage of traveling on his ship."

Hallgerd regarded her warily and then departed.

Letting out a frustrated breath, Ragna muttered, "You are foolish if you attempt to go against the Scottish king." However, this was not the time to be concerned about the affairs of this land. Ragna's quest was for only one, and she prayed he'd listen to her.

Shielding her eyes against the glare of sunlight, she blew out a short whistle and turned away. She did not have to wait long. The sparrowhawk let out a shrill cry in return and descended onto Ragna's outstretched arm. She ruffled her feathers and cast her dark eyes away from her.

"Aye, I ken you did not enjoy traveling across the sea, Oda. I require your aid on this journey. You ken what must be done. At least we did not encounter any storms."

Ragna held her breath, fearing the bird would not do her bidding. She risked much by bringing Oda on the voyage. The faithful bird had never been contained, let along confined in a cage. Yet once the decision had been made, she could not turn back. The sparrowhawk would be her eyes here in this strange land.

Ragna lifted her arm higher. "Did I not free you as soon as I spotted land? Now, seek out the wolf, my friend."

Oda regarded her for several heartbeats before giving a loud screech and flew off inland into the dense trees.

"May the Goddess watch over you," whispered Ragna, pulling the hood of her cloak over her head.

****

The journey to Steinn Castle did not take as long as Ragna feared. From what David had told her, she thought they would be spending the night among the stars and trees. When they crested the last hill, the castle stood out among the pines. The wooded valley did little to conceal the massive stone and wooden structure. Her breath caught at the sight. Never had she witnessed such a huge dwelling. The stone towers seemed to touch the clouds. Absently, she touched the amber pendant around her neck and swallowed. “You are a beauty,” she whispered.

“You would have thought differently had you witnessed the destruction many months ago. Magnar and his men have helped to secure a portion of the wall and north tower,” mentioned David, bringing his horse near hers.

“Aye, I recall how an enemy caused the fire,” she affirmed slowly.

David rubbed a gloved hand over the thick mane of his horse. “Can you not share why you wanted to travel to Scotland?”

Her mouth twitched in humor. “The importance of my message is for only one to hear. As I stated before we departed the *Orkneyjar Isles*.”

“I thought once we’d arrived you would confess your reason.”

Ragna glanced sideways at him. The only resemblance was the bluish gray color of their eyes—both traits held by their father. “Nae.”

“Important enough to journey across the North Sea?”

Sighing heavily, she cast her gaze to the valley below. “Most assuredly.”

David reached across and grasped her hand. “Then I am happy to have been of some assistance. Perchance, after you have delivered your message we can speak more."

Stunned by his touch and declaration, Ragna turned and smiled. "I would welcome the conversation. Will Jon be visiting Steinn?"

Her brother smiled in return. "Later next month. His business keeps him busy in Thurso." Lifting his hand high, he gestured for his other men to move forward.

Ragna waited until the others had started their descent and then followed. Crossing the wide valley took little time, and soon they were at the open gates of Steinn.

David bellowed a greeting to the guard along the wall, and the man responded with one of his own. They led their horses over a long, narrow bridge and entered a huge courtyard. Ragna took in the appearance of those tending to animals and of others with carts of wood and stone making their way to the other side of the castle.

She cast her gaze throughout, hoping to find the one man with whom she could speak to. The hood of her cloak fell back onto her shoulders as she twisted around to get a better view. Many smiled in passing, and Ragna returned the simple gesture.

Without waiting for any of the men to assist her, she dismounted from her horse. After giving the animal a gentle pat with soft words for delivering them safely, she moved steadily to the entrance of the castle. Her nerves twisted within her body as her steps led her inside the great keep.

Immediately, Ragna halted her progress and stared at the many tapestries lining the wall. Her gaze traveled down the entryway where she noticed two large doors, partially open. Her ears strained to pick up any familiar voices, yet none came forth. Indecision plagued her in this strange land.

Banish the fear. It will serve you nae good here.

She lifted her chin and started to move forward. When she reached the massive doors, she slowly pushed them open. Flames snapped and hissed from the large hearth at the end of the empty hall.

"*Ragna*?"

She inhaled sharply and turned around. Exhaling softly, she dipped her head in greeting. "'Tis good to see you again, Elspeth."

A frown marred the woman's features as she came forward. "We had nae news you were coming with David. Is all well?"

"The journey was only recently planned. There is a message I must deliver to one of the wolves. I can always find shelter within the trees or in the kitchens."

Elspeth clucked her tongue in obvious disapproval. Embracing Ragna, she uttered softly, "You have honored us with your visit. And the *Seer* for the *Orkneyjar Isles* will have her own chamber."

Ragna let out a sigh of relief. Though they had formed a friendship while Elspeth was on *Orkneyjar*, Ragna considered it important for the woman to welcome her into her home. The journey had allowed no time in sending a message to the leader of the wolves.

Drawing back, she studied Elspeth.

"I am happy you have finally chosen to visit us and Scotland," beamed Elspeth. "You do ken my husband told me you would *never* venture across the sea."

"That word should be banned from any

conversation. As I recall, Magnar stated the same about finding a wife. Once, I thought he had made an oath to *never* marry."

Elspeth laughed—the sound echoing within the entryway. "I declared I would *never* marry a heathen Northman."

Reaching outward, Ragna gently brushed her fingers over the woman's cheek. "You are with child."

Elspeth's good humor faded. She grasped Ragna's hand. "How do you ken?"

This time, Ragna burst out in laughter.

The woman eyed her keenly. "Aye. Now I understand. Seer *and* wise woman."

Noting the concern over Elspeth's features, she asked, "Do you not favor a child? Have you been unwell?"

"Goodness, I am overjoyed." Elspeth grabbed her arm and led her into the great hall. Glancing in all directions, she lowered her head near Ragna. "I have yet to tell Magnar I am with child."

Shrugging, Ragna wrapped her arm around the woman's waist. "Best you tell him now. Either he will detect the heartbeat of new life within you, *or* his wolf will first."

Elspeth winced. "We already have this connection within our minds. I fathom he already kens and is waiting for me to announce the good news."

Ragna snorted. "Where is the *leader* of the wolves?"

"Standing behind you," answered the familiar male voice.

Releasing her hold on Elspeth, she turned and faced the Barbarian wolf. Neither women heard his footsteps enter. One of his highly praised skills as a wolf *and* man. "Greetings, Magnar."

He regarded her with intent. "What brings the *völva* across the seas? As I recall, you declared once how much you *detested* journeying on the water."

Ragna clasped her hands together and nodded. "Aye, 'tis true." Finding the words was proving difficult for her. So much depended on aid from him. If Magnar refused…

Voices drifted by of the others entering the castle. She stiffened and glanced beyond the man. *Do not let it be him. I am not ready, Goddess.*

Magnar frowned and fisted his hands on his hips. "What is wrong?"

Ragna held back a sharp retort. His steely glare did little to calm her distress.

Elspeth went to her husband, placing a gentle hand on his chest. "Take Ragna to the solar. I shall see to our guests."

The man's features softened. He grasped her hand and placed a kiss within the palm. "Aye. Explain to our guests I will attend them shortly."

Elspeth turned to Ragna. "There is mead in the solar. Would you like me to bring you some food?"

How Magnar ever enchanted this woman to become his wife would be one she'd have to ask the Gods when she departed from this world. Giving the woman a smile, Ragna replied, "After I deliver my message, I will seek out the others. There is nae need to care for me. I will take my meal later."

The woman embraced her once again, whispering, "'Tis good to have you in our home."

After she left, Magnar started forward, making his

way to the hearth. "Follow me."

Without a word, Ragna followed the man. They veered to the right down a narrow passageway with small stairs leading upward to a door. After pushing it open, Magnar gestured her inside. Quickly closing it behind them, he proceeded to make hasty steps through a dimly lit corridor which curved, leading to another set of stairs. At the top, he opened the door and held it open for her.

Ragna entered the solar taking in the expanse of the room. A large, arched window graced the side of the room with only one shutter partially open. The fire in the hearth had dwindled to ashes, and she crossed the chamber to where a large oak table dominated the far wall. Without asking permission, she went and pulled back the other shutter. Wonderful sunlight filtered inside. She allowed the warmth to ease the tension within her body.

"For the love of Odin, *why* are you here?" demanded Magnar.

She let out a nervous laugh and turned toward the leader of the wolves. "Trust me, Magnar, there was nae other way to bring you this message."

"What message?" he snapped.

Ignoring him, she continued. "I have seen a grave vision and require your assistance. If you refuse, one of your wolves will clearly die by the next full moon." She paused to judge his reaction to part of this knowledge.

He folded his arms over his chest. "Continue."

"Unless *Rorik* permits his wolf to heal him, the man is doomed to suffer an agonizing death."

A nerve twitched in the man's neck. He turned from her stare and went to the table. Ragna watched as he poured mead into two cups and brought one to her.

She took the offering, though preferred to wait to consume the liquid until she heard his reply.

Magnar drained the entire contents of his cup and then went back to the table. Quietly, he placed the cup down while keeping his back to her. "You ken the edicts. 'Tis the one order I cannot give to man *or* wolf. What you ask is not possible."

Ragna gripped the cup tightly in desperation for more words to convince him. She knew it would be a battle with Magnar. Yet she thought by coming here herself he would be swayed to ignore an ancient edict.

"Rorik is dying," she declared softly.

Magnar shook his head.

Frustration seethed within her. "You would let your friend die? Watch him suffer? When all it would take would be one order to his wolf?"

When the man turned around, his eyes shown with those of the wolf—dark with silver flecks within the orbs. "I cannot, *Seer*, and you ken this! How dare you come before me with a request I cannot honor!"

Ragna pounded her chest as she choked on her emotions. She did not fear him. "The vision the Goddess showed me was so powerful, I felt it to my bones! For some unfathomable reason, Rorik refuses to give control to his wolf for healing. *Death* is his future, and you have sentenced him to an agonizing punishment."

Magnar stormed to her side. His rage barely in control by the look within his wolf's eyes. "There is one solution—one for another. But I ken *you* already are aware of this knowledge."

Ragna blanched. "I…I *cannot*."

The man took a step back and regarded her coolly. "You thought to come here and have me do your bidding. While we both ken you are the one to persuade Rorik to give in to his wolf's healing."

He pointed a finger at her. "I order *you*, Ragna, from the house of Maddadsson, to give your message from the Goddess to Rorik, from the house of MacNeil. You are charged with making sure he understands the wisdom of your vision. A vision, which if he ignores will be *your* failing."

Stunned, Ragna gasped and fell back against the stone bench. "Nae," she whispered, the shock of his words burying deep in her.

The leader of the Wolves of Clan Sutherland had directed an order—ancient and commanding to a Seer. Now she was bound by his law to seek out Rorik. She swallowed the bitterness and uneasiness while emotions clouded her thoughts.

Rorik will never listen to me. Therefore, death will come swiftly to him.

Chapter Three

Tempering the growing ire of having to enter Steinn was proving to be difficult for Rorik. He thought the return journey would quiet the uneasiness. The weather had changed from the biting north winds to gentle warmer breezes. Even as the pain in his shoulder diminished, Rorik was unable to settle his thoughts.

During his travels through the hills and forest, a hawk kept pace with him. He pondered the strange portent of the bird's flight. Was it a message from the Gods? His wolf refused to acknowledge his question when he presented the thought inward one evening.

He studied the commanding presence of Steinn before him. When the portcullis opened, the grating of steel intensified his distress.

Banish the unrest. Complete the task, and then you can depart.

Urging his horse forward, he crossed the bridge and entered the bailey. He chose not to dismount there but go directly to the stables. Perchance he would find solace in bathing in the river south of the keep before he sought out Magnar. He did not favor having to inform the man of his latest request from the king.

Alan greeted him at the entrance. His eyes widened in surprise. "You have returned?"

Rorik's mouth twitched in humor. "Eager to see me or Bran?"

The lad huffed out a breath. "Always for the horse."

"Why am I not surprised," muttered Rorik while he dismounted from the animal and retrieved his sword and satchel. "You will ken we had a pleasant journey on our return, and the horse was well tended to while at Vargr."

Alan gave him a skeptical glance before taking the reins. "I ken my brother would have tended to his needs, since you left in the middle of a tempest."

It was bad enough with Arnulf upon my arrival at Vargr. Must I endure another tongue lashing from his twin?

The lad clucked his tongue in disapproval of the muck covering most of his horse and uttered soothing words of comfort.

Rorik rubbed a gloved hand over his chin while he watched both disappear into the stables. Making steady strides he started for the river only to be interrupted by the approach of Steinar.

"You are going in the wrong direction," stated his friend.

Rorik bit back the curse he wanted to toss out at the man. "I thought to rid myself of the grime of my travels first."

"You ken Magnar is eager to find out why you have returned to Steinn."

Loki's balls! I should have known the wolves would have sensed my presence. "Is he in his solar?"

"Nae. He is in the north section beyond the grove of birch trees. He is making a small chapel for Elspeth to worship her God."

Rorik arched a brow in concern. "Has Magnar

turned from Odin and embraced the new religion?"

The man shook his head. "You ken how much he loves his wife. He wanted to give her a place to pray."

Love. He shuddered at the mere mention of the word. He'd go to the halls of Valhalla grateful never to be touched by that feeling. "Have you come to guide me to our leader?" asked Rorik, his tone harsher than he intended.

Steinar let out a low growl. "I suggest you temper your foul mood, once again."

"I did not ken you noticed." Rorik turned from him and started for the path leading in the northern direction.

"We have all *noticed*," snapped Steinar, keeping steady strides with him.

Rorik halted. He glanced upward and exhaled slowly. He had no wish to quarrel with his friend and grew weary of the battle within him. "Demons plague me."

Steinar stepped in front of him. "Explain."

Shrugging, he returned his gaze to the man. "Unable to speak what I cannot fathom."

His friend frowned in thought. Nodding slowly, he offered, "You have not recovered from the last battle on *Kirkjuvágr*. You must seek out a healer, a Seer, *or* permit your wolf to cleanse all wounds."

Rorik disregarded each one of those suggestions. "I do not require a healer. And there is nae Seer I trust here in Scotland. Furthermore, to give my body and mind over to the wolf for healing requires a lengthy absence. I have an important task from the king that must be accomplished."

Steinar clamped a hand on Rorik's shoulder, and he

winced in pain. "If you do not mend this, you are nae good at defending yourself, the wolves, or our king. Find a way," urged his friend. "It would be an honor to be your guardian while your wolf tends to your healing."

Softening his features, Rorik gave him a curt nod. "After I am finished here."

"Good."

They resumed their progress through the trees with Steinar in the lead. Rorik ducked under heavy pine branches. "Has the Mormaer of Caithness arrived?"

Steinar paused and glanced over his shoulder. "Aye. Does their arrival have anything to do with your task for the king?"

"A *delicate* one," confessed Rorik. "I understand David is betrothed?"

Chuckling softly, Steinar ignored his question. He stepped forward and parted the branches. "Go forth. You can discuss all with Magnar."

Rorik brushed past the man and into a small clearing. Sunlight sprinkled the ground and encircled a tiny structure. Sitting on a tree stump, Magnar worked quietly on a wooden carving resembling a woman.

Curious, Rorik asked, "What are you making?"

"'Tis a carving of the mother of Elspeth's God. She has spoken of a woman called Mother Mary. I thought to present the gift to her when I bring her to the chapel."

After dropping his satchel and sword, Rorik went to inspect the handiwork of the building and peered inside. The front of the building faced the rising sun, and more sunlight spilled within on the polished wooden floor. A lone bench and chair were the only furniture present inside. A wooden cross hung on the back wall graced by lanterns suspended on iron hooks on either side. "'Tis good. Is this where you go to in the early mornings before training in the lists?"

Magnar continued to work on the carving. "Aye."

"You never mentioned anything," countered Rorik, returning to his leader's side.

The man rubbed a thumb over the rough wood. "You never asked."

Rorik crossed his arms over his chest. "True."

Lifting his head, Magnar regarded him. "Why have you returned?"

"The king requires certain information from the woman who is betrothed to David."

Magnar narrowed his eyes. "Hallgerd?"

"Her brother has been seen in the company of King John. William believes she has knowledge about her brother's involvement." Rorik rubbed a hand down the back of his neck. "As you ken, Jorund and his father long sought the lands our king is attempting to reclaim. Lands that were taken during his imprisonment under Henry's reign."

Magnar blew out a curse and stood. "And you will use your *charm* to get this knowledge, aye?"

"Will this pose a problem, considering they are here under your roof and protection?" Rorik grew tense.

Magnar tucked the carving into his pouch secured at his waist. "I have nae concerns about your methods. Yet there is another who has traveled with them, and *she* might warn Hallgerd about you."

The air chilled around Rorik. "From the isles?" His question barely a whisper.

The man laughed, but there was no mistaking his

worried expression. "Aye, and her journey here is a first."

Nae! His mind screamed at the impossibility. Rorik clenched his jaw and began to pace. He feared to ask the next question as fury boiled within him. "*Who*?"

"Ragna."

Her name mentioned aloud shot through to his wolf, and the animal lifted his head.

Rorik ran a shaky hand through his hair. So many questions burned within him. He believed he was safe here in Scotland—away from her censure and hate. "For the love of Odin! Did the woman state why she traveled the North Sea? What could have made her leave the isles? Her home is there *not* here!" He resumed his pacing. "Is she now giving counsel to Hallgerd? Is this why they have traveled together?"

Magnar lifted his hand to halt any further questions. "I ken this is not good timing with Ragna present and your task for the king. However, she has come to deliver a message for you."

Rorik halted. "*Me*? Loki's balls! Can she not leave it with you? I have nae wish to speak to her again. I cannot worry over the words of a Seer, especially the ones *she* spouts."

"Though I ken your task is important for William, you must proceed with caution when you meet with Ragna."

Rorik shook his head vigorously. "Nae. I shall tend to the king's duty first. The Seer can deliver any pertinent information to you."

Magnar went to the chapel and closed the wooden door. When he turned to face Rorik, he smiled slowly. "This is not for me, my friend. Mend this rift you have with Ragna. She has dared to come to Scotland to bring *you* an important message."

Stunned by Magnar's declaration, he watched as the man departed, leaving Rorik unsure on how to deal with the one woman he had hoped to never see again.

****

Rorik kept his sight on the ripples of water gently flowing south. The late afternoon sun warmed his body. Bathing in the river gave him time to ease the tension thrumming through his veins. With deft skill, he wove a portion of his wet hair into a small braid on the right side of his head, securing the end with a thin piece of leather, and then did the same on the left. After he finished, Rorik dropped his arms over his bent knees.

A young doe appeared from the trees, unaware of his presence. Her steps were hesitant as she made her way on the opposite side of the river. Soon, others followed her lead and joined her. A hawk's shrill cry pierced the quietness causing him to lift his head and study the path of the bird.

If he could, Rorik would remain on this boulder by the river for the duration of the evening and into night. His stomach growled in protest, and he realized he had little food this day. He reached for his aleskin and took a sip.

Even the thought of entertaining Hallgerd left a hollow ache within. "For all I ken you might have the face of a goat."

Rorik sensed the intruder's approach behind him before the first footstep sounded. He lifted his left hand and rested it on the hilt of his sword by his side.

"I happen to cherish the faces of my goats, though they are stubborn creatures."

The ale soured in his gut. "*Seer*." He released his hand from his sword and continued to stare outward.

When silence greeted him, he dared to glance over his shoulder. Wariness from her all-knowing eyes reflected at Rorik, not the bitter coldness she often imparted to him. "Why have you come?"

Ragna lifted her chin. "I have a message you must hear fully."

Shrugging, Rorik resumed his gaze outward. "Then speak your words."

Again, the woman remained silent. Rorik pinched the bridge of his nose in frustration.

"Do you not deem it best to put on your tunic?" she suggested, stepping closer and brushing the garment against his arm.

Slowly, Rorik lifted his head to look at her. Even her words sounded different. They were almost a plea, not filled with terse venom. A rosy stain had blossomed on her ivory cheeks, and her breathing appeared labored. He pondered two things—either his naked form disgusted her or perchance appealed to her. *Surely, she despises me, nothing more.*

The barb he wanted to fling out at her became trapped on his tongue. He guzzled deeply from the aleskin. Wiping his mouth with the back of his hand, he dropped the empty skin next to his sword and swiftly got off the boulder.

Ragna gasped and clutched his tunic to her breasts. Yet she did not avert her eyes.

He dared to move toward her.

Her eyes widened, and she stumbled back, dropping his tunic.

Rorik reached out and grabbed her hand,

preventing her from falling. The contact of her skin against his sent a tremor of warmth up his arm. This time, his breathing became labored while he stared into her gray eyes. He found no hatred there—only beauty within their depths. His gaze traveled down to her full red lips, partially open and begging to be kissed. Rorik inhaled sharply. Her scent of herbs and the land filled him—raw and untamed.

"*Please* release me," she whispered.

Instantly, he dropped her hand as if he had been burned. Rorik picked up his tunic and drew it over his head. Stepping around her, he retrieved his trews and put them on. When he turned back around, her features were lacking in any previous emotions or softness, and he slammed the door on his own lust.

He gestured toward the boulder. "Would you care to sit?"

She shook her head and went toward the water.

Rorik moved to her side. "If you dared to cross the North Sea to deliver a message to me, I reckon 'tis important."

She cast a sideways glance at him. "Then you will listen?"

"I ken there is nae friendship between us, Rag—"

"I do not require your *friendship*. Simply your loyalty to me as a seer and wise woman," she interrupted.

By the Gods! He wanted to leave her standing on the edge of the river. Could they not just speak without sparring with words?

"Give me your message, Seer."

"Will you be silent until I am finished?"

Rorik gritted his teeth but gave her a curt nod.

Returning her gaze to the river, she clasped her hands in front of her. "You are traveling a dark abyss within your body and mind. If you recall, I mentioned to you weeks ago you require healing—to allow your wolf to rid you of the poisons inside you. The vision I received was *powerful*."

"And I told you I do not have time," he interjected tersely.

Her lips thinned in disapproval. "You would dare to go against a message from the Gods and Goddesses?"

Rorik folded his arms over his chest. "Which God or Goddess spoke to you?"

"How dare you!" Her eyes sparked with fury.

"'Tis a simple question, Seer."

"You are as stubborn as your father, *wolf*."

She turned from him and made to leave, yet Rorik stilled her progress with an outstretched arm. "I am *nothing* like my father."

"Was not his death a violent one caused by his refusal to heed the warning of the Seer?"

"Different circumstances," he answered smoothly.

"If you refuse to heal, death will claim your body *before* your mind." Ragna swallowed. "The agony will be unlike any you can fathom. Not only will you battle the burning pain, but the anguish within your wolf. Flames of torment will consume you both. Your wolf might sense the danger first and begin to retreat farther within you."

Stunned, Rorik dropped his arm. "I will suffer death by *Fenrir's* fire?"

"Aye," she whispered. Ragna reached out and touched his arm. "I beg you, return to Vargr immediately and choose a guardian from one of the other wolves to watch over you during your wolf's healing."

He frowned in confusion. "You risked the tempest of the sea to bring me this message when you could have sent it with another? *Why*?"

Dropping her hand, she replied, "Can you truthfully say you would have read a letter from me if a messenger presented it to you?"

Wiping a hand over his brow, he turned from her questioning gaze. "I have an important task for the king. Until 'tis completed, I cannot leave."

"Then you seal your fate, Rorik," she conceded softly.

Indecision battled within him for several heartbeats. Ragna had journeyed to deliver a vision of death to a man she despised. Unable to fathom why she cared enough to come to Scotland did little to sway him. He was honor-bound to remain steadfast in his quest for his king.

When Rorik glanced over his shoulder, he found Ragna had left as quietly as she came.

Chapter Four

Ragna rubbed the apple between her palms while staring outward from the north tower. From this vantage, she could smell the salty tang of the sea, and she yearned to leave on the next ship for the *Orkneyjar Isles*. Her task had been completed. Surely the Goddess would not be displeased with her that Rorik refused to listen. The man simply chose to ignore her pleas.

"There is nothing left to do," she muttered into the cold bite of the north wind.

Nevertheless, Ragna's emotions betrayed her words. Even though he had brought intense pain to her so long ago, she had no wish to see Rorik suffer. Or die. Yet stinging words from long ago came unbidden to her.

"Have you been eating the fresh berries in the meadow, Ragna?" asked the male voice behind her. The man rolled her name off his tongue, sending shivers down her back. She knew him well, often staring at him while she traveled into the nearby village of Kirkjuvágr.

Doing her best to compose herself, she wiped the palms of her hands down the front of her gown and turned around. "I have yet to find any. Why do you ask?"

Rorik stepped forth from the shadow of a tree. His smile came slowly as he approached her.

She tried to control the fierce beating of her heart

as the man loomed over her with a dark and hungry gaze.

"Your lips are as red as the berries that grow in abundance in the meadow," he stated softly.

"'Tis only an apple I have been eating." Unable to move away, Ragna studied the man's features—from his deep green eyes to the dimple hidden within the dark facial hair covering his chin. To suppress the urge of twining her fingers into his long ebony hair, she dug her fingers into her gown. She thought the warrior had to be chiseled from the Gods.

Rorik lifted his hand and gently pressed his thumb against her bottom lip. "Beauty."

An ache grew within Ragna. His nearness made her weak and without breath. When his hand slipped around her waist, she collapsed into his embrace, placing her palms against his broad chest. "What are you doing?"

"I want to taste your lips, Ragna. I have thought of nothing else these long summer days."

She tried to breathe, finding it difficult within his strong embrace. "Why me?" she blurted out on a gasp.

He lowered his head near her ear. "Why not you?"

His breath was hot against her skin, and she fought the desire to place her hand against her neck.

Ragna swallowed. How she yearned to kiss the man. He made her body tremble like no other. But what if one kiss was not enough? What if she was the one to take more? The air warmed and filled with the scent of Rorik.

He licked the soft skin below her ear, and Ragna let out a moan.

Laughter in the distance cooled her passion. She

peered around Rorik at the man making long strides toward them.

"Kiss her and take her to your bed, Rorik!" bellowed the intruder.

Rorik's hands tightened around her. "Leave, Father!"

Durinn MacNeil stood glaring at her. "How long did it take for my son to sweep you into his arms? I bet his wager was less than it would take him to piss out into the stream."

Ragna blinked as if coming out of a trance. "Wager?" she echoed, slowly turning her attention to the man who only moments ago she would have given much more than a kiss.

"Do not listen to the old man," whispered Rorik.

Yet Ragna saw the truth within his eyes. Did he think her foolish enough to believe the lie even with his charming words? "Give me your true account."

He shrugged. "Would you believe my truth or the wild words spouted from a man addled with too much mead?"

Durinn belched. "If he claimed a kiss from the Seer, I'd grant him a barrel of mead to take with him on his return to Scotland."

Rorik remained silent, studying her. Finally, he released his hold.

Fury boiled inside of Ragna. "Am I not worthy of more than a barrel of mead?"

"Would there have been more than one kiss?"

Ragna let loose her anger and slapped him with all her might. The man never flinched, yet his eyes flashed with those of his inner wolf.

Rorik rubbed his fingers over his cheek. "Then

your answer is nae?"

Hurt swelled uncomfortably and lodged like a stone in her throat. When she responded, her voice was tight with strain. "Never speak to me again, wolf."

As she departed past Rorik, his father's laughter filled her head. It took all her control to keep the burning tears from spilling forth. However, the moment she dashed into the cool enclosure of the trees, she let them fall freely down her cheeks.

Ragna tossed the apple far over the wall and into the dense thicket of trees below. A lone tear had trickled down her cheek, and she brushed away the moisture along with the agonizing memory from so long ago. She swallowed the bitter bile within her mouth. Turning around, she found her path to flee blocked by the massive form of a man.

Sweet Freyja! This wolf moves too silently. "Magnar."

"Did you ken many seek this view when they are troubled?" He crossed to the ledge and braced his forearms on the stone. "If you turn to the left, you enjoy the quiet of nature. Yet if you glance to your right, 'tis a great vantage point to look upon not only within the bailey but outward at any who are arriving at Steinn."

Drawing her cloak more firmly around her, she peered to the right. "I had not noticed."

He glanced sharply at her. "What troubles you, Seer?"

"Nothing," she lied, keeping her gaze fixed on the children running after one of the dogs.

"Have you spoken with Rorik?" he asked quietly.

"Aye." Ragna glanced at him. "He has decided to listen to my advice but will tend to his healing *after* his task for the king."

Magnar's brow creased. "Does he have time?"

"The Gods *may* favor him with more." She blew out a frustrated breath. "I cannot say for certain. I reckon he is already fighting the blinding pain."

"You have done all you are able for the man. If he chooses to wait, then 'tis now in the hands of the Gods." Magnar pushed away from the wall. "Furthermore, if he does die, I shall curse his wretched soul all the way to Valhalla."

Smiling sadly, Ragna offered, "You can add my words as well."

Laughter floated up on the cool breeze, and Ragna bent forward. Rorik led Hallgerd into the bailey and along the path leading to the gardens. The woman's hand rested securely in the crook of his arm. Each time he said something, she laughed in response. Though Ragna could not hear Rorik's words, she had nae doubt he was charming her with some story or commenting on her beauty. It was always the way of this wolf.

Her stomach clenched, and Ragna turned away. "Foolish man. Does he not ken Hallgerd is promised to David?"

Shrugging, Magnar crossed his arms over his chest. "As you ken, Rorik has his own set of rules."

She gaped at the man. "Both David and Jon have fierce tempers—"

"Which they inherited from their father, Harald," interrupted Magnar.

"Fortunately, I did not have to suffer his wrath, but I have witnessed the fury from my half-brothers when another man attempts to take their women."

Again, Magnar shrugged, only adding more to her

anger. All the wolves of Clan Sutherland abided by their own private rules. Even the barbarian who stood in front of her conducted business on his terms.

Turning away, Ragna departed the haven of the north tower.

****

When she first entered the hall, Ragna was prepared for an enjoyable meal and willing to relax. But all her plans were quashed when she noticed Hallgerd whispering to Rorik. They appeared to be lovers deep in conversation, and Ragna instantly searched the hall for David. After finding her half-brother not in attendance, she let out a sigh of relief and crossed to the opposite side of the hall. Before she had a chance to take a seat next to one of the other women, Elspeth reached for her arm.

"Please come sit with me at the main table," pleaded the woman. "We have not spoken much since your arrival."

Unable to think of an excuse to remain at this table, Ragna allowed the woman to guide her across the hall. "Where is your husband?"

"He is with Erik in the stables. They are tending to a new foal. David is with them as well. Your brother was intent on seeing our horses. Knowing my husband, I do not expect him to return until late."

Ragna gave her a smile. "I find your gardens and surrounding land soothing for speaking with the Goddess."

Elspeth beamed. "Have you been down by the river? I try to escape each morn for some quiet time." Her face took on a rosy glow when she added, "Magnar often finds me there."

"Aye," she responded slowly. "'Tis a lovely place." Images of Rorik's naked form on the boulder by the water flashed within her mind, and Ragna swallowed. As she'd thought before, he appeared to be a man chiseled from the Gods and something of a magician. Each night he slipped into her fragmented dreams, and each morn she shoved them aside.

Elspeth pulled out a chair, forcing Ragna to sit across from the man she tried desperately to avoid.

Rorik lifted his cup and stared at her from across the rim.

Shifting in her seat, she clasped her hands together. *What game are you playing at, wolf?*

His smile came slowly as if he heard the words within her mind. After taking a drink, he said, "Hallgerd has spoken of the strong arm of David. Can you confirm his strength, say, over mine?"

Hallgerd leaned against Rorik. "Surely Ragna has never seen her brothers in training. David mentioned she was not allowed in their father's home."

"Harald was a boar's ass," muttered Rorik and took a long draw from his cup.

Elspeth gasped. "Is this true, Ragna?"

Reaching for a jug of mead, Ragna filled her cup with the honeyed liquid. She took a sip to settle her nerves. Rarely did a conversation surround her or her father. The Seer always had the respect from others. To speak thusly was not acceptable. She fought the growing ire. "Hallgerd is correct," she confirmed, taking another sip of the cool liquid. "Furthermore, my mother had nae desire to send her only daughter into a home ruled by a tyrant of a man."

"A wise decision," Rorik acknowledged.

Hallgerd touched the man's arm. "I say your strength might be a challenge to David."

"Why don't we ask him," suggested Ragna, lifting her cup toward her half-brother striding with intent into the hall.

Hallgerd slipped her hand into her lap.

Ragna smiled inwardly as the woman's features paled. *Do not tempt the beasts within men, Hallgerd. Your guiles will only incite a war between them.*

David approached and took a seat next to Hallgerd. The woman tried to draw him into a conversation, but he ignored her touch and words. Worry creased his brow as he reached for a trencher filled with salmon and wild onions.

"How is the new foal?" asked Ragna.

After stabbing a piece of fish, he responded, "Weaker than normal." He turned to Elspeth. "Your husband will join us after he has determined the foal is gaining strength. And Erik has requested to keep him company."

Elspeth nodded slowly. "My thanks for your message. His concern for the foal is mine as well. We lost a colt, six months old, several months ago. Many of the horses were lost or became trapped in the fire from the attack. Each one birthed is now a blessing. My husband is seeking others to trade for more horses to add to Steinn."

David gave her a smile. "Aye, so he shared with us. Magnar has sent a message to Carlsten Castle for my brother to send four of our finest mares." He devoured the fish in one bite.

"This is good news!" exclaimed Elspeth.

Taking another stab at his fish, he added, "Your

brother—the young chieftain—made the suggestion. I see strength in this young warrior, and I ken Jon will as well. Erik has a sharp eye and listens. Moreover, he is not fearful of offering his own advice."

"I observed this the moment I met Erik," interjected Ragna. "His journey has already been fraught with grief and dangers. Many a young lad would cower. But this has strengthened him."

"I am in agreement with your insight," declared David while shoving another piece of fish into his mouth.

Hallgerd reached for the jug of mead. Instead of pouring some for David, she filled her cup. Giving Rorik a slight smile, she sipped her drink.

David regarded her coolly. "Is there a reason you drink heavily without eating the food our host has supplied us?"

She lifted her chin. A flash of fury shone briefly in her eyes. "I ate earlier."

"'Tis correct, David," remarked Rorik, placing his cup on the table. "I fetched some ripe berries from the bramble growing outside the castle, and she ate them with some of my cheese."

Hallgerd bent her head as she tried to stifle a giggle. "They were indeed delicious."

David's hand stilled, and he leveled a hard glare at Rorik. "Your manners are sorely lacking when it comes to my future *bride*."

"I take great care when it comes to my conduct with those who are intended to another." Rorik folded his arms over his chest and dared to wink at Hallgerd.

With a loud thud, David thrust his knife into the wooden table. Standing abruptly, he pointed a finger at him. "When the first light creases the morning sky, meet me on the hill above Steinn."

"Why not the lists?" asked Rorik.

The man's lip curled. "Let us keep the other *wolves* out of our fight, aye?"

He gave a shrug. "Your reason is sound."

David gave him a curt nod and reached for Hallgerd's hand.

The woman's shoulders slumped, but she complied.

After the couple departed, Ragna clucked her tongue in obvious disapproval. "Stirring the ire of a Maddadsson is not wise."

Rorik leaned his forearms on the table. His features were taut with strain. "Why do you care?" he asked softly.

Her heart screamed to say the words within, but her mind forbade her from speaking them aloud.

He continued to stare at her, waiting, until he shook his head in resignation and leaned back.

The sound of raucous laughter broke the moment as Erik came rushing in with Magnar following closely behind him.

Elspeth stood and embraced her husband. "Our new foal is faring better?"

"For now," Magnar confirmed, taking a seat next to his wife and reaching for a jug of mead.

Ragna picked at the food on her trencher with a fork. The conversation continued to flow as heavily as the mead, yet she remained silent during the remainder of the evening meal. Come the morn, she would cast the runes and prayed the Goddess would permit her to see a vision of Rorik's destiny.

If not, she feared death would claim the one man who once left her heart in shards of broken glass.

Chapter Five

Holding his sword up to the gray light of dawn, Rorik studied the steel. It was fashioned by the blacksmiths in the small town of *Kirkjuvágr*. The men there were known for their highly skilled work, forging and melding the iron into weapons worthy for any warrior. The blade was presented to him by his friend, Berulf the Axe, when he entered the brotherhood of the wolves for training on his fifteenth summer.

Rorik traced the engraving of the words down the length of the blade. Courage, strength, and honor—all sealed with a blessing from Odin.

A tremor of unease slithered down his back. He frowned and sought out his wolf. The beast continued to remain indifferent to his concerns. *Is this a warning? What do you sense?*

His wolf snapped at him and turned away.

He fought the bitterness and anger over his inner beast's refusal to answer Rorik's questions. Hissing out a curse, he resumed his focus on the impending fight with a certain man.

"Watch over my blade and my body, All Father. Give me strength, though let nae fatal blow come to my foe or me. 'Tis a battle of wits between two men." He brought the blade to his lips and pressed a kiss against the cold steel. "Hail, Odin," he whispered.

Footsteps rustled in the leaves behind him, and

Rorik smiled slowly. The male scent mixed with wild garlic filled his nostrils before he set eyes on the man. He picked up his shield from the ground.

Turning around, Rorik pointed his sword outward as David entered the clearing between the trees. "You are late."

The man snarled in return. "I found it difficult to leave the comfort of soft flesh."

Rorik arched a brow in amused contempt. Stirring David's ire proved interesting. How far could he provoke the man into making a reckless move? "Was the *soft flesh* Hallgerd or another?" He dared to take a step forward. "Or did you have *both* in your bed?"

"You bring dishonor to her name!" shouted David, lunging forward with his sword.

Too easy, mused Rorik as he swiftly stepped to the side and pounded his shield with the hilt of his sword. "Then by your actions I can conclude it was the soft flesh of Hallgerd? You should have remained silent about your carnal appetites."

"You are nothing but a wretched animal!"

"And a man who can entice *any* woman into his bed," added Rorik.

With a great roar, David charged forward, and the battle of swords began in earnest. Each man intent on inflicting bodily harm to the other. Groans and curses spewed forth from David as he leveled strong, precise blows on Rorik. He proved to be a worthy opponent with his strength, and Rorik relished the fight, maintaining his own skill against the man.

After delivering a fist into David's side, Rorik was rewarded with a kick to the knees, landing him onto the ground. He tumbled to the side and quickly righted himself. Charging forward, David lost his footing, and Rorik took advantage by knocking the blade from his opponent's hand with his shield.

David promptly withdrew the dirk at his belt and tossed it outward where it landed with a thud into Rorik's arm. The man then quickly scrambled through mud and leaves to retrieve his sword.

Rorik's roar of displeasure echoed in the morning air, along with the sound of his wolf's. In an attempt to rid himself of the pain, he called for the animal. The ground rumbled beneath him as pain seared into his body, leaving him unsteady.

The beast refused his pleas.

Rorik barely had time to yank the offensive blade free before David came charging at him with his sword. As he slumped to the ground and rolled to the side, Rorik narrowly avoided having his guts spilled from the slash of his foe's blade. Blood gushed forth from his arm as he crawled to the nearest tree. Gasping for breath, Rorik fought the burning agony coursing through his body.

"You are done, MacNeil! Finished," taunted the man. "Let this be a lesson if you ever come near Hallgerd again."

Lifting his sword in front of him, Rorik snarled. "*Never* tell me what to do. You shall fail. My orders do not come from you." His hand shook as he continued to hold his weapon upward.

David spat on the ground. "The next time I see you with Hallgerd, your life is mine to take. And since she is my future bride, I can give you that order."

Determined to be the winner in this sparring match of words, he countered, "Worried I can give her more pleasure?"

The man pointed his blade at Rorik's chest. "Do not tempt me to remove your heart where you sit bleeding, wolf."

With the last amount of strength he possessed, Rorik stood and dared to take a step against the man's outstretched blade. The cold bite of steel tore into his tunic as he stared into the heated gaze of his foe. "If you kill me, King William will have your neck *and* lands."

A flash of unease replaced the fury within David's eyes. He took a step back and then abruptly stormed away.

When the man vanished into the dense pines, Rorik finally slumped back down against the tree for support. Dizziness clouded his vision, and weariness crept into his body. He wiped a shaky hand over his brow and encountered moisture. Raising his hand in front of his face, he watched in stunned horror as blood oozed from the skin within his palm. "*Nae*," he muttered, clenching his fist.

He dropped his sword and closed his eyes. Searching—seeking for his beast.

"Where are you?" he rasped out. The effort cost him sorely, and he coughed, tasting bile mixed with the coppery tang of blood.

Within the murky recesses of his mind, Rorik could not find his wolf. The beast had retreated deep within his body, leaving him alone in agonizing torment.

Rorik judged death had finally come to claim him and his beast.

****

The wolf's howl of agony reached Ragna, piercing

her heart and head with cries of the animal's torment. She stumbled and dropped to her knees, losing control of the herbs she had recently gathered. The stench of blood came on the wind. Gasping for breath, she tried to maintain her focus. Pain overtook her senses, and she rocked back and forth as great spasms ripped through her body.

On a guttural cry, she dug her fingers into the muddy ground and closed her eyes. Calling forth the power of the land, she attempted to thwart the assault within her body with its soothing strength. With great effort, Ragna brought her breathing to a steady rhythm and slowly opened her eyes.

"*Rorik*," she called out on a choked sob.

She had no time to dwell on her connection with the man's wolf. They both were dying.

Lifting her hands upward, she blew across her palms. "Oda, *Oda*! Come forth."

The sparrowhawk let out a screech from a nearby tree and flew to her side.

Her hands shook as Ragna withdrew the small blade tucked within her belt at her side. After wiping the mud from her hand, she made a small incision across the tip of her finger. Blood pooled from her skin and spilled onto the ground. "Hear me, *Lady Freyja*. Do not take your warrior. Give me the strength to see through this hawk and find him so he can be healed."

Again, the ground rumbled beneath her, and the wind lifted the tendrils of hair around her face. Time slipped by as she waited for a message from the Goddess. When nothing came, she closed her eyes, daring to risk her life by not remaining patient. Chanting the ancient words of magic, Ragna prayed the

Goddess had heard her cry for help while she drew the magical signs of sight into the cool air.

"Go find the wolf, Oda," she whispered.

Her heart pounded fiercely in her chest while she opened her eyes. Clouds rumbled in the distance when the bird took flight.

Ragna stood slowly and blinked. The power filled her. Holding her palms upward, she flew within the mind of the bird. Over the meadow, across the river, and onward over the thick forest, she soared with Oda until they spotted the man lying at the base of a tree high on the hilltop. Blood and bruising appeared on his face and hands, and she swayed from the sight. "*Nae*."

Ragna took in the surrounding landscape, committing each detail to her memory. Certain she could lead the others to Rorik, she lowered her hands and severed the connection in her mind with the bird.

"Stay with him, Oda," she commanded. Fisting a hand to her mouth, she squelched the cry threatening to spill forth.

Nae time to dwell, nae time...

After retrieving her blade from the ground, Ragna took off running for Steinn.

When the entrance of the castle loomed before her, she shouted, "Where is Magnar?"

One of the guards gestured toward the stables, and she dashed across the bridge and into the bailey. Dogs barked in greeting, following her on her quest. Elspeth stepped along her path and tried to hamper her progress, but she shook her head at the woman.

"Need Magnar," she gasped.

Worried creased the woman's brow, and she dropped the basket she held.

The leader of the wolves emerged forth from the entrance of the stables in time to take a hold of Ragna. His firm grip steadied her uneasiness.

"Rorik?" he asked.

She nodded. "On…on a hilltop. Large standing stone."

Magnar directed his gaze at his wife. "Steinar is in the lists with the others. Have someone fetch him to the stables. Do so quietly as well."

"Aye, husband."

He returned his attention to Ragna. "Return to your chambers. I ken the place through the forest."

Ragna lifted her chin in defiance. "Nae. I shall go with you."

"We have a healer," he offered.

"Not one who kens the wisdom of the ancients as well as I do." She paused, trying to calm her thoughts and breathing. "Blood oozes from his skin. 'Tis the start of what I warned you about—his death."

Magnar released his hold on Ragna. His jaw clenched as he turned away and slipped inside the stables.

Rubbing her hands together to ward off the chill, she shoved aside the distress battling within her. No matter her feelings for Rorik, she could ill afford to allow her uneasiness to cloud any decision she'd make in regard to his healing.

Magnar strode forth, leading three horses outside.

She quickly stepped out of his path. "Which one is mine?"

He motioned to the sable-colored animal.

Quickly retrieving her blade again, she made long slits in both sides of her gown.

Magnar arched a brow in question.

"I have nae time to change." Shoving the blade back into the sheath belted at her waist, she quickly mounted the horse.

Steinar made long strides toward them. He glanced sharply at Ragna. "Do you have any healing herbs on you?"

Giving him a heated glare, she lifted the pouch on her belt. "As you well ken, I never travel without some kind of herbs."

After Steinar mounted his horse, he turned toward her. "You may tend to his wounds, but I have spoken with Rorik and will be his guardian while he heals in his wolf form."

"We waste time speaking. Let us go to him," she said in a strained voice.

Without waiting for either of the men, Ragna urged her horse forward through the bailey and across the bridge. Relief coursed through her knowing the man had appointed a guardian. She'd prayed Rorik had shifted into his wolf when they reached him.

Dark clouds hovered in the far distance. The scent of rain filled her as the lash of wind slapped furiously across her face. She held off the curse she wanted to spew forth and urged her horse faster. Relying on the images within her mind from earlier, Ragna traveled across the rugged landscape. Thunder clapped overhead, and she shook aside the doubts creeping into her thoughts.

As she approached the edge of the forest, the ground dipped into the trodden path.

Magnar stormed past her, with Steinar taking up position behind her. They kept at their steady pace, weaving around trees and ascending higher toward the injured man.

Oda's shrill cry reached her. They were near.

A tree limb smacked at her, and Ragna winced from the stinging pain. When the path opened before them, Magnar slowed his horse and dismounted.

"Steady," she urged her animal, coming to a halt before a large pine tree. After dismounting, she took off running toward Rorik.

"Nae!" bellowed Magnar, collapsing to the ground in front of the man.

Her heart hammered fiercely against her chest as she drew near. The scene before her stole the breath from her lungs. Ragna shoved a fist to her mouth to squelch the scream lodged within. Blood pooled from his skin onto the ground—from his face, hands, and most likely other parts of his body.

"Does he live?" asked Steinar in a hushed tone.

While she ignored the man's question, she tugged at the pouch on her belt. Fury rose within Ragna. She refused to let this warrior die. "Move aside, Magnar!"

The man gave her a glaring look but promptly did as she ordered.

Crouching down in front of Rorik, she fought the wave of uneasiness. With a shaky hand, Ragna placed her palm over the man's chest and waited. Despite the slow heartbeat, the man continued to live. On a sigh, she lifted her gaze toward Magnar. "He lives, though barely."

The leader of the wolves cast his hand outward. "Can you save him?"

Her lips thinned, and she shrugged. Uncertainty filled her answer, and she turned away from him. She could offer no words of assurance.

Ragna's fingers trembled while she moved carefully over his body, trying to determine if the man had any other injuries. *There is so much blood.* When her hand slid upward on his left arm, she encountered the wound and let out a hiss.

Ragna quickly removed her small blade from the belt at her waist. Again, she sliced away portions of her gown and handed the scraps to Magnar. With steady movements, she cut through the fabric of Rorik's tunic. After securing her blade, she drew forth the herbs from her pouch and pressed them along the jagged flesh. Not one word of complaint passed from Rorik's lips while she tended to him. How she longed for him to open his eyes and spout a curse at her. She'd give anything to see the fire in his eyes, even if they sparked hatred toward her.

She held her hand outward to Magnar for the bits of her gown. "Hear me, Goddess, bind the wound and staunch the blood flow. Allow this warrior to heal."

While she continued to chant her words to the Goddess, Ragna bound his arm with the cloth. She placed a hand over his heart, hoping to see any change from the man.

When the first drop of rain splattered across her cheek, she pulled back. "Storm is here."

Magnar glanced at Steinar. "Help me get him onto my horse."

Without a word, the man went and lifted Rorik from the ground.

Magnar took a hold of her elbow to assist her to standing. His steady gaze held hers for a few moments. She knew the leader of the wolves had questions, yet she had no answers to give him.

He gave her a curt nod and went to help Steinar secure Rorik over the horse's back.

After wiping her bloody hands across her gown, she swallowed the bitterness threatening to heave forth through her lips. Never before had her attention drifted. Furious for allowing her emotions to sway her focus, she bit her lip. Ragna feared if this happened again her power to heal would surely slip away into the mists.

Even as she studied Rorik's limp body over the horse, tears stung her eyes.

With an indrawn breath, Ragna forced the feelings for this man far into the deepest region of her heart. On the exhale, she straightened and went to her horse.

Chapter Six

When they arrived at Steinn, Ragna rushed past a stunned Hallgerd. The woman gaped at her like a forlorn fish at the entrance, and Ragna had no time to stop and explain her appearance to the woman nor Rorik's.

Once inside, the torches on the wall flickered, casting ugly shadows along her path. Whispering a word of protection, she continued onward. *Stay focused and calm. Help me, Freyja. Banish those who desire to come for the warrior. Now is not his time, I beg you, Goddess.*

She steadily moved along the corridor and made her way to her chamber. There was no time to change out of her soiled and torn gown. Quickly retrieving her small chest of healing herbs and salves, Ragna dashed back out.

Her steps faltered, and she leaned against the wall. Hysterical laughter fought for a scream within her throat. "Where did they take you, Rorik? I do not ken where I am going."

Without waiting for another to assist her in her search, Ragna proceeded to start opening doors. Her hand paused on the bolt of one of the doors. The lone howl of a wolf pierced her thoughts, and she whipped her head around half-expecting the animal to be behind her.

Ragna retreated farther along the corridor following the sound within her mind.

Light flickering from a partially closed wooden door led her forward. Her fingers grasped the cold steel, and she opened the heavy oak door. Golden light spilled out into the corridor. When she went inside the chamber, her gaze drifted to the man spread out on a massive bed. Magnar was taking great care in stripping the torn tunic from Rorik's body.

She glanced around the expanse of the chamber. Noting a table by the arched window, Ragna crossed the room and placed her chest down. Picking up a jug, she sniffed the contents and grimaced. What she required was fresh water not sour ale.

Turning toward Steinar, she handed the jug to him. "I require fresh water to mix a healing tonic along with more betony. I dread he won't be strong enough to fight a fever."

The man stepped from the shadows of the room. As he removed the item from her outstretched hand, he whispered, "Why has he not changed into his wolf?"

Bitterness clawed at her. She had warned Rorik. Told him the consequences if he continued on this quest and not permit his wolf to heal his wounds.

Ragna glanced at the bed. "Rorik holds the answer, not I."

"Did you not see this in a vision?" he snapped.

Returning her attention to Steinar, she glared at the man. "He refused my warning. As with all the wolves, you tend to seek your own wisdom most of the time."

"Enough!" ordered Magnar, coming to her side. "Fetch the Seer some water."

She watched as Steinar quickly departed, and then

she faced Magnar. “This is not my fault.”

The man’s features softened. He gripped her elbow and led her toward the bed. “Do what you can for Rorik. I ken you advised him. He chose not to listen.” Magnar dropped his hand. “I sense there is more damage within the man.”

Confused, Ragna asked, “What are you saying?”

He shrugged. “For many moons I have sensed his inner self ebbing away. He has spoken nothing of what ails him.” Magnar pounded his fist against his chest, adding, “But I ken ’tis growing and rotting within Rorik. Even my wolf can smell the sickness within the man.”

Ragna’s shoulders slumped. “Along with the demons he battles within his mind.”

“But they are battling inside his body. His wolf has abandoned him. In time, both will die.”

“Then I must do all I can for him,” she added softly. “Any physical wounds cannot heal if the mind is damaged.”

The leader of the wolves nodded slowly, rubbing a hand over his chin. “The blood stops at his waist. Do you ken why?”

“I have heard it mentioned the sickness travels from the head slowly down the body. This is only the beginning.”

“Have you sought out the runes?” he asked.

She laughed bitterly. Countless times, she’d begged wisdom from the Goddess when she tossed out her runes. The response continued to be the same. Nothing. Digging her fingers into her gown, Ragna responded, “You would ken more than my runes.”

Steinar returned with a jug of water and placed it

on the table. "I shall stand guard outside the door. Inform me when he shifts into his wolf."

"I fear that day will never come," she whispered as sorrow spilled into her voice.

Magnar placed a firm hand on her shoulder. His strength seeped into her. Ragna lifted her head to meet his gaze. "I trust you to heal him, Seer."

"And if I cannot?"

"Did we not agree to curse him all the way to Valhalla?"

Quickly turning away, Ragna tried to hide her emotions from the man. "He will not die." Yet the words she spouted rang hollow inside her. She gave the man one more passing glance and went to the table to spread out her herbs and salves.

"Though I am curious, *Ragna*. How did you ken Rorik was in danger and where to find him? You would have nae reason to venture far away from the castle. Was it a vision?"

Her hand hovered above a small vessel. Did she dare tell the man the truth? Until she sought her own answers, a lie ached to be released. However, being dishonest, especially to the leader of the mighty Wolves of Clan Sutherland, was a risk she did not wish to undertake.

She met his intense study of her from across the room. "I heard the cry of his wolf."

The man arched a brow but refrained from asking any more questions. He held her gaze and then gave her a curt nod. Quietly, Magnar departed the chamber.

Ragna let out a long sigh as the door closed softly behind him. "Either the man does not believe my words, or he has chosen not to offer any more insight of knowledge."

Gathering some bandages and the jug of water, she went to Rorik's side. "Goddess, help me to heal this man."

Ragna worked in silence for the next several hours tending not only to the wound on Rorik but also his skin, wiping the blood that continued to ooze forth. Each time she thought her task complete, more blood appeared. Her fingers trembled as she took the damp cloth mixed with herbs across his skin. Her feelings betrayed her, and she found herself studying each scar and marking on the man. Aye, she had heard the whispers spoken around the fires about the battles the Dark Seducer fought. Many times she grew curious until one of the men would hasten to add Rorik's conquest in the bedchamber after a battle.

She brushed a dark lock of hair away from his face. Even in his deep slumber, the man captivated her. "Will you not wake, Rorik from the House of MacNeil? What I would not give to hear biting words from your lips," she whispered while she drew her hand back.

After dropping the cloth back into the bowl on the small table, she reached for her wooden jar of salve. Dipping one finger inside, she swiped out a small amount. Carefully, Ragna traced a pattern of healing in a circular motion across his forehead, down his cheek, and over his jaw.

"From the air, I seek to banish the sickness. From the land, I seek to bind your wounds—stitch and mend. From the fire, let the burning flames destroy the plague that consumes you. From the north, remember who you are, Rorik MacNeil."

Ragna bent near his ear and uttered softly,

"Remember your binding vows to both—Odin and your wolf. Do not cross the void into the next. Face your demons and fight, warrior."

With one final smudge of the salve over his heart, she drew back and waited for any sign from the man. Returning the jar to the table, she pursed her lips in thought and then hastily gathered more herbs from her pouch.

Walking to the hearth, Ragna held her hand out toward the flames. "Goddess of healing, seal this chamber as I work to mend this warrior. Let nae other come to claim him from across the otherworld." Tossing the herbs into the fire, she added, "From north, east, south, and west, I, Ragna, fasten and protect those within this room."

The flames hissed, and tendrils of smoke drifted into the room, weaving their way to the injured warrior.

Her skin tingled with the power skimming across her face and down her body. She bowed her head. The Goddess had heard her plea.

Now she must wait.

****

When the first star shone in the evening sky, Ragna reckoned she could do no more for Rorik. His skin burned with fever. The bleeding had lessened giving her time to ponder what else to do for him. Her healing salves and herbs slowed the process, but she did not ken for how long. A day, perchance two? Even the magic she surrounded Rorik with would eventually leave the man.

Flames from the hearth snapped. She wiped her hand over her brow, slick with sweat, and rose from her chair by Rorik's side.

Wandering to the arched window, Ragna stared at the landscape below. A cool breeze brushed against her cheek, and she inhaled sharply. Closing her eyes, she let the scent from the land fill her, along with the sea breezes.

The door to the chamber opened. Glancing over her shoulder, she smiled weakly. Elspeth stepped inside carrying a trencher of food and a fresh gown over her arm.

The woman's smile eased the strain from Ragna. "How kind of you."

"You should let another tend to Rorik while you seek some rest and change out of your soiled gown," suggested Elspeth.

Moving away from the window, Ragna shook her head slowly. "Until the bleeding stops I do not trust another. Your healers do not hold the wisdom of the ancients."

Elspeth set the trencher down on the table and held out the gown to Ragna. "I have offered up prayers to our Lord. I hope you do not find fault if I offer my own."

Ragna understood the woman followed the path of the new religion. Once, she had heard Gunnar speak of the healing tales of this man they called Christ. He performed great deeds while he walked the land and counseled the people.

Reaching for the gown, Ragna nodded. "If your God considers Rorik worthy of your prayers, continue to offer them for his healing."

A serving woman entered, followed by a young lad. Each brought jugs of fresh water. They quickly placed them on the already crowded table, taking the empty ones and departing as silently as they entered. Another lass dashed inside the chamber and handed Elspeth a small package. She gave the girl a wink before she darted back out.

Elspeth approached Ragna and took her hand. Placing the package within her palm, she disclosed, "'Tis rose-scented soap. At least bathe and change into a fresh gown. What if Rorik wakes and finds you in this manner?"

Ragna snorted and took the offering. "Then my task here is finished, and I can leave for *Orkneyjar*."

The woman folded her arms across her chest. "Are you certain you would leave him in the care of another once he wakes?"

Finding the woman's questions annoying, Ragna went to the table. While searching for a clean bowl to dump the fresh water into she fought the growing ire inside her. She could sense Elspeth's gaze boring into her back.

"There is fresh water and a bowl in your chamber. I shall stay and wait for you to return," suggested Elspeth softly.

Glancing over her shoulder, Ragna gave the woman a weak smile. "I only require a few moments."

Elspeth lowered herself into the chair by Rorik. She pointed a finger at the man. "If he wakes, I will scream for you."

She burst out in laughter, along with Elspeth. They both glanced at Rorik. Not even their outburst had stirred the man.

Ragna hurried out of the chamber. Her steps hastened along the dimly lit corridor and to her own chamber. Dashing inside, she closed the door behind her and placed the clean gown on her bed. She stripped the soiled and tattered gown from her body, letting it tumble to the ground.

Going to the table, Ragna dumped the water from one of the jugs into a large bowl and proceeded to wash the grime from her skin. The scent of roses assailed her senses, and she gave silent thanks to whoever thought of mixing such a potent flower in the soap. Most times, she bathed in the stream near her home. Her soaps were a mixture of herbs and the wildflowers that covered the ground.

Within moments, images of long ago tumbled forth within her mind.

"You are hurt," she exclaimed, moving past the group of angry men and coming to a halt by Rorik's side. The blade had slashed along his back, ripping apart his tunic.

"Nae," argued Rorik, glancing over his shoulder. "Simply a scratch."

One of the men gave him a scathing look in passing. While he spouted a curse, the man shoved a fist into the air.

"May the Gods look down favorably on your house, old man!" shouted Rorik.

"Why did they draw their weapons?" asked Ragna while inspecting the wound. "You are fortunate it was not deeper." She tugged on his arm. "Follow me."

He waved her away dismissively. "There is nae need."

"Do not be foolish," she protested, not willing to let go of the stubborn man.

"Where are you taking me, Seer?"

How she hated when he used that tone with her.

Her mind told her to drop her hold on him and walk away. Better to let his wolf heal him than use her precious herbs and magic to bind the wound.

However, her body overrode the decision, and she continued to lead him toward the stream. As they approached, Ragna released her hand and pointed to a fallen log. "This will not take long. Then you can return to your life of battles."

The man blew out a frustrated sigh and slumped onto the log.

Withdrawing a small cloth from the pouch at her side, Ragna went to the stream and dipped it into the cool water. By the time she returned, Rorik had removed his tunic. Heat instantly blossomed within her body. The man held her captive with his gaze. Surely, he must have been carved from the Gods. No man should be so perfect, even if magic surrounded him.

Water trickled down her arm, dripping onto the ground.

"Are you unwell, Ragna?" His question was laced with mirth.

The way he uttered her name—slow and hushed—made her body heat more. She blinked and hastened around to his back.

Ragna tried to calm her breathing while she focused on cleansing the wound. How could she have forgotten her vow to banish this man from her feelings? I should have let you bleed.

Rorik inhaled sharply. "You smell like the spring wildflowers that grow in abundance, filling the meadows with their sweetness."

She shifted her stance. Do not fall into his trap. "I smell like any other woman who uses the flowers in soaps for bathing," she countered. "Hold out your hand."

Shaking his head slowly, he complied, adding, "You are the only woman that smells like you have bathed in the land. 'Tis heady, Ragna."

Dropping the soiled cloth into his hand, Ragna then removed a small bundle of herbs mixed with her healing salve. Doing her best to finish her task so she could move away from the man, she asked, "Are you not going to tell me why those men are angry with you?"

"Untruths were spoken, and I challenged them to take them back."

"What untruths?"

He turned his head to the side to look at her. "They claimed fire will cause a wolf to run in the other direction."

Studying the side of his rugged face, she yearned to trace a path from his forehead down the broad slope of his nose and across his full lips. Her fingers tightened on her bundle, causing the salve to seep into her hand. "But do not all wolves fear the flames from a fire?"

His mouth curved into a slow smile. "Aye, you ken they do." He tapped a finger to his chest. "Yet I will not confess to anyone, especially within the hearing of my wolf."

Ragna's lips twitched in mirth. She smoothed the salve over the wound. "So, you argued against to the point of stirring the fury from these men." Stepping around in front of Rorik, she then removed the cloth from his hand. "Often times, 'tis better to remain silent."

"Like Magnar?" The man burst out in laughter.

"Nae!"

She put her hands up in surrender and went to the stream. After soaking the bundle and cloth in the water until they were clean, she deposited them back into her pouch. Rinsing her hands one final time, Ragna returned to his side to make sure the bleeding had lessened.

"Have another from the brotherhood check for redness or swelling."

His brow furrowed as if he wanted to say something.

Giving him a curt nod, she made to leave.

Rorik reached out and grasped her hand. His fingers were warm and rough as he drew her near him. "Why do you care, Ragna?"

There it was again. Her name rolled off his tongue—the sound skimming over her skin.

Unsure how to respond, she shrugged.

He lowered his head to her wrist and inhaled. "'Tis a wonderful scent."

When he finally released her hand, Ragna darted away from the dangerous warrior.

Ragna shook her head, forcing the image away. Placing her hands onto the table, she blinked several times. Even though it was only a memory, she could feel the heat of the man's breath against her wrist. She lifted her hand and placed it against her racing heart. "Why does he torment me, Goddess? We are not meant to be. The man hates me, so why am I plagued by him?"

She bit her lip, tasting blood, and went to her bed. Frustration seethed inside her while she stepped into her gown. The flames snapped—an echo of her mood.

When one of the logs crackled and split in half, Ragna turned toward the hearth. Her eyes widened with the knowledge, and she fled from the chamber.

Ragna charged inside Rorik's chamber toward the table. Grabbing one of the jugs of water, she crossed to the blazing fire within the hearth, tossing the water onto the flames.

"What are you doing?" asked Elspeth in a shocked tone, coming to her side.

Handing her the empty jug, Ragna went to retrieve the other one. She tossed the water into the dwindling flames. Turning toward the stunned woman, she replied, "'Tis only a guess, but I have heard wolves do not like fire. Rorik's wolf will not emerge if the room is blazing."

"But Magnar must ken this wisdom, aye?"

Ragna shrugged, uncertain of anything. "Perchance your husband's wolf is different. If Rorik's wolf is dying, he might fear the burning heat and light."

Elspeth took the other jug from her hand. "Then we need more."

Ragna nodded and turned toward the bed. She went to Rorik's side and rested her hand against his chest. "If you can hear me, *wolf*, I shall make sure all is safe for you to come forth."

In the far distance, Ragna swore she heard the soft whisper of a wolf's howl.

Chapter Seven

One day bled into the next, and Rorik's wolf had not shown himself. Worry infused Ragna. During the first night, she kept a constant vigil at his side, ready to command Steinar to stand guard by the bed. When the new morn arrived, there was nothing.

Ragna wanted to scream and shake the injured man.

"Stubborn man," she hissed into the cold, dark chamber.

Hugging her arms around her body, she went to the window. Brittle rain slashed along the land, and she shivered more. Watching the others move about their chores within the bailey, she leaned against the stone arch for support. Weariness seeped into her with each passing hour Rorik remained unmoving.

Her gaze drifted upward. "What more can I do, Goddess? Even the runes do not speak to me. I beg you to hear my plea, though there is something else I have not done." Ragna rubbed the heel of her palm over her heart. "A piece of him lives in me. Many times I have tried to banish the feeling." She swallowed the fear lodged within her throat. "Bring him back…to me. I ken our lives are in separate countries, but a part…a part of me shall break if you take him away."

Never had she confessed her thoughts about the man aloud. Would Odin strike her down with lightning for refusing Rorik a seat at his mighty table? What if Odin was calling him forth now? The elite guards belonged to him and not her. She listened with intent, yet only the rain mixed with the other voices drifted by her.

On a sigh, Ragna lowered her head and turned around.

Did her vision deceive her? After scrubbing her eyes with her hands, she focused on the bed. There spread out in the middle of the furs was Rorik's wolf staring at her. His silver fur glistened in the early morning light, and she dared to take a step toward the animal. Never had she witnessed the man's wolf. His shoulders were massive, along with the length of his body. It was a wonder how many spoke in respect *and* dread after witnessing these wolves.

The animal followed her movements as Ragna took hesitant steps forward. She halted a few spaces from the edge of the bed. Smiling, she clasped her hands together. A lone tear trickled down her face. "You have found your way back, my friend."

The wolf studied her intently and then yawned. He lowered his head onto his outstretched paws.

Doing her best to compose herself, Ragna brushed aside the tear from her cheek and strode across the room. Quietly opening the door, she noted Steinar rooted at his place on the chair. His gaze lifted to meet hers.

Smiling fully, she nodded. "He has shifted into the wolf."

"'Tis about bloody time," he muttered. Rising from his position, Steinar stripped his tunic from his body. He stepped past Ragna and entered the chamber.

With a low growl, the wolf lifted his head and gnashed his teeth at the intrusion.

The man halted. Confusion marred Steinar's brow. He knelt on one knee. "Hear me, friend. I am here on orders from Rorik as your appointed guardian." He tapped a fist against his chest. "My wolf is ready to stand guard."

The wolf continued his protest while baring his teeth at the man. He attempted to rise from the furs.

"What is wrong?" asked Ragna in a hushed tone.

"Uncertain." Steinar made to stand. Fisting his hands on his hips, he glanced at her. "You can leave. There is nothing more for you to do. Go seek your rest."

She would not be dismissed so easily. Ignoring the man's order, Ragna went past him and stood at the end of the bed.

"Nae, 'tis unwise to get near his wolf, Seer," warned Steinar.

Ragna regarded the wolf but made no effort to draw nearer. Within moments, the animal sprawled back down. Her presence appeared to have calmed him, and he lowered his head once again onto his outstretched legs.

Steinar blew out a curse while scrubbing a hand over his face. "An interesting fate has been decreed by the wolf."

Ragna frowned. His words left her unsteady. "What do you mean?"

He dipped his head toward her. "You have been chosen by the wolf to be his guardian."

Rendered speechless, she took a step back. Uncertain over this new role, she stared at the man.

Steinar turned to leave. "I shall inform Magnar that Rorik has shifted and is now under the protection of the Seer."

Ragna glanced at the wolf and then at the retreating form of the man. She hurried across the room and grabbed Steinar's arm. "Wait."

The wolf howled in anger. The fierceness of the cry startled her, and Ragna released her hold.

The look Steinar gave her burned right through her. The color of his eyes changed to those of his wolf.

"First lesson, *Seer*, never venture outside of this room while the wolf is connected to you. Even in his weakened condition, he can wreak destruction on those he considers the enemy. Second, he has acknowledged you and nae other. He kens I am a wolf but will allow only you to remain in this chamber."

"You will leave me alone? With him?" protested Ragna, adding quickly, "How long will the healing last?"

The man smirked. "Somewhere inside the wolf is Rorik. I am certain he wishes you nae harm, so I judge his wolf feels the same. 'Tis evident by his selection of you for his guardian."

Ragna snorted and looked away. "We are not talking about the same man. Rorik once cursed me to sit at the table of the mighty beast, *Nidhogg,* and allow the dragon to feast on my flesh."

"What did you do to cause such an outrage from him?"

How could she explain the constant battle of words between her and Rorik? It was always thus between them. Watching over his wolf was far more settling on her nerves than seeing the man.

Returning her attention to Steinar, she responded, "I told him he was the ugliest man in the brotherhood, and I would rather kiss an eel than his lips."

The man tried to contain his mirth but failed miserably. Shaking his head, he departed the chamber. Pausing at the door, he glanced over his shoulder at her. "The wolf *and* man have chosen well, *Seer*. As for your earlier question regarding the healing process, 'tis entirely up to the wolf. He is now in control."

Ragna collapsed onto the bed. What possessed her to share her disputes with Rorik to him? She wiped a hand across the back of her neck in a feeble attempt to ease the tension.

Sweeping her gaze toward the massive animal on the furs, she found sleep beckoned her to join him.

"You do ken I am not a great warrior, so if someone storms the chamber, I might not be able to protect you. However, I am good with tossing out a blade."

Black eyes etched with silver throughout studied her.

"Would you mind if I rested? All of this has left me troubled."

The wolf rose slowly and moved away from Ragna, giving her more room to lie down.

Her mouth gaped open and then snapped shut. "You ken my words," she whispered. *Do not misjudge the magic within these animals, especially woven from Odin.*

Scooting off the bed, Ragna went and retrieved her dirk. Quickly returning, she lowered herself onto her side on top of the furs. Unsure if she should keep her back to the wolf or the door, she decided it best to face anyone who may enter the chamber.

Her nerves skittered in the darkened room. Each time she closed her eyes, she darted them open and peered over her shoulder. The wolf had no issue with finding his slumber, and she watched the steady rhythm of his breathing.

Heaving a long sigh, she turned away from him. Within moments, Ragna surrendered to the dark embrace of sleep.

****

Rorik trudged along the bank of the river following the sound of music and boisterous laughter. Twice, his steps stumbled, as if someone had called out his name. When he looked over his shoulder, nothing but darkness clouded his vision. He resumed his focus on the path in front of him, trying to recall how he came upon this place. Or what led him to travel without his horse, weapons, or even a tunic.

Pausing, he took in the ebb and flow of the water. He judged the river not too deep, so he'd be able to swim the distance. Should he cross here? Or should he make his way toward the merry gathering? Was there something he was required to do first?

Hesitant on making any decision, Rorik bent and retrieved a rock. Tossing it outward, he watched as it splashed into the river creating a beauty of glistening ripples. The water always soothed him. It allowed him to dwell on nothing else but the sound. He yearned to strip his trews and dive into the river.

"Why am I here?" he muttered with frustration.

"Are you fraught with too many decisions, Rorik from the House of MacNeil?"

Stunned to hear the melodic voice behind him, he

lost his footing and fell into the water.

After wiping the water from his eyes, he stood and glared at the stunning woman sitting on a white horse. "Who are you, and how do you ken my name?"

She arched a fine brow. "I ken all who journey along this river."

Taking in her appearance, he noted she appeared more a warrior than any woman he had encountered. Her gown barely covered her creamy thighs, and a sword was strapped to her back. The golden shield attached to her horse glinted in the sunlight streaming through the thick canopy of trees. Had she been studying him and his movements? Was she from another clan farther north?

Aiming her spear at him, she asked, "You have not answered my question."

Rorik held his arms out wide and smiled as the water lapped gently against his legs. "Do you always confront travelers with a weapon aimed at their chest? Or is it just men? As you can see, I carry nae weapons."

Her mouth twitched in humor while she lowered her spear. "Even as you walk the path to *his* table, your words carry those of the Dark Seducer."

His smile faltered, and a chill seized his bones. He stepped out of the water. "Who are *you*?"

The woman tilted her head to the side as if listening to someone.

"I journey with those on their final path, especially when they continue to question why they are here."

Doing the best to temper his growing ire, Rorik fisted his hands on his hips. "Explain!"

Her laughter surrounded him. "You are the first, Rorik from the House of MacNeil, to give me an order.

Nevertheless, I do not take orders from your kind."

"*My kind*?" He looked at her in disgust. Obviously, the woman hated all men. Therefore, he'd be unable to charm her.

"It is an easy question to answer, warrior."

He grumbled a curse. "Have you suddenly forgotten my name?"

"If you speak your questions aloud, an answer may pose itself on the breeze."

With his sense of direction twisted, he returned to the river's edge. If he ignored her, perchance she would take her leave. He had no desire to banter words with her. Waiting for several heartbeats, he stole a glance over his shoulder.

She continued to study him from atop her horse—a horse with a golden mane. Why did he not notice this detail before?

Rorik turned fully around and faced the warrior maiden. "If I am to join the feasting at the table of *All Father*, I am without my sword. I have nae wish to bring dishonor."

"Is this your decision, Rorik? You desire to journey to the hall of warriors and take your place at Odin's table? If so, your weapon should *already* be in your hand."

Burning pain surfaced behind his eyes, and Rorik massaged his temples to ease the agony. He found the maiden's words troubling. "When did I die? From what battle?" he demanded in a terse tone, trying to bring forth any memories.

"I made no mention of your death."

"Then why am I here?" he pressed.

The maiden shrugged. "Only you can answer this

question, Rorik."

"Why can't you help me?"

"Because it is not my path. As I have stated, I merely keep pace with you until your questions have been resolved."

Outraged, Rorik waved a hand dismissively. "Then leave. I shall seek my answers elsewhere."

A light breeze lifted the hair from the nape of her neck. She gazed upward and closed her eyes. On a smile, she opened them slowly. "Odin favors stubborn warriors, but the doors to his hall are now closing. Your quest is not finished. Either sit and dwell a while by the river until you are no more than bones or be the man *and* wolf you were destined to be."

Her words challenged him, and Rorik dared to take a step toward her. "Can you at least tell me why I am here?"

The maiden shook her head solemnly. "You chose this path. Find the reason for withdrawing from your world—your fate."

"I cannot remember," he confessed quietly. Even his memories of this wolf she spoke about troubled him. Did they travel together? *I should remember something.*

The laughter lessened in the far distance, and Rorik turned toward the sound. Part of him yearned to join them. He'd no recollection of the events that brought him here, and this troubled him. Perchance, he should sit briefly by the soothing water.

"Do not dwell in that direction, Rorik from the House of MacNeil. Often the darkness is where the answer is hidden. Return and seek another path."

Snapping his attention to her, Rorik watched as she gave a nudge to her horse and retreated through the forest.

Stillness surrounded him.

When he dared to glimpse into the darkness, Rorik found the eyes of a wolf staring back at him. Instinctively, he placed his palm over his heart.

The steady beat of man and wolf greeted him. He gasped—his eyes widening with the wisdom. On an exhale, Rorik smiled and closed his eyes.

Chapter Eight

Warmth invaded Rorik's limbs, along with the scent of wildflowers. The shrill cry of a bird brought him more out of his deep slumber, yet he found himself unable to open his eyes. Heaviness rooted within his body as he attempted to move. Even the mere action of flexing his fingers proved daunting. He struggled against succumbing to the dark abyss.

With calm breaths, he allowed the slow process of his body to become fully awake. Images of what happened to him slammed into his mind, even the ones of Odin's warrior. Did death almost claim him? Did he somehow yearn for death's embrace?

His earlier actions were foolish and almost took the life of him and his beast.

Searching inward, he immediately found his wolf. The animal regarded him, and Rorik smiled. Peace settled inside him, understanding the beast had healed his wound.

A soft snore escaped near him, and he tensed. His guardian? Steinar?

Nae. He would have sensed the wolf nearby.

Rorik attempted to swallow. His tongue stuck to the inside of his dry mouth. Unable to call out, he focused on strengthening his body. With each moment that ticked by, a surge of healing seeped into him. Alertness replaced the weariness. His breathing became strong and steady.

His wolf rose to a sitting position.

Slowly, Rorik opened his eyes and took in the shadows. In his blurred vision, he had to blink again.

Ragna.

The beauty lying next to him stole the breath from his lungs. Her hair had come unbound from her braids—the ebony tresses framing her face and body. Curled up on her side facing him, she had placed one of her hands near him. Rorik observed her sleeping form. Dark lashes graced her ivory skin, and he became captivated.

Yet why was she here? In his bed?

How many nights had he craved to have Ragna in his arms? He had buried those feelings to the darkness many moons ago when she first spurned his advances. Now to wake and find her near him caused his wall of defense to crack. Feelings he had banished long ago surfaced with ferocity. He grew weary of the bantering of words with her.

Can we not start anew? Would you consider giving me another chance?

His fingers twitched, longing to brush one of them against her skin. With tremendous effort, he raised his hand slowly and touched a lock of her hair. "So…*soft*," he announced in a garbled tone.

Her eyelids fluttered open and grayish-blue jewels peered back at him. Rorik found himself enchanted whenever he stared into her eyes. He considered them rare gems, especially on the woman lying next to him. Others feared the intensity of this woman's eyes, but not Rorik. Never.

His heart started to beat rapidly against his chest as

if beating for the first time. If only he had the strength to bring her into his arms.

Ragna's face transformed into a bright smile—one he had not been granted in such a long time. "You have returned to us," she whispered.

"Aye," he acknowledged, though his meaning was for her alone. He had returned to her.

Ragna removed herself from the bed.

Rorik felt the loss keenly. Unable to let out a protest, he followed her with his eyes.

She quickly returned with a cup and placed it gently against his cracked lips. "Drink," she urged, adding, "'Tis water."

Cool liquid seeped through his sore lips, and into his parched mouth. After taking as much as he could, he gave her a weak smile.

He watched as she placed the cup on a nearby table and picked up a small wooden jar.

"This will help to soothe and heal your lips," she explained, bending over him.

When her finger traced the salve over his lips, Rorik let out a moan—more from the pleasure of her touch.

Withdrawing, she gasped, "Forgive me."

"Nae," he mumbled. "More."

Again, she gave him a smile and continued to anoint his lips with her healing touch. Once finished, Ragna inspected his arm. "Your wound has healed nicely. 'Tis barely a scar."

Rorik studied her under hooded eyes. Her every movement, sound, and scent spiraled inside of him, bringing forth the lustful beast. Clenching his hands at his sides, he allowed her to continue. He found his strength greatly improved, and when a lock of her hair trailed across his chest, he inhaled sharply.

Ragna drew back. Bright red splotches stained her cheeks. She placed the jar on the table. Clasping her hands together, she straightened. "I shall go fetch some broth for you." She bit her lip as if she wanted to impart something else and then suddenly turned and fled across the chamber.

"Ragna?" He burned with so many questions. However, only one thought he wished to profess to her.

Her hand stilled on the door's bolt. Without glancing his way, she responded, "Aye, Rorik?"

"My thanks for your kindness," he whispered, his voice catching in his throat.

Turning around slowly, she gaped at him, but not a word came forth from those lips he yearned to taste.

This time, Rorik smiled fully as she darted out of the chamber like a frightened mare.

Steinar appeared in the entrance, making no effort to enter. "'Tis good to see you have healed."

Rorik gave him a slow nod. Before he had a chance to say anything, the man promptly left.

His gaze drifted around the room, noting the hearth barren of any heat and no lit candles. A trail of light crept in through the windows, along with a cold draft. He frowned, unable to fathom why the chamber was lacking in warmth and light.

You have many answers to give me, Ragna.

As his strength grew, Rorik stretched out his limbs. After finding no more stiffness, he tried to sit up more fully against the pillows. Beads of sweat broke out along his forehead, but he was determined to make the effort. His wolf moved forward within him, giving him more added power. Satisfied with what he had achieved, Rorik allowed his body to relax.

When Ragna returned, she halted at the entrance. The trencher of a promised meal slopped over the sides as she stared at him.

"I find I am gaining more strength," he admitted.

Magnar coughed behind Ragna. "Then you can find the effort to pull the fur over your body. I doubt the Seer needs to see your manhood."

Rorik glanced down and grimaced. In his feeble attempt to move himself into a better position, the furs had traveled to his thighs. He bit out a soft curse and flung the coverings over his cock.

A flushed Ragna turned and handed the trencher to Magnar. "Need more fresh water."

The man chuckled softly. Making long strides through the chamber, Magnar loomed over him. "Can you manage to feed yourself?"

"Aye," he grumbled, letting the man place the trencher across his thighs.

Rorik kept his focus on the broth while taking slow and steady sips. Savoring the sustenance, he ate his meal in silence while Magnar dragged a chair to his side and sat down.

When he judged he'd had enough, Rorik settled back against the pillows.

The leader of the wolves flexed his hand—a sure sign the man wanted a conversation or was in an irritated mood.

Deciding it best to begin, he probed, "Why was Ragna here? Why not Steinar?"

Magnar arched a brow. "You need to ask your wolf."

Frowning in confusion, Rorik simply shrugged. "Why would my *wolf* hold the answer, unless..." His eyes grew wide with sudden clearness. "*Nae*."

The smile came slowly from Magnar. He pointed to Rorik's chest. "Your *wolf* chose Ragna as his guardian during your healing." Then in a more somber tone, he added, "If not for her wisdom to douse the blazing fire in the hearth and candles, your wolf would not have come forth. You and your wolf were at death's embrace, and *Ragna* saved you both. Why your wolf chose her is a question we have all been discussing."

The broth settled uneasily in his gut. This was not the answer he expected. Stunned into silence, Rorik looked away from the intensity of the man's eyes. He noted the small dirk lying at the end of the bed. Was it hers? "How long did she remain at my side?"

"Ten days."

Rorik returned his attention to the man. "That explains Steinar's refusal to enter the chamber."

"Your wolf made it clear nae one could enter, even in his weakened condition. Even though you have healed, Steinar will not enter." Magnar folded his arms over his chest. "You waited too long to permit the animal to heal you."

Rorik scratched at the beard on his face. "'Tis a regret that shall haunt me." The one woman he had avoided for years now had become his protector by forging a bond with his beast.

"When you fought with David—"

"Loki's balls," muttered Rorik, forgetting about the battle with the man. "No doubt he wished to see my death."

Shaking his head solemnly, Magnar stated,

"Whatever quarrel you had with the man, I can assure you he asked about you daily, including Hallgerd. All at Steinn worried for you."

"I tempted fate with David's intended. It was reckless."

Magnar rose from his chair. Going to the hearth, he began to toss in wood and kindling. "And your plans for the woman? Will you move forward to secure the information?"

The fire snapped to life—flames dancing upward against the stones, and Rorik weighed the choices.

"Unsure," Rorik answered hesitantly. "I have not been able to get the information I require for the king. I fear I moved too fast to gather what I required so I could leave Steinn."

Humor danced within Magnar's eyes when he returned to his chair. "It will be difficult to pursue Hallgerd, when another woman has shared your bed day *and* night."

Rorik waved him off weakly. "Ragna was there for healing, and Hallgerd should understand. She is from the isles and kens the old ways. Ragna shared the bed with my *wolf* and not the man."

Magnar snorted and folded his arms over his chest. "Are they not one and the same—beast and man?"

He refused to respond.

"Nae matter. A woman is a woman. You have tempted the lass, and I do not mean Ragna."

Growing weary of the current conversation, Rorik turned away from his friend, keeping his gaze fixed on the door. Ragna had not returned with any water. He glanced inward at his wolf. *Will she return for us?*

His wolf stared back at him.

Now that I am healed, she will most likely leave.

"Pay heed to your wolf's healing more often," suggested Magnar. "I have nae desire to see you walking a path to Valhalla."

Amused, Rorik confessed, "My path led me halfway to Odin's table."

Magnar leaned forward, bracing his forearms on his thighs. "Truth?"

"Aye," he affirmed tentatively. "One of Odin's warriors met me on my journey."

"I have fought many battles, but I have never ventured near the void of nae tomorrows," admitted Magnar quietly.

"A path I do not want to travel again for some time," Rorik confessed with a sigh.

"Why did you wait so long? Can you now discuss what has been troubling you?"

Rorik remained silent. He could give the man no answers. Bitterness had clawed its way into his soul many moons ago. Perchance it was always there—biding its time to crawl forth and claim him.

Magnar stood. "When you are ready to speak, I am here. Furthermore, you must give me your word you will not allow your beast to remain apart from you. If so, you are nae good to the brotherhood."

Casting his gaze at his friend, Rorik replied, "I give you my vow as a warrior *and* wolf."

Magnar nodded slowly. "Good. I have nae wish to have my friend die."

Curious, Rorik asked, "Did you notify the king of my condition?"

His friend gave him a pointed look. "And disrupt all of Steinn with the arrival of King William and all the other wolves? The king most likely would have wanted to stay and inspect the training, or worse, consider Steinn his *new* fortress to call home." He paused and shifted his stance. "You might have been near death's embrace when we placed you in this bed, yet the moment your wolf came forth I grew confident in your healing. I shall send a message telling him of your injury. This will give you time—*time* to consider how you want to move forward with any plans."

Rorik smiled and looked beyond Magnar.

Ragna stood poised at the entrance with her hair back in braids and wrapped around her head like a crown. Her face showed no emotion. The woman had vanished, and the Seer stood in her place.

His smile faltered.

"I shall leave you in the healing care of our Seer," declared Magnar as he took his leave from the chamber.

She lifted her chin and gave him a curt nod as she stepped inside, making room for Magnar to pass. Ragna spared Rorik no glance when she went to the large table. Quietly, she poured some water into a cup and brought it to him.

Rorik took the offering. As he sipped the cool liquid, he kept his gaze fixed on her face over the rim of his cup. She continued to busy herself within the chamber. The trencher had been removed to the table, and she lit several candles. Light and warmth infused the place, casting a glow around her.

How could he get the woman to emerge again? For all his wisdom when it came to charming any female, he found the path unclear with this woman. It had always been thus with Ragna. He swallowed the rest of the water and put the cup on a nearby table. He did not want to speak with the Seer. Rorik wanted to talk to Ragna.

His wolf padded closer, and an idea presented itself.

"How did you draw forth the wolf?" he asked.

Her eyes widened in surprise, but she quickly masked the emotion. She lifted one shoulder as if she knew the answer all along. "I took a chance in believing the wolf feared the heat and light within the chamber."

Intrigued, he pressed, "A vision?"

"Nae, *nae*. There were none." Averting her gaze, she arranged the small jars in a neat order on the table.

"A wise decision. I am honored you stayed."

Her back stiffened. "There would have been nae honor in your death," she uttered softly.

Rorik scowled. *My death would have been foolish. Nae battle was fought, so I would not have been worthy to feast with the other warriors at Odin's table.*

How he longed to throw off the covers and go to her. Attempting to find the right words with her was proving difficult. He pinched the bridge of his nose in frustration, trying to sort out a plan. Rorik required more time with this woman—time to undo years fraught with tense conversations and strife between them.

On a sigh, he lifted his head. *The king can wait.*

Rorik dared to ask the question. "Will you leave for *Orkneyjar*?"

Startled, Ragna lifted her gaze and clasped her hands together.

Silence reigned between them like an unwelcomed companion, and Rorik held his breath, fearing her reply.

Her features softened. "Why should I stay, Rorik?"

Because we are not finished, Ragna, and you are curious.

Smiling broadly, he answered smoothly, "So I can show you the parts of Scotland that will steal the breath from your body."

Chapter Nine

"Are you certain you are strong enough to ride a horse?" demanded Ragna while securing a few provisions on her horse for the journey through the hills.

Rorik folded his arms across his chest. "And for the third time this morning, *aye*!"

Averting the intensity of his stare, she concentrated on her task. Why did she even agree to remain at Steinn?

Because you let the man tempt you with his words.

She dared to sweep a glance toward him. Running a hand over the golden mane of her horse, she explained, "Three days to regain your strength is to be commended. You must understand my concerns—"

"*Concerns*?" he echoed, arching a dark brow. His eyes danced with mischief, and she yearned to brush away a lock of hair from his eye.

Nevertheless, Ragna would not be dismayed. "Of course. If you fall from your horse, I would not be able to assist you. Worse, I do not ken the land, so I won't be able to find help." *Why am I babbling this drivel?*

He blinked as if he didn't understand her words. Then his face broke into the most glorious smile. "You *care* for me."

Sweet Goddess! How the man continually irritated and intrigued her. He might be correct about her concerns, but Ragna would never admit to those feelings. From the look of the man, he appeared fully capable of going into any battle. His strength and appetite had returned with vigor. No trace of his illness remained. She had always marveled at the rapid speed these wolves were able to heal their men. Thank the Gods and Goddess Rorik relented and gave over the control to his wolf for healing.

She gave one final pat to her horse and moved around to the left side of the animal. “I *care* if anything should happen and I am unable to reach Magnar.” The lie tumbled free from her lips.

As she prepared to get onto the animal, Ragna froze when he placed his hands at her waist and lifted her into the saddle as if she weighed no more than a newborn lamb. Heat from his touch seared into her body, traveling to places she yearned to have him touch. Ragna quickly grasped the reins while mumbling her thanks.

“Does not your hawk follow you everywhere?” he asked, promptly getting onto his horse. “I overheard Magnar explaining to Elspeth how the hawk warned you to my position on the hill.”

You are clever, Rorik. Her mouth twitched with humor. She shielded her eyes from the intense sunlight, searching for the sparrowhawk. “Oda prefers to keep her own company. Often, I cannot summon her for days.”

Rorik chuckled softly. Nudging his horse forward, he challenged, “I find that hard to fathom, Seer.”

Ragna followed his slow movements across the bailey. Though he called her *Seer*, there was a tone of respect.

Smiling, she urged her horse to follow.

The warm day infused her spirit as they crossed under the portcullis and over the bridge. While he maintained a steady lead, Ragna kept her focus on the warrior's strong backside and smiled.

When he came to her chamber earlier in the morn, Rorik declared it was a rare autumn day—one filled with warmth—and announced it was time for her inspection of Scotland. Dawn's light had barely graced the morning sky as he professed the journey would last all day and to meet him in the kitchens. Unprepared, she merely nodded and quickly readied herself.

Ragna cupped a hand over her mouth to stifle the laughter, recalling how he raided the fresh, warm bread from one of the ovens. The cook clicked her tongue in obvious disapproval. Yet when Rorik took her hand and placed a kiss across her knuckles, Ragna thought the woman was going to swoon into her pot of porridge.

The man's charm extended to every female at Steinn, including her. However, Ragna saw beneath the layer of smooth words and smiles. Rorik was a haunted man. She had witnessed this within his eyes long ago.

They ambled along at a steady gallop. Noises from the daily life within the large castle faded and now were replaced with gentle breezes, birdsong, and the crunch of dead leaves under their horses' hoofs. Ragna's shoulders relaxed, allowing the rhythm of the land to seep into her.

After an hour, Rorik brought his horse to a halt near a dip in the land. He waved his hand outward. "Have you ever seen such beauty?"

The gasp lodged in her throat. Here, the vast beauty of Scotland surrounded her in a lavender blanket of heather extending even to the nearby hills. A light tug of power brushed over her skin, temping Ragna to delve farther.

Dismounting from her horse, Ragna followed a moss-covered path to the heather moor. Bending down on one knee, she brushed her palm over the tiny flowers. The ancients regarded her from deep inside the ground. They were the old ones of wisdom with each passing season. Very few were able to sense them. Fortunately, her grandmother's gift with nature extended to Ragna, and when her feet touched the ground, she opened fully to the whispers from long ago.

"Greetings," she acknowledged quietly, unsure of what more to say.

Laughter escaped her as the magic of the land responded by showing her a deeper hue within the flowers. The air shimmered, and she longed to venture across to another realm. Time no longer concerned her while Ragna absorbed the wisdom from the land.

She acknowledged the response with her own magic and blew across the expanse of the moor.

Rorik's presence loomed from behind her, casting a shadow over and around her. So absorbed in what she was doing, she had forgotten about him.

Standing slowly, Ragna mused, "Scotland has its heather, but our *Lyng* flowers cannot compare, unless you journey high into the hills on one of the isles."

He stared outward. "But there is more peace here."

Could he sense the magic, too? "Is all of Scotland like this?"

Pursing his lips, he shook his head solemnly. "From what I have found, simply a few corners of land with connections to the ancients. If you cast your attention in all directions, you will find many do not travel near or through this part of the land. Those who dwell nearby speak in hushed tones of the fairy folk. This was their land before others arrived." He stooped down and plucked a tiny flower.

"Nae," pleaded Ragna, shocked at his destruction of the sacred land. Glancing around him, she half-expected the old ones to appear and seek their wrath.

Placing a warm finger over her lips, he silenced her protests. "I asked permission while you were speaking to the land. They granted my request."

Her mouth gaped open in shock. "How, *how* do you ken?"

Rorik reached for her hand, placing the flower within her palm. "Did you not feel the air warm around us, or the shift in the colors of the land—from the flowers to the sky? If you are silent, they will speak to you."

"But 'tis a rare gift to sense the ancients within the land," she returned, glancing down at the offering he presented to her.

"You once said," Rorik began tentatively, "that I was nae better than my father, but you forgot, my mother belonged to a lineage of seers *and* druids. Even now, many across these lands still believe in the Pict Gods and Goddesses. I carry part of my mother's gift inside me."

Embarrassed to have him mention her words from the past, Ragna turned away. There were so many bitter words between them. How could they manage to have any hope of a conversation with all they had done to each other? Her intention was not to demean his own power, nor to dishonor him. She was simply shocked at his declaration.

What shall I do, Goddess?

A soft breeze caressed her cheek, and her gaze followed the path of a small butterfly. It flitted along without a care in the world. A rare beauty as it disappeared from her vision. The tension in her eased, and she swallowed.

It is time to close the door on the past. Choose your words and make amends.

Turning around, she gave Rorik a weak smile. "Forgive me. I had forgotten about her. Your mother left this world too soon. My mother spoke her praises often when I worked with her on the land collecting herbs and flowers. Once, she mentioned you had been gifted with the sight, but it was not a path for you. You were destined for the brotherhood."

Rorik cupped her chin—the contact sent a jolt of pleasure over her skin. Lifting her head, she stared into his emerald eyes, studying his intent. With his other arm, he grasped her around the waist.

Her mind screamed to step out of his embrace. Nevertheless, her body betrayed her.

Lowering his head, he murmured. "There is nae need to make amends, *Ragna*."

His breath was warm against her skin. She shivered from the roughness of his light beard against her cheek. If she turned her head slightly, his lips would be against hers. The air warmed more, leaving her dizzy.

Gently, Rorik guided her lips to meet his. The first brush of his mouth sent a stirring of desire coursing throughout her body. Ragna wrapped her arms around his neck, twining her fingers into his thick hair. He drew forth her moan and answered with one of his own, kissing her more deeply. The savage intensity of her passion for him consumed her, and Ragna surrendered fully to him.

His kiss became urgent as his tongue sought entry into her soft mouth. His hands gripped her waist firmly, and he slowly walked her backward until her back hit the rough bark of a tree.

Breaking free from her mouth, he placed his forehead on hers. His breathing came out in small gasps.

Ragna's body burned for this man—only him. No other. Did he have regrets for kissing her? She grew weary of the battle between them. She understood who and what he was—seducer and wolf.

Raising her hand, she brushed her fingers across his full lips and was rewarded with another moan from the man. She dared to meet his heated gaze. Lust shimmered back at her within his eyes, along with confusion.

"Kiss me again, Rorik," she challenged.

He bent his head and trailed a path with his tongue from below her ear down along her neck. "You dare to tempt me further?"

Even though she ached for more from the man, she responded, "I only asked for another kiss."

His smile came slowly as he cupped her face within his hands. "One more kiss. Anymore and I shall strive to give you more pleasure, and my restraint is failing."

Ragna trembled from his words.

With a fierce growl, he took possession of her mouth. His tongue sought entry again, and she responded with her own fiery passion. A pulse of need thrummed between her legs, and she rubbed against his hard length. She'd always felt wild and untamed around Rorik—yearning for him to teach her about the private pleasures between a man and woman.

When he parted from her mouth, Ragna let out a cry of displeasure.

Rorik's breathing came out in uneven breaths, and he took a few steps back. He raked a hand through his hair. "You sorely tempt me to take your maidenhood here on the ground amongst the beauty."

And I would give it freely. Her nails bit into the rough bark of the tree behind her. Confusion ripped through her.

"But not today, *my Ragna*. Not today." He held out his hand to her. "Come. There is more to show you."

She swallowed the lump lodged in her throat and took a hesitant step forward. *Am I truly yours, Rorik? Or are you charming me like so many?*

Swiftly closing the door on her troublesome thoughts, Ragna trembled when she took hold of his outstretched hand.

As he placed it securely in the crook of his arm, he moved them steadily back to their horses. When she stole a glance over her shoulder, the magic of the land had faded.

Hours passed as they continued their travels. Along their journey, Rorik had referenced the skirmishes fought between their people and those who dwelled here. Peace in this northern region continued to remain unstable with occasional outbursts of fighting. She listened in rapt attention, watching as his features lit up when he spoke of his deep love for Scotland.

The rugged landscape surrounded her as he guided

them deeper into the hills, keeping them at a slow trot that bended around the pines and through a narrow path.

Curious, she asked, "Does this country mean more to you than our *Orkneyjar Isles*?"

Rorik brought his horse to a halt. Shifting on his horse, his troubled gaze looked beyond her. He lightly tapped his chest with his fist. "*Orkneyjar* is a part of me. 'Tis in my blood. Each time I return, I honor the land. Yet there are too many bad memories that haunt me there. Here"—he gestured outward—"is where I found my true home."

Stunned by his confession, Ragna remained silent. Would he share more with her? Never did she imagine the man had scars from a place that brought her peace and wisdom.

"I would like you to meet someone," he uttered quietly, dismounting from his horse.

His words interrupted her thoughts. Peering through the dense foliage, she couldn't foresee how any person could dwell in the area.

Rorik came to her side. She held out her arms, allowing him to ease her off the horse. After her feet landed on the ground, he grasped her hand. Brushing aside heavy tree limbs, he guided her along the winding, rough path.

"How can you ken the direction?" She tugged on his hand.

The man never stopped his stride when he glanced over his shoulder and gave her a wink.

Onward they traveled. Several squirrels scampered playfully out of their way, and Ragna smiled. Sunlight streamed down through the thick canopy of trees. He brought them to a halt by a giant yew tree.

After placing her hand on the tree, Rorik bent near her ear and whispered, "The mark of a druid."

Ragna studied the strange markings while tracing the edges with her fingers. Warmth seeped into her, and she quickly withdrew her hand. "Is this who you wanted me to meet? Does a Goddess of the land live beneath this tree?"

Laughter burst forth from him, and he leaned against the giant. "Nae, *nae*, my Ragna. Someone more important."

She eyed him skeptically. The man confounded her with his remarks.

"Surely you do not mean me?" inquired the low male voice. "I ken others would disagree with you."

Startled, Ragna peered around Rorik. Eyes resembling another stared back. A sliver of familiarity wove through her, but she could not recall if they had met. The man wore a simple long tunic, belted at the waist, leather and fur-lined boots, and he carried a staff as he approached.

"Greetings, Rorik."

"Hail, Uncle!" acknowledged Rorik and went to embrace the man. Turing around, he maintained his arm around his uncle's shoulder. "Ragna, I would like you to meet—"

"Declan the Brave!" Clutching a hand to her chest, her eyes went wide. "Nae. Is it truly you?"

The man gave her a wink and pinched his arm. "Aye. 'Tis me in the flesh."

"But we thought you died in a battle," she declared, taking a step forward. "There were witnesses who spoke of seeing you slain by the hand of another. Many young warriors left the isles to avenge your death."

Rorik released his hold on his uncle and came to her side. "A necessary falsehood for him to stay alive."

"But why?" she asked in a rush.

"Hence, I would not be forced to kill my brother," explained Declan.

"*Forced*?" echoed Ragna.

The man brushed a hand through his beard while arching his brow at his nephew.

Rorik gave him a slight nod to continue.

"My brother—Rorik's father—made it known we had become enemies. Since I was destined for Scotland to follow the path of other druids, he considered this an act of betrayal within our kin. My intent for leaving was also to assist in training my nephew. Durinn expressly told me to oversee another in the brotherhood. We argued, and he banished me from our home. If I had remained on the isles, he would have demanded a final battle between us—to the death."

Ragna shook her head solemnly. "You were indeed brave, Declan, but why did you not return to the *Orkneyjar Isles* after the death of your brother?"

He tapped the leaf-filled ground with his staff. "This is now my home. Even if I returned, there are some who would demand justice for the strife I caused within the brotherhood."

"You were not responsible for my father's actions," argued Rorik. "Many at Sutherland debated on his position within the clan."

"Nevertheless, I now call Scotland my home. Come, I have a fine stew over the fire that requires tending and more vegetables." Declan retreated and picked up a basket filled with mushrooms.

Ragna hastened to walk by his side. "Your nephew is correct. The slaughter and violence Durinn inflicted on our people and those here had nothing to do with you leaving. The man brought nae honor to our people. None dared challenge him, so he continued with his pillaging—all in the name of our king. The runes spoke to me before most of his vile deeds were done. You ken this."

His smile held sadness, and he halted his progress.

She turned toward Rorik. "I am sorry to speak thusly about your father."

"Your words are truth to many, including me." Bitterness laced Rorik's words. Fisting his hands on his hips, he stared at her. "What I find worrying is why you never spoke them aloud? Your words could have swayed the council on *Kirkjuvágr*."

Ragna stiffened. *You must confess the truth.* "My error so long ago made it impossible. I—"

"I made her vow not to say anything," interrupted Declan.

Rorik dropped his hands to his sides. Confusion replaced the bitterness within his eyes. "Explain."

"Ragna came to me first regarding Durinn. She had seen a vision in the runes of a great darkness he would bring to the isles if he stayed on this violent path. Ragna advised me to speak with him. Instead of my brother fearing the words of a Seer, he sought to cut out her tongue if she uttered one word to anyone. After our conversation, I blackened his eye and then went to deliver his message to Ragna."

"And I being a young Seer, worried he'd take out his revenge if I went against him," she explained further, hoping Rorik would understand.

Rorik came to her side.

She twisted her hands within the folds of her gown. “I should have been stronger *and* wiser. Perchance his wrath might have ended—”

“With your death? Nae,” Rorik expressed quietly, reaching for her hand and placing a soft kiss along her knuckles. “Often times, honor comes with being silent.”

Chapter Ten

Rorik had never desired another like the woman he had pinned against the oak tree earlier in the morn. She had spoken of the power in the land, but she did not understand the hold she had over him. She was an enchantress—stirring the blood throughout his veins and causing him to either lose his tongue or utter harsh words. He found himself unable to be in control, and this bothered him.

The Dark Seducer charmed others to do his bidding. Yet the woman who laughed and played chase with his uncle's deerhound amongst the trees had Rorik under her power.

Studying her with intent from inside his uncle's small dwelling, he allowed his shoulders to relax and smiled. The urge to join her in the merriment a heady power. Gone was the Seer. In her place, the woman he longed to possess.

And his anger toward his dead father returned in force. The man had destroyed too many lives, including his own. How many more secrets were left to uncover?

"An interesting woman," commented Declan, coming to his side. He held out a cup to him. "Mead."

Rorik took the offering, sipping slowly. "Mmm…"

His uncle nudged him. "Are you referring to the mead *or* the woman?"

Glancing sideways at the man, he answered,

"Both." Lifting his cup outward, he added, "Honey from your beehives nearby?"

"Aye," his uncle acknowledged. "News reached me about your recent troubles. Have you fully healed?"

"I can assure you I have *fully* recovered from all injuries, Uncle." Rorik took another sip of the mead while keeping his focus on the lively scene outside.

"Why is Ragna here in Scotland?"

Unsure how to respond, Rorik offered the simple truth. "To save me from death."

Declan choked on his mead. Quickly recovering, he blurted out, "The Seer of the *Orkneyjar Isles* journeyed across the sea to save you? Why not send another?"

Rorik peered into his cup and swirled the liquid. "I would not have listened to a messenger from the Seer."

"Therefore, the *woman* came to you?"

Snorting, he turned to meet his uncle's interest. "Your questions are filled with answers, *Druid*."

His uncle's eyes creased with humor, but he remained silent.

"Our past is…thorny," Rorik began. "I blame myself for many harsh words and actions."

Declan scratched the side of his face. "Aye. If I recall, there was nae friendship between you and her. Now?"

Rorik sighed heavily and went to the table. After placing the cup down, he brushed a hand down the back of his neck. "*Now*, I am uncertain but do not wish for anymore harshness between us. During my dark sleep, I had walked a path to Odin's table—"

"Loki's balls, nae," grumbled Declan and moved away from the window. "If your wounds were so severe, why didn't Magnar send for me?"

Chuckling softly, Rorik leaned against the table. "Sadly, my wolf would not have allowed another near me while I was in the deep sleep of healing."

Declan spat out another curse and waved his hand outward. "I have many healing balms and tinctures. Furthermore, I am your uncle. I should have been at your side to place your sword in your hand, if death claimed you."

Crossing to his uncle, Rorik placed a hand on his shoulder. "With the severity of my wounds, you ken my wolf is the only one who can fully heal me."

"Hmm…" He eyed him skeptically. "Then who was worthy to be your guardian?"

Rorik dropped his hand and took a step back. "I chose Steinar. Though my wolf decided on another."

"Who?" demanded Declan, his eyes widening.

Rorik swept his gaze out the window. "Ragna."

When silence cloaked the room, he stole a glance at his uncle. Rorik let out a bark of laughter then apologized. "Trust me, you are not the only man who found it hard to fathom. Even I cannot explain the conduct of my wolf."

"For the love of the Gods, I have never heard of any woman becoming a guardian for the wolves," muttered Declan, shuffling toward the hearth.

Ragna is not any woman, Uncle. But Rorik would not disclose how much more he considered Ragna. No. Those words would never be spoken aloud.

"What about this connection with you and the Seer?"

Startled from his thoughts, Rorik heard only one word and turned fully around. "Connection?"

His uncle nodded while removing a large spoon off the hook near the pot of stew.

"There is none," he asserted in a rushed tone.

Declan gestured him to come forward.

Frowning, Rorik complied.

"Tell me if you think this needs more herbs." His uncle presented a spoonful of the stew broth in front of his face.

When the hot liquid seared past his lips and entered his mouth, Rorik fought to spit everything back into the pot. He swallowed and then coughed—the broth burned a scorching path to his stomach.

His uncle pounded his back. "'Tis what I thought."

"What?" gasped Rorik, reaching for one of the jugs off the table to ease the fiery agony. After sniffing the contents, he guzzled the cool water.

Dropping the spoon into the simmering pot, his uncle replied, "You lied."

"Lied about what?" asked Ragna, entering through the front door, followed by her faithful deerhound companion.

"Different opinions," responded Rorik dryly, noting the flushed color in her cheeks and the dark strands of curls that had escaped from her braids.

His uncle chuckled softly, and the animal lumbered to Declan's side. "I see you have found a new friend, Haldor."

Ragna laughed. "I commend you for the choice of his name. The *Rock of Thor* kept me from reaching his prized stick until the end of our game."

Ruffling the gray fur on the animal's head, Declan remarked, "The beast refuses to allow even me to claim victory in retrieving the stick." He raised his head to meet her gaze. "Do all animals acknowledge the Seer as well?"

Her good humor transformed to one Rorik had seen often. He marveled at the sudden switch—from conversing as a simple woman to one who held vast wisdom. The Seer had returned.

"As I am certain they do for you, Druid," she proclaimed.

His uncle nodded slowly. "Aye, at times."

She glanced around him. "Can I offer my help with preparing the meal?"

Declan waved her off. "My thanks, but 'tis almost ready."

"Then I shall go cleanse my hands and face in the stream behind your home." Ragna swiftly departed.

Reaching for the empty jug, Rorik added, "I'll fetch some water for the meal."

"Nae. Surely you will want mead," declared his uncle, attending to his stew.

Ignoring the man, Rorik made hasty steps outside. He followed the rough path around the stone and wood structure to the stream, pushing aside heavy limbs along his path.

His steps slowed as he came upon Ragna. Her back was to him while she stared across the expanse of the water. The ever-present warble of the stream had always filled him with contentment. Looking beyond the Seer, he understood her fascination. The trees were decked in their golden autumn colors—a breathtaking scene he'd witnessed many a time traveling in Scotland but never took the time to value their majesty.

Then again, the woman standing before him held a greater beauty.

Approaching by her side, he uttered softly, "'Tis a wonder."

"I have never seen so many colors," she admitted. "They fill the land with such magnificence." She turned toward him and placed a hand on his chest. "How I envy you living here amongst this beauty. My thanks for showing me what Scotland has to offer."

Again, her smiled speared a light into his hardened soul.

Rorik shifted his stance. Her eyes misted with unshed tears. Words he yearned to profess lodged like a dry bannock in his throat. Fear kept them there, and he found himself unable to say anything. He stared mutely at her. Turning away, he went to the stream and filled the jug.

Hearing her approach, he stood slowly.

"Have I offended you, Rorik?" Her question tight with strain.

Guilt plagued him. After dropping the jug onto the ground, the water splashed everywhere. He grasped her firmly around the waist and stared into her jeweled eyes. "Your kind words left me without an offering of my own."

A smile tipped the corners of her luscious mouth. She tilted her head to the side. "Ah. We are better at harsh and bitter words but are not at ease with kind words, aye?"

He blew out a frustrated sigh. "Agreed."

Standing on her toes, she brushed a kiss along his cheek. "Let us return to Declan before he sends Haldor to fetch us."

Rorik did not want to leave. His chest ached with unsaid thoughts—so many he had kept within. Yet the daylight was now fading and Ragna correct.

He cupped her chin, warm and soft within his palm. Lowering his head, he placed a feather-light kiss along her lips. When a sigh escaped from her mouth, Rorik deepened the kiss, drinking in her sweetness. Ragna tasted of the land, and he ached for more. A fierce need to possess and protect her overtook him. Confusion battled inside him as he wrenched his mouth from hers.

With the Dark Seducer, there was always a plan. Emotions never stirred him.

Until now.

Taking a step back, he picked up the jug and went to the stream. The icy water stung like nettles on his hand, but he gave no care. He let the coldness settle over his skin, quenching the burning fire coursing through his body.

A low growl came forth from the trees. Rorik stood abruptly and glared at the intruder. "Have you been spying on us, beast?" Never had he known the deerhound to challenge him.

Ragna cupped a hand over her mouth to stifle the laughter and failed miserably. "I sense Haldor is not happy you have kissed me."

He shrugged, trying not to return the growl with one of his own. "Is he now your protector? From me? Might I remind *Haldor* that my beast is larger."

Clucking her tongue in disapproval, Ragna went to the animal's side. "I have witnessed the man's wolf. Tame as a kitten."

Rorik's wolf gnashed his teeth.

"My *wolf* is not pleased," he announced, walking toward her.

Haldor padded in front of Ragna.

And Rorik took a step back. His wolf shook with fury. Doing his best to reign the animal, Rorik allowed the deerhound the advantage. He dipped his head. "I shall permit you to escort the Seer back to the house."

Confusion settled over Ragna's features. "Is there a problem? Why have your eyes shifted to those of the wolf?"

"Simply a battle over who shall protect you. My wolf is most demanding it should be him."

Moving in front of the deerhound, she pointed a warning finger at Haldor. "I am honored by your loyalty, but you must respect the wolf, as well."

The deerhound brushed his head against her leg as if offering an apology.

Ragna returned her attention to Rorik. "I expect your wolf to understand my love extends to all animals. Though I am grateful for the bond we had shared, your wolf does not claim possession over me."

A great howl filled Rorik. Was it him or his beast? Uncertain, he took another step back.

"Why are you backing away from me?"

"Return to my Uncle," he ordered in a low voice.

Fear replaced confusion, but she quickly nodded. "Come, Haldor."

The fading sunlight danced off her hair as she slipped from his sight.

Turning toward the stream, Rorik exhaled in a rush and tossed the jug far out into the water. He forced the guttural cry he craved to let out back within his body.

His wolf had bonded with Ragna. Aye, he understood this, but his wolf had claimed *possession* for Rorik. And he was the fool for not sensing it sooner.

He glared inward at the beast. *'Tis not in our future! Do you not understand? My oath cannot be undone! You have made decisions not allowed.*

The beast howled in fury, filling his head with protests, and Rorik cupped his hands over his ears. *Enough*!

Instantly, his wolf ceased and turned away.

Thunder rumbled in the evening sky, and he cursed. No amount of reasoning with the wolf would sway him to cease his actions. Why did Rorik not see this sooner? Why did he suggest showing Ragna Scotland? A great shudder wracked through his body. Chaos ripped through him like the approaching storm.

"I escaped the clutches of death only to walk back into the abyss," he muttered in contempt.

Could he plead his case to the God of Justice, Forsetti? *Nae, but possibly another.*

Rorik slumped to the ground. Lifting his hands to the first star of the evening, he pleaded in a firm voice, "Goddess Freyja, hear my plea. I pledged my vow to you many moons ago after I sought your aid. You granted my request and saved Ragna from the clutches of my father. In return, I swore never to take her to my bed. I ken I have failed, since 'tis all I want to do when I am around the woman. A bond has formed with my wolf without my consent. I cannot undo what has been done."

Lightning seared the sky in an arc all around him. The wind slapped at his face, mocking him. Was the Goddess displeased with his words?

He gritted his teeth. "All I have left is my honor, though many would profess I had none."

Rising slowly, Rorik glanced back, recalling

Ragna's image one last time. There would be no regrets in his feelings toward her, nor what his wolf had done.

Removing his sword from its sheath behind his back, Rorik raised his arm over his head. "If you find your warrior unworthy to remain in this world for my actions, strike me down." He gripped the hilt of his sword tightly, ready for death's embrace.

The ground rumbled, and leaves swirled in a tempest around him, but Rorik stood firm in his stance. If he had failed the Goddess, death would be her victory. "Do what must be done!"

The lightning and thunder ceased, along with the threat of the approaching storm. The clouds parted, and the evening star shone with a brilliance that lit up the sky. Warmth filled Rorik while he steadied himself. When the starlight entered his body, he gasped as the power centered around his wolf.

His heart pounded like the beating drums on a longship, and Rorik fought for breath. The beast lowered his head in fear and acceptance. Rorik pondered if the Goddess would remove the wolf from him. Fisting his left hand, he pounded it against his heart.

"We live as one! We die as one!"

Musical laughter and the scent of roses surrounded him. When a soft breeze kissed his cheek, he stumbled from the touch. An unexpected sense of peace stole through him, along with her wisdom.

In a great flash of blinding light, the evening star returned to its former glow. All traces of the Goddess had vanished, and he sheathed his sword.

Rorik remained rooted to the forest floor for several moments, listening to the nocturnal animals emerge and traverse through the thick foliage. No longer fraught with uncertainty, Rorik smiled broadly and hastily made quick strides back to the house.

As his steps drew him near the dwelling, Rorik paused. In the thin sliver of moonlight, Ragna stood regally. Had she witnessed the glow in the sky?

"'Tis a beautiful evening," he announced.

She blinked as if coming out of a trance. "Aye," she admitted softly. "Have you and your wolf made peace?"

Holding her with a relaxed, steady gaze, he responded, "Most assuredly."

"'Tis good to hear, Rorik." She bit her lower lip.

He moved forward. "And?"

"*And*," she echoed, taking a small step toward him—a frown creasing her lovely face.

Rorik grasped her hands before she had a chance to clasp them together. "I sense there was more to your words."

"For a moment, I feared—"

"Nae, *nae*," he reassured in a low voice. "Never fear us, Ragna."

"Why?" Her question barely a whisper on the breeze.

Would you run if I spoke what was in my heart, Ragna? Would the Seer banish me? "Because I—"

"By the hounds of Odin! Did you forget the water? Or were your intentions elsewhere?" Declan bellowed from the entrance of his home.

Quickly dropping her hands, Rorik winked at Ragna, and pointed a warning finger at his uncle. "Lost the bloody jug in the icy stream when your beast charged at me."

Sweet laughter bubbled forth from Ragna, and once again Rorik found himself captivated by the beguiling woman.

Chapter Eleven

Hallgerd crouched low to the ground, stumbling along the leaf and mud-filled path to avoid the flap of wings over her head. Darting her gaze in all directions, she held her breath, waiting for the bird to either appear or take flight away from her. When she judged it safe to continue, she rose from her position and hesitantly prodded forward through the thick pines.

With only a sliver of the moon showing, it was hard to determine the direction. The rising moon and last rays of fading sunlight gave her small sense of relief, but when would she come upon the aging, scarred tree?

Hallgerd paused and went to inspect a large pine. Her fingers skimmed the rough bark. *Nothing!*

Shivering slightly, she pulled the hood of her cloak more firmly over her head. Fear kept her moving onward. She could not deny his summons, no matter the time of day.

Why did you not wish to speak with me earlier?

Clenching the handle of the basket so tight in both of her hands, shards of straw sliced into one of her fingers. Hallgerd let out a sharp hiss and drew her hand forth, watching as the blood trickled in a grisly pattern down to her wrist.

"By the Goddess," she muttered in frustration, wiping the injured finger against her cloak.

While she made her way deeper into the trees, Hallgerd kept her focus on each of them as she slowly walked past. When another bird darted out along her path, she bit out a curse.

"Shameful. Did not our mother beat you enough for your foul tongue?" scolded the familiar male voice behind her.

Hallgerd twirled around so fast she almost smacked the man with her basket. The hood of her cloak fell back. Cool air slapped against her face causing her to grind her teeth. "You accursed beast!" she spat out in disdain.

Sinister laughter followed. "Is that anyway to speak to your *brother*?"

Hallgerd dropped the basket. She clenched her hands at her side, lest she be tempted to pound a fist against his chest. "What do you want Jorund?"

Stepping forward, he yanked on one of her braids, and she flinched.

She lifted her head and gazed into eyes that reminded her so much of their mother. Warmth never seemed to reach them, even when they both smiled. Her mother was cruel. However, Jorund far worse in his cruelty.

Without releasing his hold, he answered, "Information."

I will show you nae fear, Brother.

"Is there a reason I had to come this late in the day? 'Tis almost dark."

Jorund tugged harder. "Do you wish me to be seen? This place reeks of wolves." He glanced behind her. "Were you careful nae one followed you?"

"Aye, nae one saw me leave. But David will

become suspicious if I am found gone from the castle," she protested.

"I care not about your future husband. I am certain you have already charmed him into your bed, so nothing you do can stir his anger." Without releasing his hold on her braid, he bent and retrieved the basket. "Furthermore, you got lost searching for flowers, aye? This can be your tale."

She took the basket from his hand. *How wrong you are with David. His distrust of me is growing.* "What information are you seeking, Jorund?"

Finally dropping his hold on her braid, he brushed a hand over his chin. "There is a certain document that is not at the keep of the MacNeil—"

"I thought it was destroyed in a fire," she interrupted, confused over this new direction of his.

"Let me continue!" he snapped.

Hallgerd clenched her jaw but kept silent.

Again, her brother swept his gaze around her, as if he expected another to come passing through. "The document I am currently searching for deals with lands surrounding the keep and bordering your future husband's. The MacNeil's grip on that area of land is substantial. I desire to take it back. For our father."

You mean for our mother. This has always been her plan. Never Father's. If only he were alive to see your corruption.

"With this valuable document," continued Jorund, "we can seize what is rightfully ours."

Hallgerd dared to further stir the anger in her brother. "Did not father make a bargain to give the lands to the MacNeil for his support in a raid on our lands in the west?"

The slap came without warning. She staggered back, slamming into a tree. Pain shattered her thoughts, and Hallgerd struggled to keep the burning tears from spilling forth.

"Lies! All of them lies spouted by Rorik's grandsire. Are you daft? You heard the tale witnessed by our mother. The elder MacNeil forced the document. By rights, 'tis mine. You should have paid more heed to her words!"

The scream lodged within her throat while Hallgerd nodded. *They are malicious lies to get you to do our mother's bidding, and you are the fool, Brother.*

Jorund pounded his fist into his palm. "Rorik must carry this document with him. Therefore, *you* must procure it by any means. Use your charms, take him to your bed, or sneak into his chamber. I do not care which method you plan to use. Get me that document."

"It might prove difficult. Rorik's attentions are elsewhere," confessed Hallgerd.

His face contorted in the pale light. Their mother's hatred of the MacNeils had transferred to Jorund.

"What do you mean?" he demanded tersely.

"Ragna traveled with us to Scotland. Her intentions were to deliver a message, but she did not share the name of the person. When Rorik became ill, she tended to him and nae other."

His eyes widened in disbelief. "The Seer is here? On Scottish soil?" Jorund thrust his fist against the tree in fury. Leaning his head against the aging giant, he raked his fingers along the rough edges of the bark. "Her arrival alters everything."

Curiosity spurred her to ask, "How?"

Jorund glared at her. "'Tis nae concern for you," he

scolded.

Hallgerd straightened fully. Doing her best to keep her voice steady, she pressed, “And what about the information King John seeks? Did he not want to learn the movements of King William and Magnar? Surely, with time I can procure what is needed from Rorik.”

Her brother waved a hand dismissively and moved away from the tree. “The king has other urgent matters. Your focus is now securing this document for me. I have new plans to form—ones that include a traitorous woman—the Seer.”

When he stepped near her, Hallgerd flinched. “I must return to the castle.”

His lip curled into a snarl as he gripped her chin. “You can blame the bruise on your reckless wanderings.” Lowering his head, he brushed a kiss over her mouth.

Bile rose from her stomach, and Hallgerd fought its release.

“Do not fail me, Sister,” he threatened. “When you have found the document, send for the messenger.” After releasing her, Jorund slipped silently through the trees.

Unable to move, Hallgerd remained in a rigid stance for some time. Fear and fury raged a battle within her body. How she hated Jorund. His evil and twisted ways continued to grow. And she grew weary of being a pawn in his path to power, lands, and more money. However, she could not comprehend this sudden hatred toward the Seer. And she was not about to ask him for an account. Not yet.

With trembling fingers, she traced a path over her cheek. The sting reminded her of the suffering from his constant abuse. Raising her head, she gave no care to the words she was about to proclaim. "When death comes for you, *Jorund*, may the claws of agony move slowly through your body and the doors to Valhalla remain closed to you forever."

A great shudder encased her body. The curse had been sent outward to the ancients. Lowering her head, Hallgerd turned and retreated out of the forest.

****

Drawing the hood of her cloak over her head, Ragna walked slowly toward the horses. Though the evening was cool, the meal she had eaten warmed her for the journey back to Steinn. Rorik appeared in a relaxed stance as he spoke quietly to the animals. No longer the hardened warrior, the man appeared more at ease and peace in this part of Scotland. He had opened a part of himself on their journey here, and this fascinated Ragna. Though Haldor remained off to the far side, she had earlier witnessed Rorik bending down on one knee and speaking in hushed tones to the deerhound. Was he making amends for his actions?

Halting her stride, she paused to admire this new feature in the man. *Or had it been hiding within him all along?*

Approaching by her side, Declan presented her with a package. "Here is a small vessel of honey for Elspeth, along with several packets of rue and betony for you. She favors this batch from my bees."

Taking the offering, she said, "My thanks for the herbs. I would like to return and see your hives."

The man smiled broadly, reminding Ragna of his nephew. "I would welcome another visit from the Seer. I do not get many visitors, especially ones held in high regard." He scratched the side of his face. "Though do not tell the leader of the wolves I confessed this to you."

"He visits often?" she asked.

"Aye." Tapping a finger against the package, he added, "He brings Elspeth. Her insight into herbs, honey, and candles is one I favor." Declan chuckled low. "When they do come to my door, Magnar takes a jug of mead and goes to the stream to rest. His demands are many, so I reckon this is his way of finding a few hours of peace away from Steinn."

"His responsibilities seem to have grown," Ragna mused, returning the man's smile.

"Most assuredly. Along with the rest of the wolves." Pausing, he pursed his lips in thought.

Ragna arched a questioning brow. "Was there something else you wanted to share?"

He clasped his hands behind his back. "Will your plans permit you to stay long in Scotland? The weather has been favorable, but soon the Cailleach's bite of winter shall descend."

Hesitant on her reply, Ragna shrugged. She had pushed aside any thought on leaving for home. Her reasons for staying were filled with questions. As Seer, duty demanded she return to the isles. As a woman, she sought another path.

Declan smiled, adding, "I would welcome the company and sharing of wisdom."

"What of the other Druids?" she pressed, curious about the others who held the wisdom of the ancients and the land.

Spreading his arms wide, he responded, "They are young and learning from the elders who live farther south. During the spring, I have been fortunate to have a powerful Druid spend time with me here. He usually travels to the isles. Perchance, you have heard of him?"

Chuckling softly, Ragna admitted, "The Druid, Cathal. A fine man, intent on learning much about our ways."

"Aye!" His eyes gleamed with mirth. "Then you ken him well."

"A wonder whenever he arrives on the isles, though it has been many moons," she confessed.

All traces of humor vanished from Declan. "There are troubles within a certain powerful clan. Evil has woven a dark thread around the MacKays of Urquhart. Cathal remains near their land in hopes of reuniting the brothers. They have each fled to different parts of Scotland. Until they return home, Cathal must be nearby to assist them against this growing evil which plagues their land."

Ragna tapped the ground with her foot. "But is this not your land as well?"

Sighing, he affirmed, "He kens where to find me, if he requires my help."

She lifted her head to the shining stars. "Then I will offer up my requests to the Goddess. Nae matter the God or Goddess, we are all here to fight evil, and those who wield the power, aye?"

Gently, Declan placed a hand on her shoulder. "Agreed."

Ragna met his gaze with a smile. "I shall return."

Crossing the path to her horse, she stopped and turned, giving one final wave to Declan. After securing the package in her satchel attached to her horse, she then permitted Rorik to help her onto the animal. Ragna watched as he hurried to give one final embrace to his uncle. Quiet words were spoken before Rorik returned and swiftly mounted his horse.

Their return journey back to Steinn was filled with silence between them, giving her peaceful contemplation to settle her thoughts. The day had been a revelation in so many ways, and Ragna had much to consider.

When the land opened before them with the torches of Steinn glimmering in the distance, Ragna's shoulders sagged. Their day had come to an end. Her thoughts returned to Declan's question about her stay here in Scotland. How long did she have until the skies turned against her returning home?

Unexpectedly, Rorik brought his horse to a halt and waited for her to approach by his side.

"Shall we return to our former stern selves when we pass through the gates?" she uttered softly, fearing the reply.

A frown marred his feature. "I am pleased you came with me today. It was important for you to meet my uncle." He drew in a deep breath and then blew it out into the chilly air. "Declan is more a father than my own. Once, when I was a lad, I ran away to my uncle's home. I confessed to him that he should be my father and not Durinn. Sadly, Declan declared I must not alter the path of the Gods. Afterward, my uncle led me to the stream and placed me on top of a boulder. There he left me and retreated to the shore. Fear seized my heart, and I believed I had brought dishonor to my father and uncle. Declan stood on the land, crossed his arms over his chest, and told me to close my eyes and listen to the water—not my troubling thoughts."

Ragna's chest tightened. How could this be the same man she met only hours ago? He appeared gentler, kind, not someone who would bring harm to a child. "How long did you sit on the boulder?"

Lifting his head to the stars, he replied, "One hour."

Gasping, she reached out and touched his arm. "How cruel!"

When Rorik returned his attention to her, his smile surrounded her in a warm embrace. He covered her fingers with his gloved hand. "Nae, *nae*. I found comfort in the water. The conflict raging a battle within me ceased. One of the first lessons I learned from my uncle."

Tears stung her eyes, touched by his declaration. "This is why you love the streams and rivers. They bring you solace."

"Aye. But you shall not hear me spout praises of the sea."

Ragna laughed nervously. "Nor I. You cannot hear your thoughts when you cross the North Sea." She shivered, recalling her journey from the isles to Scotland.

"You should be on a ship during a storm with the wind, rain, and lightning challenging for a chance to end your life and pitch you overboard."

"Do not speak so," she urged, her fingers digging into his arm. "For I fear I may not get on another ship to return home."

His mouth twitched at the corners. "Is this a confession from the Seer?"

Ragna narrowed her eyes as she attempted to remove her hand from his arm. Yet the man was made of steel and held his hand firmly against hers. "'Tis a secret. You are honor-bound to not tell another."

Slowly, he brought her hand to his lips, kissing each finger. "Ah, but the Dark Seducer has nae honor."

Her good humor vanished, along with the warmth as if he tossed a bucket of icy water onto her. Was this his way of telling her their time had come to an end? Ragna glanced sideways at the flickering lights from Steinn and swallowed. The question she posed earlier to him had been answered. She was the Seer and Rorik worked for the King of Scotland.

Two destinies forged in the blood and lineage of two countries. They were not meant to share more—nae, never a life together. Instead, the wolf and Seer had made their peace here in Scotland. This day would be a treasured memory in the stark, cold days ahead.

Her heart clenched with sadness at the truth.

Ragna sighed softly and squeezed his hand. "I am grateful for all you have shared with me today, but 'tis time to return home."

His wary gaze held hers for several moments, and then he slipped his hand free from hers.

Without waiting for his lead, Ragna snapped the reins and urged her horse onward for Steinn. When the morn came, she would find passage back to the isles and bury her love for Rorik in the cold depths of the North Sea.

Chapter Twelve

While he paced within the solar, Rorik tried to quell his worry as he waited for Magnar to enter. This morning the man had chosen to speak with Ragna first, only adding to Rorik's ire. He realized what she wanted, and Rorik was not ready to let her go.

As soon as they returned, Rorik had overheard her speaking to one of the stable lads. She told him to make ready her horse for the morning to the coast. It took all his control not to haul the woman over his back and storm up into his chambers, bolt the door, and plunder all her other secrets. Their marvelous day together crushed into dust the moment Castle Steinn came into view.

A troubling thought raced through his mind. "Was it something I said to hinder you, Ragna?" he muttered with contempt at himself.

Striding across the room, he retrieved a half-empty jug of ale and guzzled deeply. After draining the contents, he wiped his mouth with the back of his hand.

"Did you leave a cup for me?" inquired the male voice behind him.

Rorik lifted the object in question. "Sorry. None left." He deposited the empty jug onto the table and turned to face his leader.

After closing the door behind him, Magnar went to his table. He picked at several messages while remaining silent.

You are always the steady one. Rorik snarled.

"Temper the wolf," ordered Magnar, sifting through his other documents.

"You cannot allow her to leave," blurted out Rorik, shifting his stance.

The man's fingers rapped along the rough wood. "Who are you talking about?"

Rorik clenched his jaw. "You ken who I mean. I am not finished."

"Are you giving me an order?" demanded Magnar with deadly calm.

"To clarify, when it comes to Ragna, aye!" Rorik dared to stir the beast within his leader, but he would not relent.

Magnar rose to his full height. "When does the Seer become a *possession* to one of my men? Especially to the Dark Seducer? Have you forgotten your quest for the king? I have given you several days."

Dark Seducer. How he hated those two words and what they meant. Nevertheless, he had a duty to the clan and his king. Indecision plagued him. He raked a hand through his hair. Softening his tone, he responded, "I have not forgotten my task. But I require more time."

"Time? For both?" The man let out a hiss of disapproval. Magnar walked around the table and braced both hands on Rorik's shoulders. "You are playing a dangerous game, my friend. You walk two paths on this journey. Which one will you choose in the end?"

His words startled Rorik. He had never considered them separate. Nevertheless, the man was correct in his observation. This now became a challenge for Rorik.

Failure was not an option.

Blowing out a curse, the man released his hold and motioned for Rorik to join him by the fire. The blaze snapped as he took a seat across from Magnar. He settled his gaze into the tongues of flames, trying to find the words to convince the man from preventing Ragna from leaving.

Leaning forward in his chair, Rorik settled his forearms on his thighs. "I am not ready for Ragna to leave Scotland," he confessed quietly.

When silence reigned between them, Rorik stole a glance at his friend. Magnar stared beyond him, as if pondering an important declaration.

Moments later, the man brushed a hand over his chin, nodding slowly. "Ragna has requested a guard to take her to the coast in the morning. I have already agreed to her demand. What do you suggest?"

His wolf lifted his head, and Rorik smiled inwardly at the beast.

"Tell her a storm is coming across the North Sea."

Magnar gave him a skeptical look. "Tell the *Seer* I sense a storm brewing? Give me another plan."

Rorik gestured outward. "Nae. Tell her the information came from Steinar. She kens well his keen insight to the weather and the seas."

The man's eyes widened in understanding. "Aye, 'tis true. Steinar does possess the inner sight with regards to the storms—"

"She will believe him and remain here until the threat of the storm passes," interrupted Rorik, pressing his idea further.

Leaning back in his chair, Magnar folded his arms over his chest. "A wise plan. I see frailty, though."

He snorted. "There is none."

Barking out in laughter, Magnar stood abruptly and strode across to the door of the solar. "You have forgotten the most important thread within your plan. *Steinar*."

"Nae problem. The man will clearly accept aiding me in my plan." Rorik saw no flaw in asking his friend to do this task for him.

Magnar gave him a scathing look over his shoulder. "Have you spoken to him since you have awakened? You first chose him as your guardian."

Rorik frowned in confusion. "Not my decision."

"Hence, you will blame this all on your wolf?"

"Aye!"

"Loki's balls, Rorik! Did it not occur to you that your wolf was acting on *your* feelings? When the beast sensed Ragna nearby, he instantly chose the woman you have been in love with for years to be your guardian."

Love? Rorik swallowed the word before he had a chance to utter it aloud. His vision blurred. He did not love Ragna, simply lust mixed with a yearning for friendship. Yet were his emotions that obvious? How many others saw what Magnar witnessed? Was Rorik the fool and no one dared admit it openly to him?

Magnar tilted his head to the side. "What? Nae denial? Nae argument? Your silence speaks greatly, my friend."

Rorik rose from his chair, unable to say one bloody word in objection. His mouth as dry as the Dragon Fire mead his mother used to make. He coughed in an attempt to speak. "I-I do *not*," he finally stammered.

The man ignored his outburst. Opening the door,

Magnar bellowed for someone to fetch Steinar to the solar.

"Why are you shouting?" demanded Elspeth, sweeping past her husband while carrying a trencher of food.

"Is it not obvious in my demand?"

A smiled curved at the edges of her mouth. "Possibly, if anyone was within hearing of said demand. Most are either attending to chores in the bailey, stables, or in the training lists." Setting the trencher on the table, Elspeth then busied herself with removing the empty jug of mead and pushing aside the documents into a neat pile.

"Trust me, *wife*, at least one of my men heard me." Magnar crossed to her side and wrapped his arms around her waist.

She stood on her tiptoes and kissed his chin. "I shall fetch more mead and ale."

He nuzzled her neck. "I shall not be long here. Meet me by the oak."

Giggling softly, she argued, "Nae. I am helping in the kitchens with the breads."

A growl escaped from the man. "I have something to show you."

When her cheeks turned a rosy glow, Rorik turned away and went to the window. An ache settled within his chest, and he fought the urge to rub the spot. Ever since he had awoken from his deep sleep something shifted inside him. Aye, he had feelings for Ragna. Unable to deny those to himself, he chose to believe they were lustful. Yet why did he yearn for more? There could never be a life with any woman, especially the Seer. So why was he determined to keep her here?

His path as the Dark Seducer prevented him from taking any female into his life and heart.

Confusion raged like a storm on the rough seas. Clasping his hands behind his back, he stared outward and slammed the door on his troubling thoughts.

"You wish to speak with me?" inquired Steinar.

Rorik turned away from the window and leaned against the stone wall.

After giving his wife a deep kiss, Magnar released his hold on her and gestured for Steinar to enter.

The man nodded in passing to Elspeth as she departed the solar, closing the door behind her.

Magnar inspected the food on the trencher. He ripped apart a portion of bread and slapped a piece of dried fish on top. "Rorik requires your assistance."

Steinar wiped the sweat from his brow. Mud covered most of his tunic, and the stench of horse muck filled the room. "What do you need?"

Rorik pushed away from the wall. "First, I have been negligent in not speaking with you since my healing."

The man studied him like he had sprouted goat horns.

"Furthermore," continued Rorik. "I did—"

Instantly, Steinar's hand shot outward to halt his words. "Stop! Do not speak thusly. I am not to be charmed by your words. I understand what happened. You care for the woman. The wolf sensed your feelings. Was I concerned? Aye and nae. Nevertheless, your healing was all that mattered to the brotherhood."

Rorik took a step forward. "Aye, but I should have spoken to you afterward."

"And with a cup of mead," added Steinar. Fisting

his hands on his hips, he nodded in humor. "Now, what do you require of me?"

Rubbing his hands together, Rorik replied, "Can you tell the Seer you sense an impending storm coming from the north?"

Steinar's brow furrowed. "I sense none. Has she not requested a guard to take her to the coast?"

Rorik placed a hand on the man's shoulder. "But I *need* you tell her a tempest is brewing so she will remain here at Steinn."

Steinar's mouth dropped open like a forlorn fish, and then he promptly snapped it shut. "You-*you* want me to tell a false truth? Lie to the Seer?" He visibly swallowed and turned his gaze to Magnar.

The leader of the wolves gave a curt nod of approval while continuing with his meal.

"'Tis important to me," urged Rorik.

Steinar shifted his stance and glared at him. "Important to you, but deadly for me. The woman could have me flayed with a simple word or look."

"What can I offer to convince you?" suggested Rorik, determined to get his friend to aid him in this quest. All he wanted was a few more days with Ragna. Nothing more.

The man's lip snarled. "A battle of spears on the dragon's tail."

Dropping his hand, Rorik took a step back. The dragon's tail was simply a large fallen log the young chieftain of Steinn, Erik, had named after witnessing it unmoving across a gentle river one day in early summer. However, this was autumn and the water now a raging river.

His wolf padded closer inside him, eager for this

new trial of combat.

"Challenge accepted," pronounced Rorik.

Steinar dared to poke a finger in his chest. "Leave the wolf behind as well. Or I shall request one hand tied behind your back."

"Worried I'll use his strength?"

The man shrugged. "If you do, I can always remove your balls."

Rorik roared with laughter. The battle lines had been drawn and presented. "My wolf will observe."

"When has your beast ever listened to you?" protested Steinar and strode away from him. "Give me an hour to finish with the horses."

"Done."

Rorik watched as the man left, muttering curses about probable loss of limbs on his body from the lie.

With a renewed sense of hope, Rorik went to the table and prepared a light meal. He tore off a small piece of dried fish and stuffed it into his mouth. Certain Ragna would believe Steinar's untruth, he smiled inwardly. Hastily, he made a silent note to offer up a prayer to the Gods to seal the accord.

When Elspeth wandered into the solar, she clucked her tongue at him. "Will this be a game of wits or brawn strength? Steinar is already telling everyone about the match." She placed a jug of mead on the table.

Rorik choked on the piece of dried fish.

Before he had a chance to reach for the jug, Elspeth poured a large amount into a cup and presented it outward to him.

Giving the woman a weak smile, he took the offering and drained the contents. Wiping his mouth with the back of his hand, he watched her give Magnar a wink as she ambled out of the room.

"'Tis many moons since we've witnessed a challenge like the one Steinar presented." Magnar chuckled while he poured some mead into a cup.

"The last time was on the oars of the ship as we journeyed between *Orkneyjar*," recalled Rorik.

"And Steinar was the last man to remain standing on one of the oars," mentioned Magnar. "Your strength is far superior on land, but Steinar has the advantage on the water. Be wary. He might be tempted to scar your face."

Returning the cup to the table, Rorik rubbed a hand over his cheek as he made his way out of the solar. "He would not dare do damage. 'Tis perfection."

Magnar's thunder of laughter followed him along the corridor and down the winding stairs, and he smiled.

As he approached an alcove, Rorik slowed his steps. The torches flickered ahead of him. He halted his stride and leaned against the edges of the alcove. Inhaling sharply, he asked, "Are you lost, Hallgerd?"

Her gasp echoed within the narrow passageway. She came forth. "How did you ken it was me?"

Rorik tapped a finger against his nose.

The woman's fingers fidgeted within the folds of her gown. "Aye, your keen sense of smell."

"Are you lost, or were you waiting for someone?"

"I simply wanted to inquire about your health. You have been absent from the great hall."

Even in the half-lit corridor, Rorik noticed wariness in her eyes and tone. Indecision plagued him. If he spurned her, he might not get another opportunity to gather the information he required. In their earlier conversations, she became hesitant when discussing her brother. Perchance, she had nae knowledge about her brother's dealings with King John. He had not considered this possibility and thought to present this news to William.

Rorik pushed away from the wall. "I am grateful for your concerns, Hallgerd. Will you walk with me to the river?"

Her eyes widened in surprise at his offer.

Holding out his arm, he waited while she placed her hand in the crook of his elbow.

As soon as her fingers settled on him, Rorik moved them steadily along the corridor.

"Why are we going to the river?" she asked softly.

"Steinar has issued a challenge to me. I shall engage him in sport on the dragon's tail."

"*Dragon's tail*?" echoed Hallgerd, digging her fingers into him.

Smiling, he explained, "A fallen tree trapped in the middle of the river. Apparently, the men of Steinn stripped the branches and held tests of skill on the trunk. The name was given by the young chieftain after hearing a tale about a great dragon felling trees in the north."

"Why do you want to engage in this challenge? Is it not unwise after your injury?"

"Do not worry," he reassured dryly. "My strength has returned, and the wound is healed. Surely your brother had many such challenges."

As they made their way down the stairs, she gave out a snort. "Jorund found little time to display his strength since many avoided him at the games or combat in the lists."

"Is he a giant feared by his men?" teased Rorik, maneuvering her toward the front doors and outside.

"In truth, you are correct." Hallgerd blew out a sigh as she raised her head to the sunlight. "His cruelty was well known if he did not win."

Rorik studied her features. "And have you been a victim of his harsh ways?"

Startled, she touched her cheek. "Nae, nae!"

You lie, Hallgerd. I can smell the fear seeping through your skin. He kept them moving at a leisurely pace, eager to learn more. "Will your travels include visiting Jorund?"

Her face paled. "His tasks keep him busy. When he is ready, he will send a message to David."

"Then he approves of your marriage to a noble man, especially one with ties to *Orkneyjar* and Scotland?"

Hallgerd gave a slight shrug. "He has yet to meet with David. We have only corresponded through messages."

Rorik steered them away from the antics of two dogs. As he led her through the portcullis, he waved to a passing guard. "Ah. You did not seek his approval."

"David has money, lands, *and* power. There should be nae objection," she stated tersely.

"Agreed."

Leaves swirled around them while they walked along the path leading through the trees and toward the river.

Hallgerd slid a sideways glance at him. "Do you not own lands bordering David's?"

"Aye," he confirmed slowly. "Has David shared

this knowledge with you?"

Her laughter sounded nervous. "I do not recall."

More lies, Rorik mused. "The land is large, yet the main keep lies in ruins."

"Will you rebuild?"

Curious with the direction of the conversation, he brought them to a halt near an oak tree. He released his hold on her hand and retrieved an acorn from the leaf-filled ground. "It was my father's land. Steinn and Vargr are my homes."

"Then why not sell or find another who can tend to the land?"

Rolling the acorn between his thumb and finger, he contemplated on what to say to the woman. Her intentions were not what they appeared. Hallgerd showed no regard for anyone telling her what to do, except for one. David. And now it would appear she feared her brother. Was she also a charmer to seek knowledge or gain insight? Furthermore, her questions were about his land—*land* he no longer occupied or concerned himself with the maintenance.

Rorik tossed the acorn outward. "A plan I have not had time to consider."

Her eyes shone brightly. Hallgerd grabbed his arm. "I am certain David would want to purchase the land when you are ready." She squeezed slightly, adding, "Do keep this between us. I do not want to present this news to David before you are certain."

He snarled inwardly. Then David and Jon would control most of the north. Or was there another seeking a claim to the lands?

By the hounds of Odin! King John?

Rorik shoved aside the fury. Hallgerd was a pawn

in someone's game, and he wagered it was not David.

Giving Hallgerd his best smile, he gestured her forward. "Until then, I have a challenge to face."

Chapter Thirteen

Ragna fingered the leather pouch of runes attached to the belt at her side. “When do you reckon the storm will pass?”

Closing his eyes, Steinar raised his head to the north. “Uncertain. The winds might blow the tempest to the east *or* west along the coast.”

She studied him skeptically while sorely tempted to cast out her runes onto the ground for a more defined explanation. Inhaling deeply, she tried to pick up any sign of an impending storm. Aye, the man had a shrewd insight when it came to sensing the storms, but she did as well. Could his power extend farther out than hers? Her heart ached at having to remain at Steinn near Rorik. The sooner she put the ocean between them the better.

“Is there anything else you can discern?” she pressed.

Steinar returned his attention to her. “Nae.”

Boisterous laughter sounded from beyond the gates, and Ragna shifted her gaze to the people departing over the bridge. Shielding her eyes from the sunlight, she caught a glimpse of Magnar and Elspeth. “Where is everyone going?”

“To witness a challenge with spears near the river.”

Startled, she snapped her gaze to the man. “Between whom?”

Pounding a fist against his chest, Steinar replied, "Myself and Rorik." A smile twitched at the corners of his mouth. "I fear I cannot stay and discuss more about the approaching storm. Victory is within my grasp."

Without giving her a chance to inquire with more questions, Ragna watched as he darted across the bridge and ran past the group of people. Many cheered him onward while some lifted their fists, shouting to give Rorik another scar to match the one by his ear.

A gasp escaped from her. Spears? Maiming? "Sweet Goddess," blurted out Ragna.

Lifting a portion of her gown, she took off running toward the river, ignoring those in passing. Elspeth called out to her, but she dismissed the woman with a wave of her other hand and dashed along the narrow path.

What possessed the man to battle another wolf? Or was it simply a game? *A foolish one!* Did she not stay by Rorik's side those many days tending to him? Only to have the threat of him getting hurt again.

After almost stumbling over a tree root, she slowed her descent. Brushing aside a heavy tree limb, she tried to steady her breathing as her steps led her the rest of the way to get a view of the water.

Ragna came to an abrupt halt. She placed a hand over her thundering heart. It was not from the actions of her running through the trees but the man who stood proudly in only his trews on a giant log that stretched from one edge of the river to almost the other side.

"*Rorik,*" she uttered his name on a sigh. The corded muscles on his back flexed with each movement of the spear he waved about in a display of bravery.

Having no desire to be seen, Ragna pulled back

into the shadows of one of the trees. Her vantage proved wondrous as she leaned against the rough bark.

Steinar emerged and promptly stripped the tunic from his back. He retrieved a spear propped against one of the trees and began taunting Rorik.

The crowd gathered on the edges of the river with a few choosing to sit on the ground. Some brought parcels of food and drink while listening to an elder spout the tale of how he once mastered leaping from one oar to the next on a small ship through rivers near his home.

Another man stepped into her view and raised a drinking cup outward. "There is nae first blood drawn—"

Shouts and curses interrupted the man.

Magnar raised a hand to silence the wayward crowd.

Hushed voices descended throughout, and some gestured for the speaker to continue.

Taking another guzzle of ale, the man belched. "As I mentioned, the winner will not be decided on the draw of first blood but whoever shall be left standing on the mighty dragon's tail."

Ragna snorted. "'Tis simply a large tree trunk."

"Are you saying I did not choose a wise name?" demanded the young male voice behind her.

She pointed outward. "You are the name giver?"

Erik stepped by her side and fisted his hands on his hip. "Aye. Can you not see the long tail curling back into the forest?"

Arching a brow, she suggested, "Perchance, you were meant to see the dragon's shape, aye?" She regarded the aging giant contained within the water's grasp.

"Others can also see the tail," he offered.

"Because you are their chieftain, and they are in agreement."

He frowned in obvious thought. "They seek to please me?"

Ragna lifted one shoulder. "To gain favor, aye. But 'tis also a sign of respect."

The lad smiled broadly. "I am learning with the help of Magnar and the other wolves. They ken great wisdom."

Her gaze riveted to the scene below. The sparring of words continued between Rorik and Steinar. She sighed. "The wolves are an ancient order woven by magic. There is much you can learn from them, but do not forget the wisdom from others."

"I thank you for sharing *yours* with me, Seer."

Startled from her thoughts, she glanced down at him. Respect shone brightly within Erik's eyes. She dipped her head in respect at the young chieftain. "Why are you not sitting with the others? I would have thought you to be first amongst those gathered."

The lad wiped a hand across his nose. "I had to attend to my studies. Rorik is in charge while Gunnar is away. I do not want to bring dishonor by thwarting their orders."

You have discipline for one so young, brave chieftain. "A wise decision," she conceded.

"Will you join me?" he asked, holding out his hand.

Though the lad's offer tempting, she judged it wiser to remain hidden. "'Tis better if I stay here."

Erik nodded slowly, giving her a small smile.

She watched as he darted down the hill, jumping over boulders and small tree stumps until he settled next to Elspeth and Magnar.

Hushed silence descended below. Ragna averted her gaze to the two men who had now engaged in a battle to knock the other from their place on the log. Steinar proved to have the advantage with the number of strikes, yet none had drawn any blood. When the man smacked the end of his spear against Rorik's healed arm, Ragna let out a hiss.

Rorik reacted as if the blow did nothing to him. He didn't even flinch, and she pondered if he had bonded with his wolf to deflect the blows with the animal's power. When Rorik threw a hard blow against Steinar's shoulder, the man remained standing, deflecting another swift blow with one of his own.

You both are cheating with the power of your wolves. She shook her head at the folly.

Grunts and curses spewed forth from both men. If she had been closer, she would not have been surprised to hear a growl in the mix of curses either.

A few of the men began to shout out their suggestions. One proposed each man take a drink from his horn of ale. Another spouted the use of tripping or using the spear to maim certain male body parts. Each plan was met with an argument from others.

And so the battle raged on. Both men were relentless in their quest to prove the winner.

Ragna strained to hear more. The water lapped furiously against the bark on its journey downstream. A gust of wind blew past her trailing dead leaves along its path.

She stepped from the shelter of the tree's shadow.

Sunlight wrapped her in its golden warmth, and the tension eased from her shoulders and the rest of her limbs. This was simply a battle of strength, nothing more. She need not fear its outcome, though her heart pulsed rapidly against her chest.

Blow after blow was struck between the two men. Steinar lunged forward with one foot, slashing across Rorik's chest. A great howl of fury exploded within her mind. Uncertain if it was Rorik's wolf or her own cry of terror, she shoved a fist against her mouth to suppress any sound.

With trembling legs, Ragna moved forward and halted near one of the large boulders. Settling down on the smooth surface, she tried to calm her racing heart. She should not be here. She should not watch this dangerous skirmish. Aye, she had witnessed many such displays of strength and endurance on the isles, but this was different. Feelings she had locked away with a stern will seeped through every action of hers while watching Rorik.

This is why she wanted to leave Scotland. Her love for him so great, Ragna was unable to contain it within. If she were not careful, others would soon notice.

Ragna's heart shattered with each blow against the man who held her heart.

After ducking a blow meant for his head, Rorik rose and leveled a hard fist against Steinar's jaw, sending the man into the river.

Without thought, Ragna abruptly stood, shouting victory for Rorik. Realizing her mistake, she clamped a hand over her mouth. Thankfully, her cheer was drowned out by the resounding shouts of the others below as they stood. Many went to Steinar's aid, and the remainder of the crowd waited for Rorik to retreat onto land. He was met with hard thumps on the back, kisses from some of the elder women, and a huge embrace from Magnar.

Laughter bubbled forth from her, and she pressed a hand to her chest. "You were magnificent," she murmured.

As if he heard her, Rorik raised his head from those gathered around him.

Her breathing hitched as their gazes locked. Rorik's smile came slowly while she fought the urge to clasp her hands together. Her fingers itched to wrap around his neck and pull him closer to her mouth for a heady kiss.

One of the men nudged Rorik while pressing a jug against his chest.

Rorik gave her a wink. Returning his attention to the man, he then took the offering. He guzzled the entire contents within moments. As others continued to offer him praises, he nodded or gave the occasional laugh at a response.

Ragna started forward, then hesitated.

Hallgerd had appeared near Rorik's side. Although David stood only a few paces from the woman, Ragna's heart still seized with jealousy. Unfamiliar with this feeling, she tried to banish it aside. Confusion settled like a swarm of bees. She drew in a large breath of air and released it out on a rush and turned away.

With unsteady steps, she retreated into the shadow of the trees.

****

Wisps of smoke trailed around her like the claws of a raven. The stench of death filled her nostrils, hampering her ability to breathe. Did she bring dishonor to the Goddess and now her life was forfeit?

"I cannot help what is within my heart!" Ragna choked out on a scream. "I beg you to show me another path—another way out of this madness."

Blackness crept through her vision. Holding her palms outward, she tried to fight the horror approaching her. It slithered across the expanse of darkness with its menacing steps.

"Why do you not answer me? Tell me how I have wronged you?" She tried desperately to search through her clouded memories, but to no avail. Somehow, she had doomed her fate with her actions.

Ragna lowered her arms, unable to stop the inevitable. Her lungs fought for breath.

In a glint of light, the sword's steel lashed out at her.

I have failed you, Rorik.

Ragna woke on a scream while clutching her head within her hands. Shoving the fur covering from her trembling body, she turned and spewed what little food she had in her stomach onto the floor. Tears spilled down her cheeks as she tried to bring air back into her body. Curling up onto her side, she waited for the burning pain in her head to lessen. Moments slipped by in agonizing torment. She forced her eyes open, searching the chamber for any sign of danger. Golden embers from the hearth flickered like a menacing animal. When she judged all was safe, Ragna turned away.

Her vision had been so powerful she still could feel the lash of the blade against her skin. With shaky fingers, Ragna trailed a path across her neck. She curled her hand into a fist and rose into a sitting position on the bed.

"I cannot fathom my death at your hands, Goddess, or of another," she declared into the cold chamber.

Was it evil that had woven a thread inside her? If this were daylight, she'd seek counsel from Declan.

Moonlight dusted the floor of her chamber through the cracks in the wooden shutters, urging her to come forth. After rubbing her eyes with the heels of her palms, she scooted off the bed toward the arched window. Drawing back the shutters, she relaxed in the moon's soothing light.

Her heart calmed.

"I seek more answers, Goddess," she pleaded softly. "Only magic can help me with your guiding hand. Show me the path—be it my own or Rorik's. I shall abide by your decision."

Ragna turned from the window. She fetched a cloth and empty basin. Quickly cleaning up the mess on the floor, she deposited the items near the hearth to be dealt with later. She wandered to the table and poured a small amount of mead into a cup. The honeyed liquid helped to settle her stomach. Slices of apple remained on her evening trencher, and she hastily shoved one into her mouth. She took one more sip of the mead to settle the tremors still coursing in her body.

Going to her trunk at the end of the bed, she drew forth a simple, coarse gown. After dressing, she retrieved her cloak and wrapped it around her shoulders. She crossed the room to the table. Her fingers glided over her pouch of runes. What she required was more powerful magic.

Ragna reached for the small blade. Tucking it

securely within the belt around her waist, she glanced at the open window. "Make me a shadow, Guardians of the night stars, so others shall not see me pass."

Drawing the hood of her cloak firmly over her head, Ragna quietly departed the chamber.

As her steps led her near the great hall, she paused before the entrance, listening for any voices within. What greeted her were the snores of sleeping men, and she smiled. In a quiet whisper, she stole past the entrance and toward the massive oak doors.

Placing her hand on the rough wood, Ragna gently pushed one open. A blast of cold air hailed her when she stepped outside. Determined to move swiftly, she followed the path which led to the gardens. If her memory served her correctly, there would be a wooden ladder hidden within. Apparently, the young chieftain had boasted of fleeing Steinn with his Aunt Elspeth after it was attacked and set on fire many months ago.

She prayed the ladder still existed.

Her steps were cautious, steady, until she noted the entrance to the kitchen gardens. Slipping past the open gate, she paused. *Did you not mention the apple trees by the stone wall, Erik?*

Moving carefully, she twisted around a group of rosemary bushes, following the path to the outer castle walls. Hope flared within her when she approached the trees. Ducking behind them, she crept along carefully.

An owl screeched above her. Ragna halted, unsure if the ladder could be found in the darkness. Determined not to give up, she started forward and almost tripped. Her foot encountered a rough object. She held back the curse and bent down. Her fingers sought and found the precious item.

After retrieving the ladder from its hidden spot, she placed it against the wall and climbed to the top. Reaching for a nearby tree branch, Ragna started her descent. Her cloak snagged on one of the branches. Quickly freeing herself from its grip, she continued to make her way down. When her feet touched the soft ground, she let out a sigh of relief.

She pushed back the hood of her cloak to listen. The river was south from her position. Grateful for the moonlight, she followed its path slowly. As she passed each tree, Ragna pressed her palm against the rough bark, whispering ancient words of protection on her journey.

No one would find her. No one would harm her.

By the time she reached the river, her body burned with the power from the land. Uncertain of how much time she could maintain control, she pushed beyond the limits of her own power, seeking more. Heat flared in every pore of her skin, and Ragna removed her cloak, along with her shoes. After tossing everything aside, she undid her leather belt and stripped the gown from her fevered body. Ragna unraveled her braid, letting her hair trail down her back.

The words she whispered now became a chant as she removed the small blade from its sheath off the ground. Ragna stepped near the water's edge, allowing herself to bathe in the glow of the moon. With a swift slash across her palm, she watched the drops of blood splattering into the water.

The air swirled around her, and Ragna clutched the amber pendant around her neck. The Goddess called her forth.

Stepping into the water, she raised her hands

upward, and a song of power came forth from her lips.

"From the land of my ancestors to the land of the ancients, I, Ragna, from the house of Maddadsson, beseech the wisdom to see beyond the veil. Come through me to clear away the confusion and indecisions. Banish the vision and replace them with your guidance."

As Ragna dug her feet into the sandy soil of the river, she felt her body drift along the current of the water, journeying far beyond this time and place.

Chapter Fourteen

Rorik leaned forward on the north tower, bracing his forearms against the rough stone ledge. Unrest had plagued him. His attempts at sleep were haunted with dreams of a certain enticing woman. Seeing Ragna amongst the trees after his challenge with Steinar gave him hope. She had not fled to the coast. Therefore, when he entered the great hall for the evening meal, his gut soured at finding her not there. Elspeth informed him she had favored taking a light meal in her chamber. Rorik's good mood had vanished, and a great amount of mead had become his meal.

"Do you seek to avoid me, Ragna? Should I let you slip away again?" His question full of bitterness and confusion.

Rorik's cloak flapped furiously around his legs. He ignored the bite of wind slashing across his face. Scrubbing a hand over his forehead, he fought leaving the cold emptiness of the tower.

The scent of another swept by him from beyond the walls of Steinn. Who would dare leave the protection of the fortress in the middle of the night? Or was it another attempting to enter?

Nae, 'tis only the ghosts that haunt the land.

He dismissed it, believing it to be the night animals taking flight or the weariness from lack of rest. He closed his eyes and tried to settle his troublesome thoughts.

An owl's hoot stirred him, and Rorik opened his eyes. His wolf rose from his sleeping position.

Rorik narrowed his focus.

Whoever had ventured near the outer walls and trees of Steinn was long gone. He sighed, prepared to leave the solitude of the tower when a faint tremor rippled through him. Rorik braced his hands on the ledge and inhaled deeply. Merging his powers with the wolf's, Rorik inhaled again, more strongly.

He let out a sharp hiss and slammed his fist against the hard stone ledge. *Ragna!*

Though he was furious she had abandoned the safety of Steinn, Rorik also grew curious. How did the woman leave, and why would she depart? The castle had been secured before the first evening star ascended the sky.

Did she not trust Steinar's account about a storm coming across the sea? Did she think to journey to the coast all alone?

Fear seized him at the thought.

Rorik turned swiftly and dashed through the open door. Descending the stone stairs two at a time, he made his way out of the keep. His steps led him along the back entrance toward another way of leaving the castle. He had no intention of signaling anyone with the raising of the portcullis.

A guard approached from the protection of the trees. As soon as the man noticed him, he stepped aside.

"I have business to attend to," Rorik declared in a hushed voice.

None of the guards questioned the reasons of the coming and goings of the wolves. Many from the brotherhood chose to roam the land during the dark hours. Magnar had given strict instructions to the guards to allow any of the wolves to leave and enter without his permission.

The guard nodded and unbolted the heavy lock.

Rorik slipped silently through and took off running in Ragna's direction, pausing several times to catch her scent within the trees. When he realized his movements were leading him to the river, he slowed his pace. The air warmed greatly as he neared her position. Soft light flickered beyond the trees, luring him forward.

When he emerged near the bank of the river, he froze at the image before him.

Beautiful light danced around Ragna's naked form while the water lapped gently across her thighs. Her ebony locks fell in gentle waves down her back, ending just above her heart-shaped bottom. She was a Goddess of the water, calling forth the ancients with her song.

You are my Goddess, Ragna.

Desire slammed into Rorik with such force, he stumbled back. His heart hammered against his chest. Heat built inside his body, and his cock strained against his trews. He was too confined, unable to breathe with the garments sticking against his skin. He tore the cloak from his shoulders. After ripping the tunic free from his body, he stripped from his boots. On a sigh, he sank his toes into the bliss of the cool ground.

Rorik did not fathom her reason for being here, nor did he care. He no longer battled against wanting Ragna. With each word she sang, the hard metal around his heart splintered away. Years of resisting this woman had now vanished.

His pressed the heel of his palm against his wildly

beating heart. *I shall claim you, Ragna. You are mine.* Rorik's hand clenched and unclenched. He wiped the sweat from his brow. Unable to control being silent, he stormed across the ground and stood at the edge of the water.

"Come to me, Ragna," he demanded in a hoarse voice.

She glanced slowly over her shoulder. Shock briefly turned to a heated stare. "'Tis really you," she uttered softly.

His breath caught. Her eyes shone like starlight as her gaze traveled the length of him. Rorik's cock swelled even more. He held out his hand. "Do not deny me, *Ragna*."

A smile teased the corners of her rosy lips as she turned around fully.

This time, Rorik gazed upon her lush body, taking in her full breasts and rounded hips. Hers was a body to worship—to give pleasure. Her pert nipples reminded him of berries—to be suckled and tasted. And how he craved to taste the sweet nectar hidden behind her dark nest of curls.

"Will you take me here on the land?" she asked gently, striding forward.

Holding out his hand, he responded, "Aye. Here on the land of my ancestors, I shall claim you."

She tilted her head to the side and bit her lower lip. "For this night? For the next? How many?"

Heat seared into him when she slid her fingers across his palm. How Rorik craved to answer her fully. Emotions warred inside him. Would she spurn him again? Would she even believe him? He crushed her against his body and felt her tremble when he cupped her chin. The touch of her skin against his sent him spiraling. "What would you have me say, *my kærr*?"

Her shoulders sagged on a sigh. "The truth, Rorik. *Always* the truth."

Rorik traced a delicate path over her bottom lip with his thumb. Lowering his head, he teased his tongue between her parted lips, tasting the honeyed sweetness of mead. "I want you forever." He breathed the words against her mouth. "Only you." He drew back to study her response.

A great shudder wracked her body. Ragna pressed her fingers deeper into his shoulders. "Make love with me, Rorik."

"Do you understand what I am asking of you, Ragna? What I require is your heart *and* soul. Once I have taken your maidenhead, you shall be mine—completely."

Tears brimmed within her eyes, and her lip trembled. "What happens come the morn? Shall the Dark Seducer—"

Rorik took possession of her mouth in scorching passion, silencing any further discussion. Tomorrow would come as surely as the sun rose each morn. They had time to discuss their plans. Time to sort out their concerns and questions. This night was theirs.

The kiss burned through his veins, banishing the bitter coldness and filling him with a fierce need for more. Is this what he had fought against all these years? Feared she would rule his heart if he wanted more? Feared he could no longer be the man everyone had expected of him?

He slammed the door on his fears. He would take her fully. Take possession of her body. Show her pleasures that would rival any others.

When her moan resonated within him, he deepened the kiss, thrusting his tongue into her velvet softness. His hand skimmed along her smooth skin until he sought his prize. Fondling her full breast, he pinched the pert nipple and was rewarded with another moan. He smiled against her lips.

Ragna rubbed against his aching cock, and this time he let out a growl of pleasure.

He traced a path along the vein of her neck with his tongue, savoring her own womanly scent. When he reached the path between her breasts, he cupped one and tasted fully. Rorik took his time, committing to memory the delicious sweetness with each swipe of his tongue. Her skin was as heady as the land they stood upon—wild and untamed. No longer was she the controlled Seer. This was the woman Rorik had yearned for. Ragna filled the emptiness he had used as a shield for so many moons.

There was no going back.

In one swift move, he lifted her into his arms and strode into the protection of the trees.

Ragna rested her head on his shoulder while she twirled his chest hairs with her fingers. "You are magnificent, my warrior." Her breath was warm against his skin.

He bit her lightly on her shoulder. "And your beauty steals the breath from my body."

She gasped. "I need more of you."

Rorik halted before a giant oak tree. He gently lowered her feet to the ground. Sweeping his gaze behind her, he went to retrieve his cloak. Returning, he spread it out near the base of the aging giant.

Grasping her firmly around the waist with one hand, he recaptured her lips—demanding and forceful. Desire tore through his veins. His tongue sought entry into her soft heat, and he inhaled her scent. He absorbed her—the warmth and wildness beneath the Seer.

Ragna returned his kiss with reckless abandon. When she wrapped her arms around his neck, he groaned deep within her mouth. The blood pounded in his veins in a way he had never known. She had pushed past his barriers of steely control.

This time Ragna broke free from the kiss. Her smile was filled with enticement as she knelt in front of him. Tugging on the laces of his trews, she met his lust-filled gaze. "'Tis not fair," she pouted.

Arching a brow, Rorik fisted his hands on his hips. Understanding her meaning, he proposed, "Then rid the garment from my body. Yet I must warn you, my resolve is slipping. I ache to bury myself inside your softness."

The game of seduction now belonged to her, and he reveled in the pleasure. Rorik was no longer the Dark Seducer. He was simply a man, and she was seducing him. He banished all and surrendered to Ragna.

Rorik watched as she undid the laces with trembling fingers. When the last one slipped free, she grasped the sides of his trews and yanked them down. His cock sprang free from its prison, and he let out a groan, keeping his hands tightly fisted.

Ragna's eyes widened in surprise.

He held his breath, craving her touch yet fearing he'd spill his seed before he had a chance to enter her. Need and desire overrode any clear thought. Rorik grasped her hand. "Touch me, *my kærr*."

Watching in a hooded gaze, he let her explore, showing her how to stroke the length of him. When she squeezed him, Rorik clenched his jaw so tight he feared it would snap in two.

"Hard and smooth." Ragna breathed the words against him. "What do you taste like, my warrior?"

The dizzying pleasure built. How he had dreamt of having her mouth on him, taking him deep and trailing her tongue down to his heavy balls. Letting out a sharp hiss, he removed her hand from his body.

Ragna let out a cry of displeasure. "Nae—"

He placed a finger against her lips to silence any further protest. And she responded by nipping tenderly on his flesh.

Rorik dropped to the ground and cupped her face. He drank in the sweetness of her lips with each kiss. Gently, he pushed her back onto his cloak. Nipping the soft spot below her ear, he allowed his hand to stroke a lazy path down the slope of her breasts, to the dip in her abdomen, and farther until he found her womanly folds. His fingers skimmed over her soft curls, and then he delved one finger inside her hot moisture. He found her center and rubbed his thumb over the sensitive core, watching the flame of her desire build within the depths of her eyes. With each flick of his finger, her body quivered two-fold from his touch. She breathed lightly between lips already swollen from his kisses. As he roused her passion, his own grew stronger.

"*Rorik*," she gasped, closing her eyes. She squirmed and whimpered. "Aye, more," she pleaded, arching against his hand.

"Open your eyes," he demanded hoarsely. Leaning

over her, Rorik bit along the pulsing vein on the side of her neck.

Her eyes fluttered open.

"Give in to the pleasure, *my kærr*."

Ragna moved in an ancient rhythm of passion, and he gritted his teeth, aching to bury himself deep within her body. Her scent filled him. Mesmerized by the beauty in front of him, Rorik was swept into her own ecstasy of release.

With a savage growl, Rorik took her mouth in a firestorm. Nudging apart her thighs with his hand, he guided his swollen cock to her entrance.

While her fingers splayed into his hair, she urged him onward. "Take me now," she pleaded in a ragged breath against his mouth.

Taking possession of her mouth, his lustful beast drove fully inside her.

They both cried out in unison at the heady sensation. He thought he'd died when he entered her—so tight and hot. Their tongues clashed in a wild dance of passion. Ragna's warmth surrounded him—filling him completely. When she scraped her nails down his back, Rorik stilled, believing he had hurt her.

"*Nae*, do not stop," she hissed out. "Feels good…"

Smiling against her lips, he proceeded to slake his pleasure on her supple body. With each thrust, the turbulence of his passion swirled around them in a multitude of dazzling colors. His lips seared a path over her face, finding their way to her mouth. As his thrusts became urgent, more demanding, beads of sweat broke out along his brow.

While the hot tide of fervor raged through them, the fire grew within him, begging to be released. Never had he craved a woman like Ragna. No one else had cracked his hardened shield. The fortress, built so long ago, had never allowed love to enter. Until now.

Unable to hold back any longer, Rorik shook as his pleasure exploded into her. His roar of release echoed through the trees, and the ground rumbled beneath them.

The lingering passion rippled across his skin as he rolled over onto the ground, bringing Ragna against his chest. His heart hammered while he cradled his beloved. Rorik's breathing was ragged, and he tried to quiet his trembling body and hers.

As the air cooled around them, Rorik drew a portion of his cloak over their bodies. Never had he been so consumed by passion with another woman. He yearned to explore more with Ragna.

Staring upward at the stars, he spoke softly. "I have not scared you? My tastes can be demanding. You have sampled only the beginning of what I like to do."

"Scared of you?" Her question was one filled with concern.

Rorik returned his attention to her.

Raising her head from his chest, she dazzled him with one of those smiles he loved but rarely received from her. "I have never feared you, Rorik." She kissed his chin. "What other carnal pleasure do you enjoy?"

"Aye? You enjoy gathering wisdom—"

"Even when it comes to pleasure," interrupted Ragna.

Chuckling softly, he reveled in the warmth of her soft breasts against his skin, even as he craved to be inside her again. His hand stroked across her bottom.

Her lips parted on a sigh.

"I have yet to taste the sweet honey between your curls." He inhaled the scent of their lovemaking.

"What else?" she asked, rubbing her thigh gently over his growing cock.

Rorik tugged on a lock of her hair. "How I have desired to see your hair spilling over your bare skin. You must wear it down more often."

"It can be troublesome at times, especially when I am tending to chores or the animals."

He let the curl slip free and moved his hand to cup her bottom. "You are a beauty."

The smile she gave filled him completely.

"I want you again, but I fear 'tis too soon," he murmured.

Ragna leaned up and kissed the side of his mouth. "I shall not stop you, my *pleasure warrior*."

Instantly tossing the covering from their bodies, Rorik grasped his swollen cock. "Get on top of me."

Lust shimmered within her eyes. "A new way of pleasure?"

"*Aye*."

He watched in silent anticipation while she positioned herself over his swollen cock. Clenching his jaw, Rorik waited patiently for Ragna. When her hand slipped below his, he let out a sharp hiss and released his hold. Her heat surrounded him as she guided his length inside her tight body.

Ragna placed her hands on his chest and let out a long sigh, taking him in her completely.

"Sweet Goddess," he uttered in a strangled voice. He gripped her hips, encouraging her to find her own rhythm.

"Oh, my," she gasped, tossing her head back.

The tempest built within her. Rorik swiped a finger over her sensitive nub, stroking the passion even more. His body began to quake with a need to release. He continued his loving assault on her until she screamed his name as the swell of desire crashed through her.

With his name still on her lips, the liquid fire burst forth from Rorik.

Finally spent, Ragna collapsed against his chest. Wrapping his arms around her still-quaking body, he whispered the ancient words of claiming, binding them both.

In that quiet moment, the world ceased to exist, and peace entered his heart. Ragna had eased the anguish from his soul. His heart demanded he speak what had been held within, but his tongue kept silent.

On a sigh, Rorik closed his eyes. *Nae matter what shall happen, I love you, my kærr.*

Chapter Fifteen

Delicious warmth surrounded Ragna, along with the soft snores of another. With great effort, she cracked open her eyes. Rorik appeared to be in a deep slumber. One arm was flung out to the side while the other held her securely around her waist.

Birdsong echoed quietly in the forest, heralding the start of a new dawn. Glancing outward, Ragna noted the last of the stars dwindling away. She hated to wake him, but it was time to return to Steinn.

My thanks for sending Rorik to me, Goddess. I do not ken our path, but I nae longer fear your objections.

Returning her attention to him, she continued to study his features. A dark shadow of hair covered part of his face—a look she often favored from Rorik. Her fingers itched to sweep back a lock that always managed to grace the side of his face. Most often, he braided the troublesome hair on both sides.

Her heart beat fiercely for this man. He stripped away the trappings of what she was—a seer and a *völva.* Ragna simply became the woman in his arms. She had tossed aside the idea many moons ago of ever taking another man. There had been only one who dwelled within her heart. *Rorik.* As much as she despised what he had become, Ragna recognized the true man still lay buried deep inside his soul.

"Do you find my face pleasing?" Rorik asked

while keeping his eyes shut.

The low timbre of his voice sent a tremor of desire pulsing through Ragna. “Interesting.”

When he opened his eyes, mirth spilled forth from those vivid green eyes. “But not *pleasing*?”

Ragna bit her lip to keep from laughing. “I ken many have told you such. Does it matter to add one more voice to your skills?”

A frown replaced all humor. He cupped her chin with his rough hand. “Do not speak of the others. They mean *nothing* to me.”

Hope fluttered like the wings of a bird within her heart. She wanted to confess all to Rorik, yet unsure of how he would respond. The man once admitted to not loving anyone. He had no love for his father and said little about his mother, so why did Ragna expect him to love her?

Placing a hand over his, she responded, “*Very* pleasing.”

Rorik graced her with a beaming smile and withdrew his hand.

“We must leave,” she whispered.

“Aye,” he acknowledged, then added, “Though I yearn to take you once more.”

Heat pooled between her legs, craving to feel his touch, too. Before her resolve to leave slipped farther away, she said, “Then the sun will be rising across the land.”

Grumbling a curse, he took her mouth in a searing kiss. “This is not over,” he asserted firmly.

“Agreed,” she confirmed, kissing him back.

With a groan, Rorik ended the kiss and rolled away from her. “Where is your clothing?”

"Tucked near the oak behind us."

He arched a dark brow and promptly retrieved her gown and cloak. Returning to her side, he held out his hand. "Allow me to assist you."

Ragna averted her eyes from his growing length and grasped his hand.

Nuzzling her neck with his lips, he whispered, "On your next lesson, you can taste me."

The light graze of his beard against her skin caused her to shiver in anticipation of their next encounter.

After donning her gown and cloak, Ragna sought out her shoes and went to sit on a boulder by the soothing river. She watched in fascination while Rorik quickly put on his trews, tunic, and boots. As he made steady strides to her, he swept up his cloak from the ground—shaking leaves and twigs free.

He loomed over her—powerful and protective. "Before we depart, I am curious. Why were you out here? Were you planning on leaving to the coast?"

Unprepared for his questions, she stared mutely at his face.

Smiling, he held out his hand. "If you prefer to keep silent, I shall understand. The *Seer* has her secrets, aye?"

Taking his hand, she stood slowly. *I have only one secret. My love for you.*

She swallowed. Glancing over her shoulder, Ragna fought to find the words. She blew out a frustrated breath and met his questioning gaze. "I grew troubled and required answers from the Goddess."

He placed her hand in the crook of his arm. "And did you find what you were seeking?"

Nervous laughter bubbled forth from her. "Oh,

aye."

"Good." Rorik steered them away from the water's edge and through the trees.

"Since you have asked a question, may I ask one of you?" She glanced sideways at him.

He lifted a tree limb out of their way. "Only one?" A smile tipped the corners of his mouth.

"Am I allowed more than one?" she asked hopefully.

"Proceed."

"What brought you to the river?"

"I sensed your presence outside the walls of Steinn."

Halting their progress, Ragna stared up at him. "How? Did you follow me from the castle?"

Rorik tapped the side of his nose. "I found sleep elusive and sought out the north tower. While there, I noted a lone person departing away from the castle, and then I inhaled your scent."

"From the north tower?" she asked in disbelief.

A frown marred his features. "Do you not ken how powerful we are, Ragna? I have shared my ability with the land, but the wolf's power is stronger."

Slipping her hand free, she went to one of the trees. She placed her palm upon the rough bark. "My life has been spent gaining wisdom from the ancients, the Gods and Goddesses, and the land. You and the wolves were not a part of my life on the isles. Forsooth, the wolves are more legends with tales of great deeds—a secret brotherhood—men who can take the form of a wolf. Aye, some of those before me feared you and your kind, yet our people on the isles see the wolves as great heroes."

"Not even your elder Seers spoke to you about the powers that reside in each of us?"

She glanced sharply at Rorik. "Never. We did not learn the ways of the wolves, and the brotherhood did not ken our edicts and powers. Did you ken I am able to sense the heartbeat of this tree?"

Rorik joined her near the giant. "Nae," he admitted quietly. "Tell me more."

"Not only the heartbeat but its warmth travels through my skin and into my veins. If I close my eyes and focus, I can reach through the many moons of this tree."

A bird flew out from the branches above them.

She pointed upward with her other hand. "If I so wish, I can call Oda from the comforts of her perch to find another."

Placing his hand over hers, Rorik's tone turned serious. "You mentioned Oda had informed you to my position. Was there a reason? Did you have a vision?"

Regarding him slowly, she nodded. "By using magic, Oda became my eyes to search for you, and nae, I did not have a vision."

"Explain."

Desperation tightened her throat. Ragna swallowed and forced the words free. "I heard the cry of your wolf."

Giving her a skeptical look, Rorik released his hold and took a step back. He shook his head. "You must have heard my growl of pain."

Uneasiness settled inside her. She removed her hand from the tree. "Nae, Rorik." Moving hesitantly toward him, she reached for him.

Rorik turned away in silence.

Ragna's hand fell to her side. *He does not believe you. Could he be as scared of what happened as you are?* "'Tis the truth," she offered in a firm voice.

When he turned to face her, Rorik's guarded expression had eased. "How?"

Relieved, she answered, "I heard his cry of anguish within my mind."

"By the hounds, the beast truly brought us together," he blurted out, raking a hand through his hair. "I do not ken if I should be angry *or* grateful."

"Do you not control your wolf?" She grew intrigued, recalling the time she'd spent with his wolf while Rorik was in the deep healing sleep."

"Aye, but the beast wields his demands. Often, I battle between man *and* wolf."

Curious, she pressed for more. "Clearly your father would have trained you, or another from the brotherhood?"

Irritation flashed briefly within Rorik's eyes. "My father had other plans for me. He cared *nothing* for the beast, nor his. To him, the wolf was a weapon to use in attacks against the enemy."

Her brow furrowed. "What plans?"

Rorik laughed bitterly. "You do not want to ken the evil he did to me." He turned and stormed through the trees.

She would not be dismissed. Ragna followed the man. Weak early morning light snaked through the clouds overhead as she jumped over tree roots, attempting to keep up with his pace. When she came to a partial clearing, she halted her stride. Rorik's rigid stance and tense features worried her.

"Tell me everything, Rorik," she encouraged.

His lip curled in disgust. "The account is wretched and made me who I am." In two strides, he gripped her upper arms. "Are you certain you want to ken the secrets of the *Dark Seducer*? There is only one other who learned what my father did to me, and even the great leader, *Magnar* recoiled in disgust."

Ragna blanched, not prepared for this revelation. Quickly banishing the uncertainty, she swallowed and gave him a curt nod to continue.

Releasing his hold, Rorik then clenched his hands at his sides and walked away. He stopped abruptly and raised his head to the sky. "My first lesson in bedding a woman came on my fourteenth summer. My father presented me with a thrall—five years older than me and skillful in carnal pleasures. As the woman taught me what she knew, my father remained in the chamber and gave her instructions." Rorik pointed to the leaf-covered ground. "He *disregarded* my other power of the land. Told me my duty for the king would be in securing secrets for the king in this manner. He observed how women appeared to touch or comment on my good features, and this would become my future. Coaxing secrets from women's bed chambers."

Rorik's tortured gaze met hers. "To argue against my father's demands would incite his wrath. He never beat me. The man took out his fury on the women who serviced and taught me. Forsooth, I became his *thrall* and sealed my fate with my silence."

Her stomach roiled, and a tear slipped down her cheek. "I…I am sorry," she managed on a choked sob.

"Do not pity me!" he scolded—his voice taut with strain.

"To clarify," began Ragna, then cleared her throat.

"I am *sorry* for what was done to you. There is nae *pity* in my feelings." She sniffed, adding, "I confess 'tis fierce anger for the vile man who sired you."

He scrubbed a hand vigorously over his face. With quick strides, he crossed the expanse that divided them. Rorik wrapped his arms around her waist. "Forgive me. At times, my anger is barely contained when I think of him. Even in death, I pray he will *never* enter Valhalla."

Ragna rested her cheek against his chest, inhaling Rorik's scent mixed with the land. "One can only hope that Durinn's balls are eaten slowly by Odin's dogs in the other world."

Rorik roared with laughter, breaking the earlier tension. Tipping her chin up with his finger, he stared into her eyes. "Have you cursed the man?"

She lifted one shoulder. "The ancients can find nae fault with words uttered on an early morning breeze."

He bent and placed a gentle kiss on her lips. Ragna drank in the sweet and tender moment.

"Sadly, we must return," he murmured against her cheek. He drew back. "However, there is a difficulty. We cannot stroll together through the gates of Steinn, which leads me to my other question."

Ragna arched a brow. "How did I manage to escape unnoticed by the guards?"

His mouth twitched with humor. "Did you use magic to vanish within the mists snaking around the hills?"

Wrapping her hands around his neck, she confessed, "I might be a powerful Seer, but that ability is beyond me."

"I am shocked at your declaration," he teased.

She stood on her tiptoes and leaned near his ear,

whispering, "I used the ladder in the kitchen gardens and climbed over the wall."

"By the hounds of Odin! You found Erik's old escape method."

"Aye," she acknowledged with pride.

He rubbed his chin as if pondering some great secret. "We were told the ladder was removed from the gardens."

"Truth? By whom?"

"The chieftain. Erik."

"A young chieftain who likes to escape his duties and roam unseen," she mused. "He spoke an untruth."

He took her hand and placed a searing kiss along the vein on her wrist. "I am grateful it still remains safely tucked away, or else last night would not have happened."

"I have nae regrets," admitted Ragna on a sigh.

Securing her hand within his, Rorik steered her forward along the narrow path. "Nor I, *my kærr*."

As their steps led them closer to Steinn, silence reigned between them. Questions tumbled within her mind, but she was too tired to speak them to Rorik. Her life would never be the same. Her heart now bonded with this man for all eternity. Yet neither had spoken of the one word she yearned to hear and speak aloud.

Love.

In her heart, Ragna loved this man completely, even with his scars. If she shared what had remained hidden with him, she risked shattering her heart. Was she strong enough to endure the pain, though? As a woman and not the Seer?

Nae. Her love was far too powerful and fragile. And his love for her simply implied but not spoken.

"Is this the tree you descended from over the wall?" Rorik asked quietly, snapping her out of her thoughts.

Ragna surveyed the area. She tugged on his arm. "Nae. 'Tis the other one farther along the wall."

With quiet steps, he led her to the base of the tree. "I shall assist you," he offered.

"You are following me over the wall?" Surveying the branches, Ragna doubted the tree could manage to hold their combined weight.

"Nae," he reassured. "Only on the lower branch. I can watch and assist you, if needed."

Before Ragna had a chance to start her ascent, Rorik wrapped his arm around her waist and brought her to his chest. Placing her hands on his shoulders, she roamed his features. Words lodged like stale dried fish in her throat.

Tucking a stray lock of hair around her ear, Rorik trailed a finger down the side of her neck. "I shall find a way for us to be together."

Ragna's lip trembled. "How?" she managed to blurt out. "As Seer *and* Dark Seducer?"

His features hardened. "With you, I am simply the man."

"And when you're not? You are part of an ancient brotherhood whose edicts are bound to the King of Scotland."

"Agreed, 'tis an uncertain path at the moment." Rorik rested his forehead against hers. "At present, I must complete the task I was sent to do for the king."

"Does it involve Hallgerd?" Ragna held her breath, fearing his response.

His grip tightened around her waist. "Aye," he

confirmed.

Will you bed the woman to get the information?

As he if read her thoughts, Rorik whispered, "My plans do not include bedding the woman."

Relieved, Ragna sighed and drew back. Another idea presented itself. "How can I help you?"

A frown creased his forehead. "Nae, *nae*. Too dangerous."

Ragna smacked the side of his arm and pinned Rorik with a glare. "I am not a meek lass. Have you forgotten I am skilled in the bow as well as a blade?"

The man smirked. "I ken well your skill with a bow. Do you recall the time when I caught you aiming your arrow at a young boar? You missed."

She tried not to roll her eyes upward but failed miserably. "The hunter became interrupted by the sounds of a man stomping through the forest."

"Stomping?" he echoed. "I am offended. I do not *stomp* anywhere."

Shrugging, she offered him a smile. "Nevertheless, your footsteps warned the boar, and my arrow did not hit its mark." Ragna wrapped her arms around his neck. "If you require my help with the woman, please seek me out."

His other hand cupped her chin—warm and strong. "For now, I have two requests from you."

Her lips parted on a sigh. "Aye?"

Rorik took her mouth in swift possession, sending her senses spiraling. Yearning for more, Ragna opened fully to the heady sensation. Delicious warmth invaded her body, and the world faded away.

Slowly, he withdrew from her mouth and released his hands from around her waist.

Ragna pressed her fingers lightly against her mouth. "And the other request?"

His smile rivaled the early morning sunlight dancing through the branches of the trees. He turned her toward the tree and gave her a smack on her bottom. "Toss me a couple apples over the wall."

Chuckling softly, Ragna made her way carefully upward along the tree. Slipping on one of the large branches, she heard Rorik's soft curse. Laughter infused her spirit, and she cast a wayward glance over her shoulder.

More curses spewed forth from the man. "By the hounds of Odin do not make me regret my actions and follow you."

"Patience, my warrior wolf," she soothed, resuming her progress. When she reached the ledge of the wall, she gave him a parting wave over her shoulder. Returning her attention to her position, she found the ladder in the same position she'd left earlier and descended into the garden.

After choosing the best apples for Rorik, she returned to the top of wall and tossed the bounty to him.

When Ragna's feet touched the garden floor, she leaned against the cold stone. Clutching a fist to her heart, she whispered, "I love you, my warrior wolf."

As I do you.

Startled by the response, she glanced upward, half-expecting Rorik to be nearby. Yet there was no one there. Simply a whispered hope on a breeze. "A foolish thought," she chastised.

Drawing the hood of her cloak over her head, Ragna made her way to her chamber.

Chapter Sixteen

Elspeth arched a brow. “What great secret warrants us to use the back entrance leading from the cellars?” she asked dryly.

Magnar knew her skeptical expression well. He closed the small wooden door behind him. “I do not want anyone to follow us.”

She gestured outward. “Who would dare do so? Your men are breaking their fast in the hall, and others are attending to the animals. Dawn’s light has scarcely entered the sky.”

He took her small hand into his. “I have something to show you.”

Elspeth pursed her lips in thought. “Are you worried Erik will attend to us?”

“Nae,” he replied, placing a kiss on her chilled hand. He drew her against his chest. “Erik favors following another wolf—Rorik.”

Biting her lower lip, she asked, “Aye, he prefers to listen and spend time with the man. Do you reckon ’tis a wise choice?”

Magnar placed her hand over his heart and wrapped his arms around her waist. “Tell me your concerns.”

“You ken I have nae objections, but his skill as a charmer is well known.” A rosy glow stained his wife’s cheeks.

"I can assure you, Rorik has nae interest in sharing what he does in the bed chamber with your brother."

Her eyes widened. "Goodness, husband! 'Tis not what I meant to say. I have complete trust in the man to keep his…*his knowledge* about…well you ken what I am trying to say." She turned away. "At times, he appears troubled."

Magnar's good humor vanished. "You are wise in your observations. His future was destined by his father. Even though he struggles with the conflict, the man remains steadfast in his duty to the brotherhood and our king. Furthermore, you have nothing to fear with the man. Out of all the wolves, I trust him above all the others. If not for his father's brutal actions toward his son, Rorik would be the leader of the Wolves of Clan Sutherland and not I. His strength over the land is great. But his path clearly has been chosen by another, and the Gods have destined Rorik take this journey." He caressed her cheek with his fingers. "Neither the king nor anyone else kens this. You are the only person I have shared this knowledge with, and I trust you, my wife."

"If he has this great power, what do you have?" she asked.

"Wisdom, control, *and* my silent approach. I thought you knew."

Elspeth nodded slowly. "Aye, as silent as a wolf, but you've never shared all the lore behind the wolves."

"Another time, my wife," he proposed.

On a sigh, Elspeth returned her attention to him. "You once mentioned the cruelty of Rorik's father."

Anger surfaced instantly within Magnar toward the elder MacNeil. "*Aye*. His actions were so cruel toward his son and others that his death was not mourned," he confessed in a terse tone.

She cupped his cheek. "Then let us say nae more. I trust in Rorik's judgement to guide our young chieftain as well."

His wife's touch banished the gloom of their conversation. Magnar slammed the door on Durinn MacNeil's deeds and resumed his original task.

Taking her hand within his, Magnar led her along a narrow, curved path.

"Can you share where we are going?" she asked.

He shook his head.

"'Tis a new landscape to explore?"

Magnar ignored her, tugging her gently through the trees.

Elspeth snorted. "If I guess, will there be a reward? A *pleasurable* reward?"

Magnar squeezed her hand.

"Is that an 'aye'?" She giggled. "Can you not share anything?"

"For the love of Odin," he grumbled. Magnar fought the smile forming on his mouth.

Leading her down a slope along the path, he brought her against a group of pines. He turned to face Elspeth. "Close your eyes."

Excitement flared across her face. After giving him a quick nod, she complied. "Lead onward, husband."

With his heart pounding fiercely inside his chest, Magnar led her around the trees and into the clearing. Morning sunlight bathed the small chapel, and he prayed she would find favor in the stone building.

Magnar bent near her ear. "Open your eyes, *kærr*."

When her eyelids fluttered open, Elspeth gasped.

Gesturing outward with his other hand, he announced with pride, "'Tis yours to pray to your God."

She clutched his hand to her breasts. "Sweet Mother Mary of God." Swallowing visibly, she turned her gaze to him. "You built this chapel? For *me*?"

Smiling, he replied, "Aye. For you, *wife*. But do not expect me to start praying to your God."

Throwing her arms around Magnar, she hugged him tight. "My thanks," she managed on a choked sob. "'Tis the kindest deed anyone has done for me, except for your love."

He held her close, pleased with her response.

She lifted her head. "I love you."

Magnar brushed a tender kiss along her bottom lip. "I have something else for you."

Elspeth wiped away a tear from her cheek. "*Another*?" she echoed in a shocked tone.

Withdrawing the small wooden carving he made for her from the pouch at his side, Magnar ran his thumb over the smooth surface. He placed the carving into the palm of her hand, saying, "You often speak of Mother Mary."

"*Magnar*," she whispered, admiring his handiwork, and raising it up to the light. "'Tis stunning. I shall treasure this day and your gifts always." More tears brimmed within her eyes. "Before I wander into the chapel and offer up my prayers, I have a confession for you."

"Do tell," he urged.

Wariness flashed within her eyes. "I wanted to wait until I had seen the healer before sharing my news," she began, placing her palm over his heart. "I am with child."

Finally! He wanted to shout to the halls of Odin. With his voice thick with emotion, Magnar dropped to one knee and pressed his ear against her womb. His wolf leaned closer. A faint heartbeat greeted them. Joy infused him while he managed to whisper words to the bairn growing within his wife's body.

"Tell me you are pleased, Magnar. I ken there is more to learn about the wolves. If this bairn is a son—"

Standing abruptly, Magnar lifted his wife into his arms and went to a small bench beside the chapel. Cradling her close on his lap, he roamed her features. "First, banish your fears. I shall teach you the wisdom of the brotherhood. We both have a duty to our son. Aye, the bairn is a boy."

She smacked his arm. "Or a lass."

A smile twitched at the corners of his mouth. "'Tis definitely a boy."

Her humor was instantly replaced by one of shock. "You already knew I was with child? A boy?" Elspeth narrowed her eyes. "How long have you known, *husband*?"

"From the first beat of his heart. My wolf notified me to his presence. It made it difficult for me to remain silent and not listen to the first flutters of my son's heartbeat. I grew anxious waiting for you to share the news with me."

Elspeth relaxed in his arms. "Ragna warned me this might happen."

Placing a firm hand over her womb, Magnar stared at her. "The Seer kens you are with child, but you chose not to tell me?"

She ran a finger along his torc. "I wanted to be

certain." Raising her head to meet his gaze, Elspeth added in a somber voice, "It was important to *me*."

Magnar brought her head against his chest. His heart overflowed with love for his wife and for the son she carried within her womb. "Then I shall make this vow here before your God and mine."

Elspeth pulled back and regarded him.

"When you bear more sons, I will instruct my wolf to remain silent." Pleased with his decision, he waited for her response.

Smiling, she leaned near his ear. "Do not forget our daughters, as well."

Turning slightly, Magnar met her lips. "Done." Then he sealed his vow with a scorching kiss.

****

After flicking mud from his sword, Rorik then leveled it outward at the man striding into the lists. "The hour is late, even for you. We could return to the warmth of the hall and engage in a battle of wits over a game of *hnefatafl*?"

Magnar snarled in protest. "Either you spent the night in the arms of soft flesh, or you found comfort from the biting wind on the north tower?"

He grinned at his leader. "Both."

"And you think to best me after a night of nae rest?" taunted Magnar, slashing his sword into the air. Crossing to the opposite side, he retrieved his shield from a steel hook on the fence.

"Aye." Rorik tapped his chest with his fist. "I am the younger and do not require as much rest as an *older* wolf."

"You are older by one turn of the moon," argued Magnar.

Rorik shrugged indifferently. “Nae matter.”

Arching a brow, Magnar lunged at him. Rorik reacted swiftly and moved aside, smacking his leader on the back.

Stumbling slightly, Magnar turned back toward him. “Be warned, I *will* wipe that smile from your face.”

“I believe ’tis a snarl,” disputed Rorik, pounding the hilt of his sword against his shield. “Challenge accepted.”

“Do not bring your wolf into this,” ordered Magnar and shifted his stance.

“Hmm. Did not Steinar say the same to me?”

“Your victory over Steinar means nothing to me.”

For the next half-hour, the clash of blades, grunts, and curses flew out between the two men in the lists. Both were intent on becoming the champion. Regardless of Magnar’s strength and fluid movement with his blade, Rorik managed to level a blow against the man’s jaw. Yet Rorik barely missed being sliced across the arm from his leader’s sword. However, he wasn’t so fortunate, and Magnar’s fist landed a strike across his brow.

Rorik stumbled, shaking away the dizziness from the shock and returned to the battle.

With the arrival of Steinar and several other men, Rorik fought harder. Blood seeped into his eye from a cut on his forehead, causing his vision to blur. Another blow to his jaw from Magnar left him unsteady on his feet. Leveling a fist into the man’s side, Rorik was rewarded with a kick to the knees, forcing him onto the ground.

As Magnar readied to level his blade against his

chest, Rorik rolled away and quickly stood. After wiping the blood from his brow, he tossed aside his shield and withdrew the dirk from the belt at his side.

"Two blades? Fearing for your life, MacNeil?"

His opponent stalked Rorik. His eyes shifted briefly to those of his wolf. Then Magnar tossed aside his shield as well.

Rorik's expression stilled and grew serious. A low growl escaped from his wolf, and Rorik crouched in anticipation of setting his wolf free to battle the leader's wolf.

The man's lip curled. "Did I not order you to keep your wolf restrained?"

"Then rein in *your* wolf, *MacAlpin*!" snapped Rorik.

For several moments, tension shook the air. Hushed silence descended over them as thick as the gray clouds above them.

While each man continued to breathe heavily, Magnar was the first to drop his blade. A great roar of laughter burst forth from him. Finally spent, he wiped a hand across his nose to staunch the blood. He shook his head in good humor while crossing to Rorik's side.

Magnar extended his arm outward in a gesture of goodwill. "Well done, MacNeil. 'Tis good to have you back in the lists with me."

The wolf within him settled, and Rorik dropped his blades.

Grasping the man's forearm, Rorik returned the smile with one of his own. "Your wife will not be pleased with another broken nose," he remarked.

His leader leaned close and whispered, "I fear the women shall turn in horror at the bruising to your face."

Rorik winced when he attempted to smile. “There is only one woman I care about, and I shall attend to her healing touch.”

All humor vanished from Magnar. He lowered his arm and took a step back. “Be careful the road you choose, my friend.”

“Or the woman?” Rorik added, gesturing for them to depart the lists, so the other men could engage in their training exercises.

Magnar went to the well. After bringing up a bucket of water, he emptied the contents over his head. He shook his head vigorously. Handing the bucket to Rorik, he leaned against the well. “How goes the task for the king?”

Ignoring the man’s question, Rorik lowered the bucket into the well and filled it with water. As soon as he dumped the water over his body, he shook to rid most of the water from his skin. Setting the bucket on the ledge, Rorik then wiped the water from his eyes with his hands. He glanced sharply at the man. “Interested in a quick run through the forest to the top of the hill?”

A smile broadened Magnar’s features. “Man, *or* wolf?”

“Wolf.” Rorik nudged him along toward the open portcullis. “We can shift when we cross into the trees.”

Their quiet departure was met with a salute from two of the guards on the tower of the gatehouse. When they slipped into the protection of the trees, both men removed their boots and stripped the trews from their bodies.

Rorik managed to be the first. He bent on one knee and grabbed a fistful of dirt. After whispering the ancient words of magic, he then tossed the mixture into the air. Inhaling slowly, the power built within his body. On the exhale, Rorik shifted in a shimmer of gray light, transforming into the wolf.

The wolf shook off the lingering power. After listening with intent, he gave a quick glance over his shoulder.

Without waiting for the other wolf, he took off through the dense forest. With agile speed, he trampled over the landscape, swiftly leaping over tree roots and around narrow paths. Small animals quickly dodged out of his path, most likely fearing for their lives. But the wolf cherished his freedom and gave no care to their presence. He traversed over the rocky incline, steadily making his ascent. More leaves, mud, and rocks flew forth from behind him. The wind ruffled over the back of his fur, and the moist, musty scent of the land filled his nostrils, urging him onward to his destination.

When the scent of his leader reached him, the wolf slowed his progress. Giving respect to his superior, he darted to the side to allow his leader passage in front of him. He promptly resumed his journey, taking a parallel path apart from the other wolf. As the clearing came into view, he slowed his pace. He padded to the center near the other wolf. Stretching out his front paws, he then settled back onto his hind legs.

The wolf took in his surroundings. A lone eagle's cry shattered above, and he snarled at the intrusion. His ears twitched, detecting the steps of a stag foraging for food along with other smaller animals scampering through the dense foliage. He listened to the rustle of the leaves and tree limbs. Closing his eyes, he inhaled the scent on the breeze. When he judged all was safe, the wolf shimmered back into the man.

Soon Magnar joined him, preferring to remain silent like him.

Rorik leaned his arms over his bent knees, enjoying the last impressions of being the wolf. The north wind smacked his backside with its icy fingers, causing him to smile. He'd forgotten the wild freedom of being one with his beast. No troubles. No tasks to complete. No demands from others. Simply the huge landscape to wander and explore.

He placed his palm upon the cold ground. His thoughts returned to Ragna. *Can you hear the heartbeat of the land, kærr? Do the veins stretch to the seas?*

Rorik waited for an answer, though he expected none.

On a sigh, he resumed his position. He raised his head to the eagle circling above them. "I have claimed Ragna." He stole a glance at the man.

"About bloody time," announced Magnar, plucking a shaft of grass from the ground.

Stunned by his leader's declaration, Rorik blurted out, "You act as if our union was expected."

Magnar snorted and smacked him on the back. "You have loved that woman since you first made that damnable wager on stealing a kiss."

"For the love of Odin, does everyone in the brotherhood ken this knowledge?"

The man lifted a shoulder. "Would you be offended by the truth?"

"Then I am the fool," complained Rorik, standing abruptly. Picking up a small stone, he rubbed the smooth surface with his thumb.

Rising, Magnar approached near his side. "If you

recall, Durinn forced you to make the wager, aye? Furthermore, the woman has pined for you as well. Her constant harsh words about you and your wolf made me wonder as to her true feelings." He chuckled softly, adding, "I came upon the revelation many moons ago."

Rorik folded his arms over his chest. "You are certain the others in the brotherhood do not share this same belief?"

"If they do, they choose to remain silent. Also, after your wolf allowed Ragna to become your guardian, Steinar sensed there was more between you both." Magnar brushed a hand across his forehead. "What do you propose to do about your unfinished task for the king?"

"*Unfinished*?" he echoed with uneasiness, keeping his focus on the eagle.

"You avoided my earlier question," explained Magnar.

He tossed the stone lightly within his palm. "Did you ken Hallgerd was interested in my lands to the south?"

"Interesting. They once belonged to her grandfather, aye? And then to your father?"

Tossing the stone far, Rorik watched its descent. "Indeed. Whatever schemes Jorund is planning, I do not believe Hallgerd has the information I am seeking for the king."

Magnar scratched the side of his face. "What is your next plan?"

Relaxing his stance, Rorik faced the man. "I shall use the wolf to spy on the woman, even venturing to the south near Ecklund's lands. I can detect more information than charming the lass with words."

His friend arched a brow. "And the Dark Seducer?"

Rorik let out a sigh of relief. For the first time in his life, the path for his future became one he destined for himself, and not from another. Rorik had no time to dwell on the consequences from his king. Determination and love for his woman filled him. This became his focus and guidance.

"The Dark Seducer has plans for only one, *Ragna,*" he confessed with a smile.

Chapter Seventeen

While stifling a yawn, Ragna tucked her legs under her body and drew the wrap tighter around her shoulders. She never took to her bed when she returned to Steinn in the early morn, choosing to do other chores. Ragna busied herself with helping in the kitchens, tending to the herb garden, and making an herbal brew for a sick lad. Earlier, she spotted Rorik leaving the lists with Magnar. She kept her gaze on him until he disappeared over the bridge.

When the evening meal came and no appearance from Rorik, her joy vanished. The food she managed to eat instantly soured within her stomach, and she took to drinking more mead.

An ember snapped in the dwindling fire within the hearth, startling her, but the light from a lone candle on the table dispelled the gloom around her.

Rubbing her temples, she tried to ease the dull ache which had settled behind her eyes. All these new feelings left her unsteady. Ragna smacked the cold stone with her hand. "You are behaving like a forlorn goat looking for its mate," she chastised. "The Seer does not behave in this manner."

Suddenly, Ragna laughed at the foolish thought. Her feelings were those of a woman in love. Years ago, she would have never welcomed the man to her bed. Ever. Considering the pain he had caused her.

Nevertheless, her love for Rorik remained a thorn buried deep in her heart, aching to be set free.

"What would the Seer advise?" she uttered softly. "Would she cast the runes under the moonlit night? Or would she seek out the Goddess in the wildflowers bordering the stream?"

She pressed her palm over her heart. "It beats for only one man, *Freyja*, and I believe you sent him to me when I went to the river."

Biting her lower lip, she twirled a lock of hair between her fingers while staring at the starry night sky. She yawned again. Sleep beckoned her to its waiting embrace, and Ragna stretched out her legs and stood. Folding her arms around her body, she sighed heavily and took a couple steps back to enjoy the view one last time.

"Do you often speak with the stars?" asked the low male voice within the shadows of her chamber.

"Rorik?" she asked in disbelief, glancing over her shoulder. Her wrap slid from her shoulders and dropped to the floor.

He stepped into the moonlight of the room, and her heart nearly jumped out of her chest. "Does it bother you I am here?" His question was filled with concern.

The warmth in Rorik's voice skimmed over her skin. Heat flared around her neck and rose to her face. She stared at him, unable to move forward. "Nae," she managed, taking in his appearance and noting the man wore only his trews. Ragna watched as the hunter approached his prey, and a tremor of anticipation danced along her skin.

The man grabbed a fistful of her hair and inhaled sharply. "What flowers do you bathe in?"

“’Tis the herbs,” she admitted. Swallowing, she asked, “How did you get in my chamber?”

Rorik winked. “Secret passage. I followed your scent here.”

When she tried to peer around the man and discover this hidden doorway for herself, he shook his head. He pressed a kiss along her neck and dropped his hand. “Face the stars, *kærr*.”

Returning her attention to the night sky, Ragna tried to be patient. Her fingers itched to touch the man and weave them into his long, dark hair. Instead, she clenched her fists so tight her nails bit into her palms. Her mouth yearned to taste him, and her body hungered to have him inside her again.

“Do you trust me, Ragna?” His breath was warm against her ear.

She gave a curt nod.

“Say the word aloud,” he ordered, trailing a path with his finger down the slope of her neck.

“*Aye*, I trust you.”

With Rorik’s hot presence behind her, she became dizzy. Heat pooled in places she craved to have him touch.

“The passion I am going to give you requires you to surrender completely,” explained Rorik, adding, “To only feel the pleasure, I shall bind your sight with this ribbon.”

Ragna closed her eyes and bit her lip. After he secured the ribbon over her eyes, he gently pushed her chemise off her shoulders, trapping her arms at her side. “I cannot move,” she complained.

His low growl brushed down the back of her neck, followed by light kisses. With each touch, the flame of desire built within Ragna. He nibbled his way across her shoulders and moved to stand in front of her.

A cool breeze brushed over her skin as Rorik pushed the material lower to her waist. When his fingers pinched her nipples, she tingled all the way to her toes. Yet when his mouth descended over her breasts, Ragna groaned from the pleasure.

"You are a beauty," he murmured against her skin. "So soft."

Soon, her chemise pooled around her feet.

His light beard merely added to the heady sensations as he continued to press kisses over her body while his fingers teased her intimate core with light strokes. Ragna quivered, unable to stand the pleasurable assault any longer. "Rorik, need *more*," she pleaded.

Pressing a finger over her lips, he nuzzled her neck. "Shh…*my kærr*."

She rewarded him with a nip along his finger.

His growl came swiftly. Rorik's mouth descended over hers in a demanding kiss—thrusting his tongue deep into her mouth. And Ragna responded with her own fiery passion. He tasted of the wildness of the land and ale. The kiss was one of possession, and she surrendered to the man.

When he broke from the kiss. Ragna swayed from the loss. A strong arm banded around her waist and lifted her into his arms.

Licking his taste from her lips, Ragna asked, "Can I now remove this ribbon?"

"*Nae*." His response left no room for objection.

After he placed her gently on the bed, she heard him rid himself of his trews. Her breathing became ragged, filled with wanting him closer.

His fingers skimmed from the bottom of her foot to behind her knee. "You are my Goddess, *Ragna*," he proclaimed, spreading her legs farther apart. "I shall never forget this image of you."

She trembled when he moved near her on the bed. Then he placed kisses along her inner thighs. Her breath came out in short gasps when he reached her intimate area. "What…*what* are you doing?"

"Feasting on your sweet honey," he replied in a hoarse voice.

He blew against her core, and Ragna trembled. When his tongue flicked over her center, she thought she'd died. Frustrated at not being able to see him, she tore the ribbon from her eyes, challenging his order.

Propping up on her elbows, Ragna met his heated gaze—dark and compelling.

Rorik bit her inner thigh. "You must be punished for disobeying my order."

"I want to watch," she demanded—digging her hands into the furs. If he attempted to bind her eyes again, she'd insist the same for him.

Ragna tried to wait patiently—her heart beating like the wings of her sparrowhawk.

His sensual smile came lazily. Rorik lowered his head and showered her with kisses, licks, and nips with his teeth over her sensitive core. The fever of desire grew and spread throughout her. A pulse of need drummed between her legs, and she groaned deeply. Ragna longed to move, but he had placed his hands firmly over her thighs, pinning her against the furs. The tight knot within her begged for release, and she whimpered. When his moan rumbled deep against her, Ragna closed her eyes and soared on the pleasurable wave, crying out his name as the tremors shook her body.

"*Rorik,*" she protested on a sob.

"Aye, *aye,*" he growled.

Trying to regain her breathing, she opened her eyes. Ragna needed to feel him inside her.

Rorik raised from his position and loomed over her—his breathing ragged. He took his hardened length and stroked it along her entrance and continued to rub over that sweet spot. Her moans became tearful—begging him to enter.

"Does this not feel good?" He teased her breasts with his tongue.

"Stop tormenting me," she complained on a gasp.

He bit the side of her neck. "'Tis *pleasurable* torment."

She wrapped one leg around his, urging him onward.

In one swift thrust, Rorik buried himself deep inside her.

A great cry tore from her throat—while she reveled in the heady sensation of the man. Her body clenched and grew heavy with an aching need. With each thrust, the firestorm built once again until Ragna soared higher, swept away on the tide of desire. Waves of ecstasy throbbed through her.

His mouth sought hers in a frenzy of kisses. "You are mine, *forever* mine." He murmured the words against her cheeks, lips, and below the soft spot of her ear. His roar of release echoed all around her, and he recaptured her mouth in another blinding kiss.

Neither of them moved for several moments. With great care, Rorik eased onto his back, bringing her body against his side. Completely sated, Ragna snuggled close. She placed her hand on his chest, waiting for his fiercely beating heart to find its steady rhythm, along with hers.

Ragna tilted her head up and trailed her fingers through the dark shadow of his beard until they settled on his bottom lip—finally noticing the faint bruising along his jaw. "What happened?" she asked softly, studying his features and noting other bruises and a small cut above his brow.

Cracking open one eye, he smirked. "A blow from Magnar."

Her mouth opened in shock, and then she snapped it shut. "I hope you did the same to him."

She felt the rumble of his laughter against her skin.

"The man suffered a broken nose," he proclaimed, opening both eyes.

Ragna rested her chin on the arm lying across Rorik's chest. "Elspeth will not be pleased."

"His wolf will heal him. You should have seen us earlier in the morn."

"Goodness! Is this why you have been absent most of the day? So we would not worry about you?"

All good humor vanished from his face. Holding her with a relaxed and steady gaze, he asked, "Why do you care, *Ragna*?"

Her body trembled. How many years had she kept her reasons hidden? Now, the emotion unfurled like petals on a flower. Tears smarted her eyes, and she feared losing control. Feared he'd slash her heart to ribbons if she confessed everything.

You can no longer hide in the shadows, Ragna.

Shoving aside her turmoil, she blurted out the

words that had been buried within her heart, "I have *loved* you since the night you seized victory from the game of *Skinnleikr* in the hall of Rangvald the Bear. Afterward, I watched in awe as you stomped your way down the table, holding the ball under one arm and downing horns of ale presented to you."

"You were there?" he whispered in a shocked tone.

"Hiding in the shadows. My father judged it wise to marry me to Rangvald."

He scowled and spat out, "The man is as old as his dying horse."

Ragna twisted her fingers into the furs. "Despite the consequences, I could not marry him when my heart felt the first stirrings of love for another—*for you*."

Rorik cupped her cheeks on a deep exhale. "How I have longed to hear those words pass from your lips, *my kærr.*"

"Truly?" She blinked, trying to hold back the tears.

"By the Gods, aye!" With a feral growl, Rorik covered her mouth hungrily. His lips were hard and searching. When he eased back, Rorik brought her head against his chest. His fingers shook as he trailed a path down her back. "I have a confession."

Hope blossomed within her heart. She held her breath, waiting to hear the words she ached from the man.

His hand stilled. "I did make a wager to capture a kiss from the Seer. Not only a kiss but to bed you, as well."

Ragna shuddered on an exhale. "Why?" she asked, trying to mask the disappointment within her voice.

"A bad decision on my part. I heard about the beauty of the Seer upon my visit to *Kirkjuvágr*. The daughter of the Earl of *Orkneyjar* was a prize for any man. Even if she was his bastard daughter."

Ragna stiffened. "At least he acknowledged me, though from afar."

"Indeed, but only after you became the honored Seer. It was his sons who made up for his years of not acknowledging you by accepting you into their home," added Rorik.

"Which I did not accept. I decided to take the smaller dwelling on their land." This was not the conversation Ragna had intended. The past long buried, along with the stinging pain she'd endured from Rorik. One moment she was experiencing great joy within the man's arms and the next recalling bitter memories.

His fingers resumed their lazy movements down her back, though it did little to soothe her tangled nerves.

"Since I had spoken of my latest conquest in the bed chamber, several men dared me to steal a kiss from the elusive Seer. My father overheard the wager and doubled the amount, proclaiming your heart was as frozen as the Narn lake in winter."

"A challenge you heartily accepted," she mused with sorrow.

"Aye."

Ragna raised her head from his chest. "Was I not worth more than a barrel of mead?"

Grimacing, Rorik stared up at the ceiling. "There might have been coin involved, as well."

By the Goddess, save me from this wretched memory. "I should have slapped you harder."

"Agreed. But in truth, I was happy I lost." His smile held sadness as he returned his gaze to hers.

Curiosity spurred her to ask, "Why, Rorik?"

Taking her hand, he placed the palm over his heart. "On that day, *Ragna*—daughter of Harald Maddadsson—stole my heart. And on that day, I vowed to stay far, far away from a woman who frightened me."

A gasp escaped from her lips. Ragna pushed away from him and scooted to the edge of the bed. She cupped a hand over her mouth to fight the scream lodged within. She shivered, but not from the coldness in the chamber and her lack of clothing. Confusion knotted like vines inside her stomach. Her hands clenched.

"Ragna?" he asked warily. "Speak to me."

When she turned to face him, her eyes sparked with fury.

A frown marred his features. "What have I—"

She held her palm outward to halt his words. "My life has been filled with those who are *frightened* of me—fearing I will find fault in their words or deeds. Aye, they give me respect, but I ken what they think." Tapping the side of her ear with her finger, she continued, "Whispered conversations reach me as surely as the scent of flowers on a summer day. Now, I have to endure it from you?"

The man groaned and got off the bed. "'Tis not my meaning." Moving to the table, he reached for a jug and sniffed its contents.

Feeling defenseless without her clothing, Ragna stood and glanced around the chamber for her wrap. "'Tis clear to me," she protested.

Rorik downed the contents in one gulp and crossed the room in two strides.

"Do not," warned Ragna as hot tears threatened to spill forth. She took a few hesitant steps back.

Ignoring her pleas, Rorik wrapped his arms around her waist. "Look at me, *kærr*."

She wanted to take out her anger by pounding on his chest. Slowly, she lifted her head as her defenses weakened. "*Frightened*?"

Pressing his forehead against hers, he spoke tenderly, "Aye, of the *love* I felt inside my heart that day. There was nae room for love in my life. Not for the Dark Seducer. It frightened me, so I shoved it aside. My wolf knew the bond, waiting for the moment to bring you to me. I ignored so many signs along our journey. Until I said the words to claim you, I lived in the shadows of doubt and objections."

"Love?" she whispered, drawing back to study him.

"I ken you have heard the words in your mind, my beauty." Rorik's smile returned in force.

Confounded, she shook her head. "How is this possible?"

He gripped her chin, forcing her to meet his heated gaze. "Once I claimed *and* professed my love for you, a magical bond formed within our minds. 'Tis only when we speak to one another that this occurs. In time, we will learn to master our thoughts to each other."

Ragna swallowed. "I thought them hopeful dreams whispered on the breezes when I heard you in my mind."

His lips brushed along hers as he declared, "I *love* you, Ragna. I kept the love I bore for you locked under the steel of my heart. I wish to complete the claiming by marrying you. Will you have me, *my kærr*?"

A choked sob escaped from her throat, and she threw her arms around his neck. "Aye, *aye*!"

He smothered her lips with demanding mastery. The kiss and Rorik's confession healed the pain from so long ago. Her tired soul surrendered to the bliss of being in his arms.

Rorik tugged lightly on her bottom lip with his teeth. Moving his hands down her back, he cupped her bottom and rubbed it against his swollen length. She felt her knees weaken. When Ragna let out a sigh of pleasure, he recaptured her mouth with savage intensity.

Without warning, he lifted her into his arms and returned to the bed. Placing her hips on the edge, he brought her legs around his body and thrust deep inside her. Her hands clutched the furs as she watched in a sensual haze Rorik's slow and steady movements—all while he observed her under a hooded gaze.

Ragna writhed beneath him, enjoying the different position and wonderful tingling over her skin. When his hands roamed intimately over her breasts, she arched wildly, throwing her head back. Stars burst before her eyes, and she shook from the powerful pleasure.

With a fierce cry, Rorik found his release, bellowing out her name. Finally spent, he collapsed over her, breathing heavily. Several moments passed before he tugged her body along the furs to the middle of the bed.

He cradled her within his strong arms. Contentment filled Ragna for the first time in her life, yet one fear remained.

"Rorik?"

"Aye?"

"What happens in the morn?"

He brought the furs over their bodies and kissed the top of her head. "'Tis already early morn."

She blew out a frustrated breath but remained silent. Her eyelids grew heavy.

"I have a new proposition for the king and will depart Steinn in a few days, hopefully with the information he seeks. He might not favor this new plan, but I cannot continue being the Dark Seducer, especially if I am to marry."

Her eyes fluttered open. "If he is not in agreement?"

Shrugging slightly, he answered, "Banishment from the brotherhood *and* Scotland."

Worry infused Ragna. This was not what she wanted for the man she loved. He was honor-bound to ancient edicts—laws she understood well. The ways of the wolves might be foreign to her, but Ragna lived her own set of rules as a Seer and wise woman. She would not allow him to be dishonored. There had to be another way.

"Sleep, my love," he urged on a yawn. "I can hear the rumble of your thoughts in my mind."

"But I am not speaking to you," she protested.

"Nevertheless, muddled words are entering my mind," he murmured.

I must learn to shield my thoughts from you, my warrior.

A growl escaped from Rorik. *Never!*

On a smile, Ragna closed her eyes and offered a silent prayer to the Goddess that the King of Scotland hear Rorik's new plan and govern wisely.

Chapter Eighteen

The sound of boisterous laughter woke Rorik from his deep slumber. When he opened his eyes, sunlight danced like golden jewels inside the chamber. The warm scent of another filled him. He swept his gaze to the stunning beauty curled up on her side next to him. Dark eyelashes dusted her ivory skin. Her swollen lips teased him to be suckled and tasted. He found his cock swollen and eager to wake her in more passion.

Even so, the morning hour grew late, and plans needed to be made. His task for the king not quite fulfilled.

Rorik brushed a kiss over her brow. Rising from the bed, he stretched his arms over his head. He had slept fully in the bed of a woman without the threat of constant nightmares from the past. Was love truly the key? He believed himself unworthy to love or to accept love from another. Especially from Ragna. Never had he known such intense passion.

Glancing over his shoulder, he took in a deep breath and exhaled slowly. How he loved this woman. They had wasted too many years within the prison of their tormented anguish.

Determined to forge a new path, he would first present his plan to Magnar. If all did not go well with the king, at least his leader might consider taking him on as a blacksmith in the forge or another position at

Steinn. Rorik's skills were varied, but his heart belonged to the brotherhood and now Ragna.

Banishment from Scotland was not an option. Perchance, he would rebuild the crumbling ruins on the land he held in Scotland. Or return to *Orkneyjar*. Rorik firmly knew his beloved would be by his side, wherever they chose to make their home.

He went to retrieve his trews and quicky put them on.

"Where are you going?" Ragna patted the furs in invitation.

Going to her side, Rorik brushed aside a dark lock of hair and nibbled on her earlobe. "I have business to attend to. The sun is gracing us with a glorious day."

"Sun?" she mumbled, turning around to give him an abundant view of her luscious breasts.

Rorik kept his hands fisted by his side. The temptation to join her back under the furs a heady desire. "'Tis late morn, my love."

Ragna snapped her eyes open and bolted upright. "Late morn," she echoed on a squeak.

More laughter drifted upward to them from the bailey, followed by shouts from one of the men.

Her head turned toward the window. "Sweet Goddess, I require clothing!"

Sweeping his gaze around the chamber, Rorik went to fetch her chemise and shawl. Bringing them to her, he then stepped back. Rorik tried to hide his smile behind a cough. *You are wild, untamed, and a vision to feast upon. And I adore you.*

As she tossed aside the furs, Ragna blew out a curse. "This clothing will not suffice for picking mushrooms in the forest with Elspeth." Her eyes widened. "The woman might be confined to her bed. The early months of carrying a bairn—"

Rorik choked on his laughter. "*Bairn*? Elspeth is carrying Magnar's child?"

She looked aghast. Reaching for his hand, Ragna smacked his palm over his heart. "Swear by the axe of Odin you will not speak of this to *anyone*—not Magnar or any of the other wolves. *No one*!"

"You have not answered my question," Rorik replied dryly.

Stomping her foot, she glared at him. "Aye, she is carrying his child! Is it not evident with the vow I have asked you to swear by?"

Her eyes glittered in the soft light of the chamber, reminding Rorik of the sea on a cloudy day—a tinge of blue and gray. He marveled at them.

"Swear the oath, Rorik," she ordered with demanding authority.

Instead of recoiling at the Seer's tone, he smiled fully. "Aye, *kærr*."

"Do not mock me," she scolded, jabbing him in the chest with her other hand.

Rorik squeezed her hand. "You offend me. I have given you my oath. Can you share why I have made this vow?"

Snorting, Ragna released her hold and went to the trunk at the end of her bed. "Because *I* made a vow not to mention anything until Elspeth had a chance to speak with her husband. I am unsure whether she has shared the news with him." Bending over, she presented Rorik with a stunning view of her bottom. She brought forth a green woolen gown and threw it onto the bed.

Folding his arms over his chest, he fought the

growing lust to take her instantly from behind. His mind returned to the conversation. "Certainly, Magnar will announce this joyous news when his wife tells him, and my oath will be released."

His beloved frowned in concentration. She mumbled something he was unable to interpret.

Crossing the room in great strides toward the bed, he then lifted the gown and held it outward. "Let me assist you. If you do not cover your skin—" Rorik traced a path over the slope of her soft breast with his finger "—I fear I shall take you hard and swift."

Ragna's lips parted, and he required no invitation. The gown slipped from his hand as he covered her mouth hungrily. When Magnar's bellowing reached his hearing, Rorik froze for an instant. Burying his face in her neck, he breathed one last kiss along her skin.

On a sigh, he retrieved the gown and helped her ease into the garment.

She brushed her fingers over his lips. "You are a wonderful kisser, Rorik." Her brow creased. "But I am certain many have confessed this quality about you, aye?"

Rorik cupped her face within his hands. "Aye. Yet none have I loved. Only you, my beauty. *Only you.*"

After giving her a feather-like kiss, he strode to the back of the chamber. "Curious about your secret passage?"

Her eyes lit with excitement. She grabbed her shoes and dashed to his side. Quickly putting them on, she turned away from him. "Would you be so kind as to tie my tresses into one braid?"

"So lovely," Rorik whispered as he complied to her demand. When finished, he asked, "A tie to bind the mass?"

"My method is to weave it around my head, but we have nae time." She took a hold of her braid and darted across the chamber. As she searched throughout the furs on the bed with one hand, Ragna beamed as she brought forth the ribbon he'd used to cover her eyes. Returning to him, she held it outward.

Rorik withdrew the ribbon from her fingers. "I can think of other uses for this silken material."

Her cheeks turned a rosy glow before she turned away from him.

After quickly binding the end of her braid, he then steered her to the right.

She stared up at him. "There is nothing here but a wall-hanging."

Rorik winked and shoved the heavy material aside. "A wooden door awaits, beloved." He pressed against the top panel, and the door eased open.

"'Tis small," complained Ragna, peering down into the darkness.

"Once you take the bend at the corner, light from the connecting chamber seeps through. 'Tis a long, narrow passageway. I am curious why the chambers are connected. This chamber is made of stone and wood, while the other one is mainly built with wood."

"How did you ken I was in this one?"

He tweaked her nose. "Your scent drifted into my chamber."

Ragna arched a skeptical brow. "One might think Elspeth conspired to put us together."

Both turned at the sound of knocking on the door.

"Ragna?"

His beloved's eyes widened in horror. "'Tis

Elspeth. Go now," she whispered, shoving him toward the opening.

"One moment," called out Ragna.

Chuckling softly, Rorik kissed her soundly and then ducked into the murky passageway.

As soon as the door closed firmly behind him, he made his way back to his chamber. Once safely inside, he went to the small table and reached for a jug of water. Emptying the contents into a basin, he splashed the icy water onto his face.

Rorik stilled. Inhaling sharply, he detected another had been in his chamber. "*Hallgerd*," he bit out. Nothing appeared to be disturbed as he glanced around the room. Important documents that belonged to him were safely tucked away at Vargr with Lord Sutherland. His mind tried to sort out her reasons.

Was her purpose to entice him for carnal pleasures? Granted, the woman was brazen, but Rorik deemed she would not venture alone inside his chamber to warm his bed. Was there something she sought? His earlier suspicions of Hallgerd as a spy for her brother remained steadfast. But why him?

He rid his hands of the water, trying to ease the tension coursing through him.

Making haste, he found a fresh tunic in the trunk by the wall and grabbed the leather belt off the chair. As he dressed, he noted his weapons on the table and went to secure his dirk within his belt and placed the smaller blade within its sheath on the outside of his boot.

Leaving his chamber, he almost collided with David. He grasped the man's arm to steady them both and flashed David a smile. "Forgive my rush, I would have thought you to be breaking your fast, or in the lists."

David's expression was tight with strain. "Done *and* done. The hour is late. I wish to speak with you."

Loki's balls. I have nae desire to discuss your woman. "What is on your mind, David?" he asked with steely calm.

The man gestured behind him. "May we speak in your chamber? Whispered conversations in corridors have a way of reaching others."

Doing his best to temper the growing ire, Rorik turned and went back inside his chamber. As soon as David entered, he closed the door behind them.

Rorik clasped his hands behind his back. "You seem troubled."

Giving him a startled look, David crossed to the window and pulled back one of the wooden shutters. "First, 'tis good to see your health has returned—"

"If you have come to offer your amends for my injury I suffered, you can stop there," interrupted Rorik. "I had been unwell for many moons. 'Tis I who should offer amends for causing strife between you and Hallgerd."

Scratching the side of his face, David studied him warily. "Nevertheless, I wanted your death, which cannot be undone by the Gods. But there is another reason I am here. I shall share that Hallgerd did not agree to this marriage. It was an arrangement between her mother *and* brother, though I doubt Hallgerd knew about her brother's involvement." His voice hardened, adding, "Had I known the Dark Seducer stalked the grounds of Steinn, I would have proposed going directly to Jorund's castle."

Exhaling slowly, Rorik unclasped his hands. Taken aback by the man's declaration, he moved to the table near the arched window. Lifting another jug filled with ale, he poured a hefty amount into two cups.

Handing a cup to the man, he proposed, "Let us drink to peace between us."

David nodded solemnly, taking the offering. He lifted the cup outward and then took a long draw of the ale. Letting out a nervous laugh, he stated, "This journey has been fraught with uncertainty from the moment I left the isles."

Rorik observed him hesitantly. "Explain."

After placing the cup back on the table, David leaned against the wall. "A marriage between the families of Ecklund and Maddadsson would have ensured a solid bond between Scotland *and* the isles. Jon and I ken there will come a time when both countries shall be united under one king—be it here or Norway. With a strong clan, our lands would be vast."

The ale soured in Rorik's gut. "The Wolves of Clan Sutherland are loyal to only *one*—the King of Scotland. Never shall we follow any King of Norway."

The man waved a hand dismissively. "I agree, yet the battle for lands in the north of Scotland remains." He blew out a frustrated breath and pushed away from the wall. David began to pace in front of the empty hearth. "In the event of any battle between kings, I had hoped to forge an alliance. We are thinking of the future of Scotland *and* the *Orkneyjar* Isles."

Rorik emptied his cup. "This is a conversation for Magnar, not me."

David's expression held a note of disdain. "We have already spoken with your leader. But this is not why I have given you this account. My actions were to share with you that I am not going to marry Hallgerd. She has called off the marriage, and I have agreed. I judged it wise after what I have witnessed from the woman. If you want to take her as your woman, I can send a message to Jorund. Presently, Hallgerd is preparing to leave for *Hamnavoe*."

Rorik stiffened, unable to fathom the man's words. *The woman is leaving Scotland? Then I can leave for Vargr in the morn with this information for the king.*

"I assume by your silence you agree with my words. Shall I go inform her of this news?"

"Nae!" Rorik snapped, picking up the jug of ale and refilling his cup. He poured more into David's, splashing some over the rim. Unprepared for this new revelation, he sought to find a way to discuss another woman with the man. *I have nae urge to fight you again over another. Your sister.*

He handed the cup to David.

The man brushed a hand over his brow in obvious confusion. "I thought you desired Hallgerd for yourself."

Rorik guzzled the ale until the last drop. After setting the cup onto the table, he straightened. "*First*, I have nae plans on making Hallgerd my woman. Simply playful conversation. I seek another for marriage—one which she is in agreement. Though I fear you and Jon might not find favor with this arrangement."

A muscle twitched angrily on the man's jaw. "Who?"

"Ragna."

David flung his cup into the hearth. The wood shattered—its splintered fragments echoed around them. "You go too far, MacNeil! 'Tis an outrage! If you think to despoil my sister by taking her in marriage, I will not give my consent."

"'Tis not your decision. Clearly, you did not hear me when I stated Ragna *agrees* to this marriage." Rorik's tone cold and exact.

Fury blazed within the man's eyes. "When did you intend on speaking to me? To Jon? Or were we not a consideration in your plans?" He stormed to the window. "How can you expect us to honor this union—*you* whose conquests with women are many." When he returned to face Rorik, contempt for him was etched across his face. "You are not *worthy* to share a life with Ragna."

David's words slammed into him. Clenching his fists, Rorik fought the battle of the truth within. So far, Rorik had done nothing honorable to be worthy of Ragna's love. Nevertheless, he'd removed the chains from around his heart, opening fully to the love he bore for her.

Rorik approached the man. "You are correct. I am not worthy of her love. I intend to spend all my days honoring the love I have for Ragna until my last breath. Can you accept my declaration?"

His features turned suspicious. "Why now?"

"When your sister ventured across the North Sea to save me from death, she unlocked my darkest secret—my love for her. If you want to ken more, you must speak with Ragna." Rorik clamped a hand on the man's shoulder and felt him stiffen. "I have not asked for your permission, yet I pray to the Gods one day you and Jon will find me worthy."

Rorik released his hold. His steps led him out of

the chamber, but it was David's chilling words that made him pause at the entrance.

"If you ever hurt Ragna, I will slice out your heart and feast on your blood."

Without looking at the man, Rorik replied in a somber voice, "If that day comes, I will hand you my blade to do the deed."

****

The burning blaze within the hearth did little to ease the chill from Hallgerd's bones. Hugging her arms around her body, she attempted to dwell on something else other than the consequences of her forthcoming actions. It would serve her no good. The decision to leave Scotland had been made.

After her clipped conversation with David, they both agreed to end their union. Her future in this country as the wife of a jarl vanished within moments. The thought of returning to the home of her mother soured like goat's milk in her stomach.

Flames snapped at her, mocking her situation. Her thoughts drifted to Jorund's request. Unable to gather the information he sought, her brother would surely take out his rage on her. She had searched Rorik's chamber and found no document, no message, nothing. Her brother's hatred for the Seer confounded Hallgerd even more.

"Now with nae means of marrying David, I must endure the wrath of our mother as surely as yours," she uttered with contempt for both.

When the burning log snapped in half, Hallgerd took a step back. The road ahead appeared barren. With no means of escaping, she had to devise a plan. A plan which required trusted allies back on the isles—those who hated her mother and Jorund. Would they agree to her plans? Aid her in ridding them from the land?

Hallgerd turned at the soft rapping noise on her door. Shrugging aside the uncertainty of her future, she hastily went to see if it was the maid to assist her in packing her trunk.

What greeted her was not the kind face of a maid but the snarling gaze of her guard. His loyalty existed for only one—her brother.

She swallowed the bile taste within her mouth. “What do you want, Vidar?”

His mouth tightened into a thin-lipped smile, while his gaze traveled over her body. He stepped nearer. The stench of ale and onions reeked from the man, and her stomach roiled more.

“Are you inviting me into your chamber, Hallgerd?”

His voice slithered over her skin, and she fought the urge to slap the lustful intent from his face. Hallgerd balled her hands into tight fists. At present, she did not want the man to know her intentions of departing Scotland.

She raised her head high. “Nae. Either you state why you are here or leave. I am expecting my maid.”

Vidar’s lip curled. “I do not fear the weak women here, nor *any* woman.” He yanked on one of her braids. Pulling her close, he licked a path across her cheek with his tongue. “If you think marriage will save you from me—”

Hallgerd slapped him with all her might. The resulting impact made her lose balance, and he shoved her away. Managing to grab the door for support, she spat out, “*Never* touch me again, Vidar.” She shook with rage, fighting the urge to claw out his lecherous eyes.

Instantly, the man withdrew his dirk. His nostrils flared with fury. “I will not forget this day. Fear me, Hallgerd. Soon, you will be mine for the pleasure. Then I shall return you to your future husband.”

His harsh remark unsettled her. Using her fear as a shield, she snapped, “Nae! This day will be one to share with Jorund. When he hears how you have touched me, then we shall see who is more scared.”

A shadow of alarm reflected briefly in the man’s eyes. He took a step back. Withdrawing a flattened parchment from the belt at his side, he tossed it outward. “From Jorund.”

The parchment landed at her feet. “I have not procured the document for him,” she protested.

Vidar flicked his thumb along the steel of his blade. “’Tis not my concern. If you do not find what he seeks, your *brother* will defend my actions for your failure.”

Hallgerd dug her nails into the wood but kept her tongue silent.

After giving her a curt nod, Vidar sheathed his dirk at his side and retreated into the darkness of the corridor.

Hallgerd’s hands shook as she bent to retrieve the message. She quickly closed and bolted the door. Dashing to the hearth, she broke her brother’s seal and unfurled the parchment.

Unprepared for this latest demand from him, Hallgerd hissed out a curse. He no longer cared about the document belonging to Rorik. Jorund expected—no commanded her to bring Ragna to him. “What are you planning, Brother?"

Whatever reasons he had it was obvious he despised the woman. And she could not fathom his interest. Why not simply appear at the gates of Steinn and speak with her?

Unless his intention was to do harm to the Seer.

Hallgerd laughed bitterly. Tears burned her eyes, but she refused to let them fall.

"Nae," she stated with conviction. Crumbling the message within her hand, she flung it into the fire. She watched as the flames licked a path along the edges of the parchment until they were nothing but ashes.

Satisfied with her decision, Hallgerd spat out, "I am finished being your *thrall*, Jorund!"

Chapter Nineteen

"Do you trust me, Seer?"

"Why do you insist on calling me thus?" whispered Ragna, doing her best to rid the uneasiness settling into her bones.

"Because this is who I am seeing—from your rigid stance, hands clasped together, and your tresses braided and woven around your head," answered Rorik smoothly.

Ragna stared into his eyes dancing with mirth. They gleamed like the green grasses in spring on the hills around *Kirkjuvágr*. Her question appeared to have amused him.

On a sigh, she released the tension in her shoulders and returned the smile with one of her own. Unclasping her hands, she asserted, "There are many watching us."

Rorik's smile deepened into laughter. "When the Seer wanders anywhere, all eyes are fixed on her. You are respected by the people here as much as those on the isles."

The man's horse nudged him from behind. Rorik turned and patted the animal's mane. "Patience, Bran." He returned his attention to her. "Now, my beauty. Are you worried others will observe my affection for you?"

Heat blossomed from her neck to her face. "Aye—*nae*," she half-whispered.

His good humor transformed into a smoldering

look. "Your taste lingers on my tongue. And I do not care what the others think. You are mine."

"You look as if to devour me," she returned, placing her cool palm against her cheek.

Stepping mere inches in front of her, he bent his head near her ear. "When I return, I will do more than *devour* you, my love." His breath burned hot between the curve of her neck and shoulder.

She shivered but not from the cold. "Then return soon to me, my warrior."

Rorik smothered her lips with demanding mastery, leaving her body tingling from the top of her head to the tips of her toes. He broke from the kiss and grasped her hands. "I shall return in four days. Until my return, swear to me you shall not wander outside the gates of Steinn without any guards."

"Am I chained to this castle?" Ragna attempted to free herself from his hold, but the man held her firmly in his steely grip.

"Loki's balls, nae!" he hissed. "You must ken this is Scotland and not the isles where there is nae threat of battles between kings." Rorik rested his forehead against hers. "Swear to me, *Ragna*."

"I will honor your request, though I am not pleased." Her voice was resigned.

"Then these words you have spoken are your vow to me," he whispered.

"I am your ever-obedient woman," muttered Ragna.

The warmth of his laughter surrounded her. She bit her lower lip to prevent the smile forming on her mouth.

After placing a kiss across her knuckles, he

beseeched, “Send a prayer to the Gods to give me nae storms on my journey.”

Tilting her head to the side, she suggested, “The Gods and Goddesses do listen to you, Rorik. You can offer your own prayers to them.”

He snorted and released his hold. “Yours are received more than mine. My actions have not found favor with them.”

Rorik mounted his horse. After grabbing the reins, he gave her a wink. “Four days, *kærr*.”

Fisting a hand over her heart, she murmured, “Four days, my warrior wolf.”

Ragna tucked a loose strand of hair behind her ear. Her cloak whipped furiously around her body while the threat of snow lingered on the north wind. Keeping her focus on Rorik departing through the gatehouse and across the bridge, she waited until he vanished from her sight. Whispering one last prayer of protection over her warrior, Ragna tried to shove aside the growing restlessness within her.

When he announced last evening his departure for Vargr to speak with King William, her heart thundered wildly. Their hope for a future together so fragile. Would Rorik’s king allow him to seek another way to fulfill his duties for him and Scotland? What if the king denied him? Then when he mentioned his conversation with David and the man leaving to escort Hallgerd back to *Hamnavoe*, Ragna grew curious to learn more.

Instead of blurting out all her questions last night, she simply cherished being in his arms. The night belonged to them. No king. No duties. No worries. At times, their lovemaking was fierce—as if this would be their last time together. Ragna wept silently when Rorik slipped out of her chamber in the early morn before dawn.

Elspeth approached quietly by her side. “I have offered my own prayers for his travels.”

Smiling at the woman, Ragna nodded. “You are kind, though why would your God watch over those who do not honor him?”

“My Lord loves and cares for all his people,” explained Elspeth.

“I reckon he would not find favor with me casting runes and using magic,” argued Ragna. “Once on the isles, I heard a priest say my flesh would burn in the fires of your Hell.”

The woman cast her a sideways glance. “In the end, God shall judge, not a priest.”

Ragna shook her head in dismay. “But do they not consider themselves close to your God and speak for him?”

Elspeth’s laughter had a sharp edge. “And yet, many of these priests take women as slaves to their bed. One former priest who visited Steinn believed it was his divine right—thought himself above all men *and* women. My brother never sought his counsel, since he honored the old ways. However, there were others at Steinn who followed the new religion, and my brother welcomed these priests and monks. Soon thereafter, this one priest departed and never returned. When I mentioned to my brother why the priest left, he confessed he sent the man on a journey of penance for his sins.”

Shielding her eyes from a shaft of sunlight streaming through the gray clouds, Ragna grew curious. “I have heard some people make pilgrimages to certain shrines as an act of amends. Did the priest bring dishonor to a woman?"

She lowered her voice and leaned near Ragna. "There might have been a witness to the man's dealings with women in the forest around Steinn. I had heard the whispered rumblings along the corridors near the kitchens."

"Even though your brother followed the old ways, he sent you away to an abbey when you were young. Why would he do so?"

"Aye, *aye*," affirmed Elspeth, a smile tipping the corners of her mouth. "My brother thought the nuns would be able to harness my tongue and actions." She chuckled and crossed her arms over her chest. "This never happened within the abbey. To be honest, I found a new path in the ways of our Lord. When I returned home and shared my wisdom with Thomas, he did his best to avoid me."

Ragna laughed. "He should have sent you to my mother, the elder Seer."

Grabbing her arm, Elspeth's smile faltered. "Nae. Then I would not have found our Lord. Furthermore, Brother Calum visits from Vargr once a month. You would like him."

She patted her friend's hand in comfort. "'Tis true. We must walk our own journey, especially for you and Magnar. And perchance one day I shall meet this Brother Calum."

"If I may be so bold," began Elspeth. "You appear to have found favor and love with Rorik?"

Heat blossomed within Ragna at the mere mention of the man's name. Her feelings were not a subject she discussed with others. As the Seer, Ragna presented a formal appearance. Even with those she maintained friendships with on the isles.

A new road. A new country. New friendships. "I *love* Rorik." The words tumbled free on a sigh.

Elspeth beamed. "'Tis joyous to hear this news. I confess, Magnar feared you both would kill each other with your harsh words."

Arching a brow, Ragna remarked, "Aye. Harsh words due to a murky past filled with torment. Now, Rorik seeks to find another way to serve his king."

The woman nodded slowly. "David leaves tomorrow for the coast to send Hallgerd back home to her mother."

Both women stepped back to avoid being trampled by a goat, a barking dog, and Erik. Ragna skirted out of the way of another dog, snapping furiously at her in passing.

Ragna pursed her lips. "Aye, I did hear this sudden news." Scanning the bailey behind them, she sought her brother's presence. They had not had any time to speak. *I must speak with you before you depart, Brother.*

As if the woman read her unspoken thoughts, Elspeth offered, "David is with Magnar."

The pithy bleating of a goat sounded behind them.

"How many times has the goat escaped from her pen?" asked Ragna, drawing her cloak more firmly around her shoulders.

Elspeth gave the animal a withering glance. "Una is a *stubborn* goat. We have tried moving her pen with each new season."

"There is another resolution," suggested Ragna, observing the playful actions of all three involved.

"Goodness. Do you have insight into the animals?"

Starting for the castle entrance, Ragna confirmed, "Indeed. Send for me when you have placed Una back in the pen. I will tend to her in the evening."

Letting out a groan, Elspeth muttered, "Why am I not surprised."

While strolling through the open doors, Ragna smiled as her brother descended the stairs.

David greeted her with outstretched arms. "Did you hear me call your name within my mind?"

"I cannot hear another's thoughts," she lied, recalling Rorik's whispered love for her inside her mind last evening.

Embracing her in a strong hug, David chided, "A true confession from the Seer." He withdrew and placed her hand in the crook of his arm, steering her toward the great hall. "I am sorry we have not had a chance to speak. Between my duties and your absence—"

"You are leaving for the isles," she hastily interrupted. "With Hallgerd."

His sharp eyes bore into hers. "Rorik has spoken with you!"

"Elspeth mentioned the news," she declared, doing her best not to stiffen at his censure.

David moved them into the hall and led her to a table away from several others who were breaking their fast.

Gently, he lowered her onto the bench. He sat down by her side and took her hand into his. "Before we discuss my plans, *Rorik* has spoken to me of you…and him."

Ragna studied her brother. Fury and hurt warred within his eyes, and she fought the urge to pull her hand away. "I ken you are not pleased with this news."

"Nae," he spat out. "Have you truly considered what this means? Are you blinded by the man's charms? He is the *Dark Seducer*, Ragna."

Withdrawing her hand from David's hold, she placed it on the rough wooden table for support. How she despised his censure. "He is but a man to me, Brother. And I love him. Have *loved* him for years." As her words began to flow, she gathered her strength.

His features became strained. "What kind of life with him are you destined to have, Ragna?"

She studied him thoughtfully for a moment. He required the truth. "Presently, Rorik is on his way to speak with the king regarding his current position within the brotherhood."

David rubbed a hand over his forehead. "The king cannot undo edicts that are born into these wolves. Furthermore, I do not deem the man can simply walk away from who he is."

"His path was not chosen by the king or Rorik. But by his father!" A cold knot formed in Ragna's stomach. "I crossed the accursed sea to save him from death after I had a vision. Did you not consider this is what the Gods and Goddesses want for us? That this is *our* destiny? You cannot even fathom how weary I became from hiding my love for Rorik."

"You are the Seer and a *völva* for the *Orkneyjar Isles*. Can you find contentment when the man has tasks for the king? When he roams Scotland without you? Will he find comfort in the arms of another woman?" David's questions were laced with scorn.

Her resolve cracked. Within her heart, she had no doubts about Rorik's love. Then again, her brother was reminding her of her duty—a duty she presently battled with inside her thoughts. No matter the love she bore for Rorik, she had an obligation to her people, as well. Could she not love both countries—seek to serve both?

Ragna drew in a shaky breath and released it slowly. She clasped her hands within her lap. "Change comes to us all, David. Even you did not foresee what would happen between you and Hallgerd. Paths we judge are a wise course may take a sudden turn. The fate of the Gods and Goddesses are ones we cannot question or attempt to hinder. Even you must agree with my words, aye?"

The man raked a hand through his hair. "Now you are spouting words as the Seer."

"I am both," she corrected, placing a gentle hand on his arm. "This love is not new—simply now visible for all to see. One day, I hope to have yours and Jon's blessing."

A shadow of annoyance crossed his face. "Odin help me when I speak with our brother about this latest news."

"Supply Jon with good mead, and he will be agreeable to anything," Ragna suggested with a smile.

David grimaced. "The last time we both drank heavily we ended up quarreling over a woman, and swords were drawn as we fought on the Earl of Moray's table in the great hall."

"As I recall, you have fought over many women." Ragna was barely able to keep the laughter from her voice.

Her brother pointed a warning finger at her. "But not Hallgerd."

"Truth?" she asked, stunned. "The woman is a beauty. Surely, he would have granted his approval."

Shrugging, he confessed, “Jon disliked the Ecklunds, specifically Jorund. He advised me to consider another for my wife several months ago. When I pressed him for more, he refused to convey anything else.”

“Yet you disregarded his counsel,” she uttered softly.

David frowned and scratched the side of his face. Letting out a sigh, he leaned back against the table. “Her beauty and lands captured my attention. And I believed our brother let his personal dealings with Jorund affect his decision to an agreement with the marriage.”

Ragna arched a brow. “And since you are the elder, you were not swayed by his account.”

“As it should be,” her brother returned.

“I do recall the fierce dislike of Jorund on the isles. I only saw him once, yet his image of malice stayed with me.”

Her brother scowled. “There are whispers the man was banished to Scotland. Even Hallgerd had nae desire to travel to his keep when we ended our marriage plans. She preferred to leave for the isles.”

Grasping his hand, Ragna offered, “I shall say my prayers to the God of Sea for safe passage.”

“I welcome any, especially at this time of year. The seas can be fierce.” He squeezed her hand “Will you be here when I return?”

Unsure how to respond, Ragna shrugged. “Not only does my fate depend on the Gods and Goddesses, but the king of Scotland.”

David stood, bringing her along with him. “Any messages you wish me to take to the isles?”

She tilted her head to the side. "If your travels take you near *Kirkjuvágr*, seek out Berulf the Axe. Let him ken that I have delayed my return. He can get a message to the local healers and other wise women on the isles."

He gave her a curt nod, adding, "Winter is coming. If you find you are unable to remain at Steinn, you are more than welcome to stay with us in Thurso. Speak with Magnar. I am certain he can provide a guard for escort. Or send a messenger. Jon or I will come fetch you."

Ragna embraced her brother. "Do not worry. Though I find the keep full of noise and people, I have grown to enjoy being around them."

"'Tis not what I meant," he scolded, withdrawing from her.

Smiling fully, she replied, "Do not worry."

David's smile softened the curse he bit out. Striding forth from the hall, he paused at the entrance and glanced over his shoulder. His tight expression had returned. For a moment, Ragna pondered if there was more he wished to discuss. Yet his attention was directed toward a man calling out to him within the corridor.

As he slipped from her sight, Ragna sighed wearily. Their conversation had been far too brief. A trip to visit both her brothers in Thurso would be good. It would be a chance to heal old wounds and make amends for the years they had missed.

With more men entering the hall, the din of noise increased. Ragna made her way steadily out of the hall. Her steps led her out of the keep and toward the kitchen gardens.

What she required was solitude. The conversation with her brother had left her with a dull ache behind her eyes. Furthermore, she did miss the quiet times of being amongst the trees and land. The people of Steinn were kind toward her, but Ragna's lack of freedom to come and go whenever she wanted left her frustrated. She yearned to be surrounded by the soothing comfort of the land. This is where she could gather her thoughts, offer her prayers to the Goddess, and simply reflect in quiet contemplation.

A woman greeted her in passing—her arms full of rushes for the hall.

Ragna returned the gesture with a smile of her own. The dreary day had transformed into one filled with sunlight, and she raised her face to the warmth. Entering the gardens, she paused and snapped a small piece of rosemary from one of the bushes. While she continued onward, Ragna lifted the herb to her nose and inhaled the aromatic scent. Deeper she traveled until she came to the cluster of apple trees.

After dropping the rosemary branch, she ducked under the branches. Ragna regarded the ladder in its former position. Tapping a finger against her lip, she debated whether to escape once again over the walls of Steinn. Surely there would be no harm in following the path down toward the river.

There is only one flaw in your plan. You swore an oath to Rorik.

She rubbed the knot in the back of her neck and wandered over to one of the apple trees. Weariness crept into her as a chill snaked along her back. Her eye began to twitch, which did not bode well. Lights of varied colors swamped her sight. Unable to hinder the oncoming vision, Ragna stumbled forward to one of the trees. Settling down against the trunk, Ragna then allowed the land to soothe and comfort her. After closing her eyes, she stretched out her palms on the soft ground.

Within seconds, images flashed through her mind. A gust of wind swept her away. As she hovered over the carnage of men, she covered her ears to bind the screams and cries of agony. Icy winds slashed at her face, and her own screams were silenced by the crash of thunder.

A blur of gray mist swept through her body, and her lungs seized. *Nae!* Ragna's hand shook as she reached out to halt the wolf's progress. But to no avail. The wolf howled in fury as he stormed through the butchery, drenching his fur in the blood of his enemies.

When the hiss of an arrow landed with a sickening thud in the wolf's back, Ragna's scream tore from her throat in agonizing pain. With a deafening roar, the vision snapped shut.

As she fought for air, Ragna squeezed her eyes shut and rolled to her side. Great spasms wracked her body. Unable to still her ragged breathing, she dug her fingers deeper into the land, seeking the healing power.

Moments ticked by in torture. Beads of sweat trickled down her cheeks, and Ragna couldn't fathom if it was simply moisture or tears. On a deep exhale, she blinked several times and rose to a sitting position. She placed her head on her bent knees and waited for the beating of her heart to return to its steady flow.

Lifting her head, Ragna stared upward. *Not again, Goddess, please not again.*

On a choked sob, she avowed, "I swear by the

sword of Freyja and Odin, I will not let you *or* your wolf die, Rorik."

Chapter Twenty

"Snow is coming," protested Magnar, sorting through the messages on his desk.

Ragna took a step forward. "Declan's home is not far. Grant me one guard."

"Can you not wait until the morning?"

"Nae," she protested.

"Can you share why 'tis important to make this journey?"

She gave out a snort. The man would not understand the meaning of her vision, and she recalled his last refusal to help her when she first arrived in Scotland. "Nae. If snow falls, we can find shelter with Declan."

"I judge it wiser to wait."

Ragna smacked the wooden table with her palm. "'Tis urgent I speak with him."

He arched a brow in disdain while keeping his focus on the parchments in front of him. "Your anger will not alter my decision. As you ken, night comes early during this time of year. Most of your journey would be shrouded in darkness. I will not put your life or that of my men in danger. Since you are now claimed by Rorik, I have to consider his account."

"My actions do not need consent from any man," she said defensively, glaring at him.

Magnar's hands stilled over the parchments. His

nostrils flared. When his gaze met hers, she noted the muscle at his right temple twitching angrily. The man stood slowly. If he thought to scare her, then he did not ken her own fury and determination.

"Can you not fathom the bond Rorik and his wolf have made with you? If any harm comes to you while he is away, he will seek vengeance against those who caused you harm—"

"I am not a weak woman, Magnar."

He slashed the air with his hand to silence any further words from her. "Enough! If Rorik sought to expand his attack against those who brought you any harm, his wolf would be uncontrollable, and he would unleash an attack against *me*. He has tasked your protection to me and Steinar. Even though I am his leader, the bond between you and him strengthened after Rorik claimed you. 'Tis much stronger than his duty to me."

This new wisdom settled uneasy within her. *Will my movements always be constrained?* Ragna shook her head in frustration. To argue any further would do no good. "I will be ready tomorrow before the first light of dawn streaks the sky."

Magnar's features softened. "Would you like Steinar to escort you?"

"Goodness, nae!" she blurted out in a rush. "Give me a man who is not part wolf."

His face split into a wide grin. "Do you find us annoying, Seer?"

"Always," she admitted, a smile forming on her lips.

Magnar settled back into his chair. "I do not envy Rorik."

"Should I be offended?"

He reached for a quill. "Your dealings with the wolves have not always been looked upon as favorable."

Ragna flicked at a piece of wool on her gown. "And as I have stated many times, the wolves abide by their own edicts and disregard those of their people."

Shrugging dismissively, he argued, "I might say the same about you, Seer. You follow your own set of laws."

"Now I am forced to endure another set of edicts with Rorik's," she confessed quietly.

Dropping the quill, Magnar stood once again and crossed around the desk. "Do you love Rorik?"

Surprised by his question and harsh tone, she gaped at the man. Her love for Rorik consumed her. But did the man not understand the fight she battled between Seer and being a woman? She swallowed. "I love him fiercely."

His smile returned along with a glint of humor. "As I am certain Rorik does with you, as well."

She pursed her lips in thought. Wolf and Seer lore and edicts—ancient, binding, and powerful. Learning to trust another set of laws proved a difficult task. However, Ragna loved Rorik with all her heart.

Setting aside her discomfort, she stated, "Allow Steinar to accompany me on my journey."

Magnar's eyes widened. "Why the sudden change?"

Smiling, she answered, "Rorik would want a *strong* friend to see me safely to his uncle's."

"And a wolf for protection," Magnar added. "If I could not travel with my wife, I would want another wolf at her side."

Ragna nodded and did something she had never done before to the man. Placing a gentle hand on his arm, she stated, "My thanks for granting my request and your counsel."

Without giving him a chance to respond, Ragna turned and walked quietly out of the man's solar.

****

Pulling the hood of her cloak over her head, Ragna stepped out into the bailey. Wind and leaves whipped around her as she made her way toward the stables. The gray sky would surely bring rain or snow soon. *Nae storms, Goddess. Guide our travel across this land with your shield of protection.*

Another person crossed in front of her, and Ragna halted her progress. "Hallgerd," she greeted.

The woman smiled weakly. "I had hoped to see you before we departed for the coast. May we speak?"

Ragna gestured to a bench near the stables. She noted David's tense features as he held the reins of their horses. He gave her a curt nod of acknowledgment and strode toward the gates.

Hallgerd twisted her gloved hands within her lap as she sat down next to her. "I have heard the good news about you and Rorik. I am pleased for you both."

She regarded the woman, recalling their earlier conversation when they first arrived together in this country. "And yourself, Hallgerd? Will you find contentment returning to the isles? What about Scotland?"

Her expression turned pensive. "Before I can make a life here, I have to return to *Hamnavoe*."

"I am sorry about you and David," managed

Ragna. "Surely, you ken what you will confront when you return home."

Fury shimmered in Hallgerd's eyes. "Aye, Ragna. The wrath of my mother." Her hands stilled, and she stiffened. "Nevertheless, she is aging. The Goddess may favor her an early death and save me from the wicked lashing by her hand."

Frowning, Ragna reached across and grasped her fingers. "Is there not another way?"

Hallgerd laughed nervously. "Again, the Goddess may grant me her death."

"If not?" demanded Ragna, concerned for the woman's safety.

She glanced upward. "Winter is harsh on the isles. Many succumb to its waiting embrace. My mother might lose her footing on the rocky shores and take a fall. Or slip on a patch of ice while tending to her herbs." When she returned her gaze to Ragna, hostility laced her words. "Perchance, a quick snap of the neck will suffice."

Slowly, Ragna removed her hand. *So you will do the deed of killing your mother.* "Can you not flee to another part of *Orkneyjar*?"

The woman looked affronted and stood. "*Hamnavoe* is my home! There are good people there who have also suffered greatly from my mother *and* brother."

Ragna rose from the cold bench. "Then I shall offer my prayers of protection for you, Hallgerd. If you require counsel, go to Berulf the Axe. He kens the other Seers on the isles."

Her features softened. "Do not worry for me, Ragna. 'Tis time for me to take a stance against my own kin. I am nae longer their *thrall*."

Watching as the woman departed to her horse, Ragna pondered how in such a short time in Scotland Hallgerd had turned away from a lifetime of decisions made for her by her kin. "You found yourself here, but is it a wise plan you have set in motion when you return?" she whispered.

Ragna smiled at David as he waved farewell.

Steinar approached with two horses from the stables. The man glanced sharply at Hallgerd in passing. Coming to a halt before Ragna, he spoke, "'Tis good to see her return home. I never cared for the woman."

"Are there any women you favor?" Ragna asked dryly.

"You offend me, Seer. There are many women I like. She caused trouble between you and Rorik."

As the man helped her onto her horse, Ragna grew curious. "Then you find nae issue with me and Rorik? Do you find *favor* in his choice?"

Grunting a curse, he swiftly mounted his horse and grasped the reins. Wiping a gloved hand over his chin, he replied, "When the wolf chose you to stand as guardian for Rorik, I understood the bond between you both." He glanced sideways at her. "Though it took a while for you and Rorik to recognize what had happened."

Ragna looked at him in amused wonder. "And who will claim the heart of the *Pirate Wolf*?"

Steinar frowned with cold fury. "None!" With a snap of the reins, he took off through the raised portcullis.

"As I once stated as well." She gave her horse a

nudge and followed the man.

When the sun broke through the heavy clouds, Ragna's tension eased. Steinar kept them at a steady pace over the terrain. Eager to see Declan, she pushed aside the vision. She grew certain the druid would be able to give her counsel. Ragna missed speaking with other seers and druids. She'd always welcomed their wisdom and found no fault in sharing hers with them.

The autumn view presented a pleasing sight as they traveled. She smiled, catching a glimpse of Oda gliding high above them. The peaceful ride through the country infused Ragna. She noted the path Rorik had taken her to view the magic in the landscape on their first travels across Scotland. Silently, she made a vow to return with him.

Hours later, they emerged before the dense forest. Each dismounted from their horses and walked carefully along the narrow path. Her horse snorted, obviously displeased by their surroundings. Ragna turned and patted his soft muzzle, whispering soothing words.

When they emerged, Declan was there to greet them. "Hail, Steinar and Ragna."

"MacNeil," returned Steinar in greeting, taking the reins of her horse from her fingers.

The richness of Declan's voice reminded her of Rorik's. She went to greet him, embracing him warmly.

"What brings you to my door so soon?" he asked, drawing back. "And why are you here with the pirate?"

Ragna waited until Steinar had vanished around the side of Declan's dwelling. "I require your wisdom on a vision."

Nodding slowly in understanding, he gestured her

toward his house. Once inside, the scents of food cooking over the hearth assaulted her. Her stomach protested loudly.

Declan burst out in laughter. "'Tis good to ken I have made plenty."

She grabbed his arm. "You knew we were coming?"

Pointing a finger upward, he remarked, "Oda notified me of your presence."

Ragna nodded in good humor. "The hawk has made a friend."

Dragging a chair by the fire, Declan suggested, "We shall speak by the fire."

She peeked at the open door and hesitated. Her words meant only for Declan. After removing her cloak and placing it on a bench by the door, Ragna settled in a chair by the blazing warmth of the fire.

Declan handed her a cup of ale. "Steinar will be some time tending to the animals."

Startled, she asked, "How do you ken?" She took a sip to soothe her parched mouth.

Removing a large spoon off the iron hook near the hearth, Declan proceeded to stir the contents of the cooking vessel over the fire. "This particular wolf does not find favor deep within the forest or small enclosures. He prefers open spaces and the sea."

Sputtering on the ale, Ragna shook her head. "Do you ken each of the wolves' likes and dislikes?"

His features turned somber. "Since there is nae Seer here in the North, the wolves seek my counsel, including Steinar."

"Rarely do I witness a smile from the man," she complained, taking another sip of the ale.

Declan's rumble of laughter filled the home. "If you do, beware. Most likely the man is telling an untruth."

A moment of clarity struck Ragna as she recalled her conversation with Steinar about a storm coming through the North Sea. He professed all with a twisted smile. Ragna lifted her cup toward Declan. "I am grateful for this piece of information. 'Tis all becoming clear."

Declan's bushy eyebrows shot up in surprise. "Then you have witnessed his smile?"

Ragna laughed fully. "Aye!"

The druid dropped the spoon into the pot and pulled a chair near her. "Do share the account." In a more somber tone, he added, "And your vision."

For the next hour, Ragna explained everything in detail to Declan. The druid listened in rapt attention, nodding several times. After giving her account, she took a large gulp of the ale and settled back in the chair.

Declan studied the flames for a time. And Ragna waited patiently.

Folding his arms over his chest, he regarded her slowly. "With any vision, this can be a warning of a *possible* future—one thread woven on the Fates' loom. Furthermore, you do ken that the thread can be snapped, altering the forthcoming of events. Nothing we foresee is all-knowing. Often, what we witness is muted with sounds and colors making it unclear for you or me to determine its outcome. Does it involve you? Not even a Seer can accurately foresee events meant for them. You are convinced you are involved in these happenings?"

She clenched her fist. "The wolf went right through

me."

"And you are worried for Rorik?"

"I let my feelings unsettle me during the vision," chided Ragna, rising from the chair and placing the cup on the table. "Too much blood on the wolf to determine if it was Rorik."

"Another possible perception is there are many visions within the one you have experienced." The druid stretched and peered into the pot. "Do you love Rorik?'

"Aye" she blurted out.

He smiled and turned back to her. "With love comes new concerns. You must train all over again how to stay focused during a vision. 'Tis a difficult new road you walk in your life—one of the Seer and one who has discovered *love*."

Ragna found comfort in the druid's words. *I must return to the lessons my mother taught me.*

A shadow appeared in the doorway. "Snow is falling," announced Steinar.

"Stay the night," encouraged Declan, motioning for the man to enter.

When Steinar appeared to be considering his offer, Declan added, "Even if you ate a meal and left thereafter, your journey would be cloaked in dark. The snow is light. I do not foresee the threat of a storm."

Steinar shifted his stance.

"For the love of Freyja," hissed Ragna and marched to the man's side. "Would you feel better if I sent a message with Oda to Magnar?"

His features brightened. "Aye."

"'Tis settled," Ragna affirmed. "Now please enter. You are letting the warmth escape from the house."

He stepped past her and went to warm his hands by the fire.

Ragna fetched her cloak and walked out into the trees behind the druid's home. She knew Oda had perched herself high in the dense forest. Grateful for the druid's counsel, she lifted her head to the falling snow. Several flakes touched her cheeks causing her to smile.

Ducking under heavy limbs, she halted. She swept her gaze upward. Giving two short whistles, she waited for the greeting from the hawk.

Silence ensued, and Ragna trudged onward.

When a twig snapped to her right, she paused. Animals roamed easily through their home within the forest. She blew out another two whistles and resumed walking more carefully along the narrow path. The quiet stillness enfolded her, and a prickling of unease slipped down her back.

"Steinar?" she called out, peering over her shoulder.

Leaves crunched, and another twig snapped, pulling her attention to the right.

The screech of her hawk and the howl of a wolf warned Ragna to the presence of an intruder. And then she witnessed evil approach—one she never expected to encounter. She stared into the eyes of hatred.

Before she had a chance to utter another word, someone struck her over the head. Searing pain exploded inside her, and the impact sent her sprawling forward onto the ground. Dizziness clouded her vision as she fought for breath, along with the scream that became lodged in her throat.

When another blow slammed against her head, Ragna slid into the void of darkness.

Chapter Twenty-One

Elspeth approached her husband's side inside the gatehouse. "You are worried."

"Aye." Magnar wrapped an arm around his wife while staring out at the expanse of the landscape. "If they had planned on staying, Ragna would have sent word."

She leaned against him. "How?"

"The woman's sparrowhawk. Yet there has been nae sign of the bird."

"They might have stayed with Declan because of the snow," explained Elspeth. "Did you not mention to Steinar to go easy on the animals if snow descends?"

Magnar frowned and waved his hand outward. "Even if they lodged the night with the druid, they should have returned to Steinn hours ago. I ken the man. He would have departed before the first light of dawn on the following day. 'Tis almost dark, and the snow has been light."

Nudging him with her hip, she remarked, "Would it be so wrong if they prolonged their visit with the druid for a few more days?"

He blew out a frustrated sigh. "You do not ken Steinar. If he planned on remaining longer than what he professed, he would have found a way to notify me. The man grows eager to return to his love of the sea."

"There is nothing you can do until the morn,"

offered Elspeth softly. “Let us take our meal in our chambers this evening.”

Magnar cupped her chin. Images of another time flashed through his mind, reminding him of when his beloved was taken prisoner. “My fear is greater with Rorik returning. If Ragna has fallen into danger, I will not be able to control him or his wolf.”

Alarm crossed her features. “Is this what happened to you when I was taken by your brother and Halvard? You have not spoken of that time with me.”

“Aye!” Anger laced his words. “It took all my control and the words of the other wolves to prevent me from shifting and slaying all in my quest to reach you.”

The smile Elspeth gave him eased the agony of the memory.

Gripping his hand, she placed it firmly over her heart. “It was many months ago, and you rescued me. ’Tis not good to dwell on bad thoughts. Let us offer our prayers that Steinar and Ragna return *before* Rorik.”

He bent and kissed his wife soundly. Her love filled him completely.

When the bellow of one of his guards reached him, Magnar lifted his head. Barely making out the two riders heading toward Steinn, he noted one of the men was slumped over his horse. Quickly releasing his hold on Elspeth, he leaned out the tower and shouted for the guard to raise the portcullis.

After assisting Elspeth out of the gatehouse, Magnar charged toward the entrance. A chill of foreboding slammed into him watching the two riders approach. Their gallop was muted over the snow-covered bridge, yet it was the sight of Steinar’s horse being tethered to Declan’s that undid him. He looked beyond for another rider.

Magnar clenched and unclenched his right hand.

"I shall fetch the healer," stated Elspeth, giving his hand a quick squeeze before dashing inside the castle.

Weariness marred the druid's features along with a large bruise on the side of his jaw. The man dismounted slowly from his horse.

"Where is Ragna?" demanded Magnar, rushing to Steinar's aid. Several other men came over to assist him. Not a sound passed from the man as they eased him from his horse.

Declan brushed a hand over his brow. "Taken by a group of men. Steinar sensed the men and went after them as a wolf. He took an arrow in the shoulder, and another grazed his leg."

"Give me your full account once we get Steinar settled into a chamber," ordered Magnar, shoving aside his fury and fear.

Once inside, they managed to get the injured man to a chamber near the stairs. A fire burned low within the hearth, and only a few candles were lit within the darkened room.

Declan positioned himself on the bed, keeping Steinar on his side. He slipped the cloak from the man's shoulders. "Should you not build up the fire?"

Magnar shook his head while inspecting the damage the arrow had caused through the torn and bloody tunic. "We have recently learned the wolves emerge faster if there is nae fire nearby."

"From Rorik's time of deep sleep?"

"Aye." Retrieving his dirk from the sheath on his side, Magnar shredded the tunic in half.

Each man worked carefully to remove the garment

from Steinar's body.

"How long has he been this way?" asked Magnar, easing the man onto his stomach.

Declan shifted off the bed. "Since the first hill leading to Steinn. He refused to have his hands fastened to his saddle."

Magnar grunted a curse. "Wolves *despise* being bound."

"As he informed me, as well," muttered Declan, darting a glance at Steinar. "He fought to stay upright the entire journey here. Even refused my support to bandage the wound after I sliced off most of the arrow's shaft last evening. He kept thrashing about trying to leave, which only made his injury worse. Thankfully, he collapsed for several hours. We left in the early morning. The snow and darkness made it difficult for us, but the Gods eased our passage through the forest."

The healer entered, bringing his basket of herbs and salves.

Another lad followed behind him with a jug of water. After dumping a portion into a large basin, he brought it over to a small table next to the bed and quickly left the chamber.

Going to Steinar's side, the healer probed the damage done by the arrow. His brow furrowed as he observed and touched the jagged skin. "'Tis good to see the steel barb did not go through his shoulder."

A low growl came forth from Steinar.

"Be careful, Munro. The wolf is protecting him," warned Magnar.

The healer's eyes widened. "Should I wait until they are both in the deep sleep?"

Steinar gnashed his teeth in protest.

"Nae. Remove the barb." Magnar placed a firm hand on his friend's head and bent near him. "Hear me, wolf. The healer will remove the unpleasant bit of steel. Once done, I shall be your guardian, and you can complete the healing process."

Steinar exhaled loudly.

Magnar gave a curt nod to the healer, and the man resumed his task. Beads of sweat broke out along Steinar's forehead, but he uttered no sound of complaint, even when Munro dug the arrow spoon deeper within the shoulder to find and retrieve the barb.

Long moments bled into the next while Magnar maintained his hand on his friend's head. If the wolf suddenly emerged, he was prepared to stand between the healer and Steinar's wolf to take any angry blow from the animal.

Elspeth entered quietly bringing more cloths and bandages. After giving him a weak smile, she slipped out of the chamber.

"There is the beastie," Munro announced, holding the barb outward.

Magnar removed the steel from the healer's fingers. Striding toward the hearth, he then tossed it into the dwindling flames. "I will find the man who did this to you. You shall be avenged, Steinar."

While the healer finished tending to Steinar, Magnar motioned for Declan to join him by the window. He drew back one of the wooden shutters and inhaled deeply. The brittle air cooled the fiery temper coursing through his veins.

"Give me your account, Declan."

The druid leaned against the stone wall. "Steinar sensed others approaching. He also heard the cry of a hawk—"

"Most likely Oda, Ragna's sparrowhawk," interjected Magnar.

"Aye. Steinar did mention this to me right before he shifted and stormed outside. I followed his lead, which led me along the back of my dwelling into the forest. Arrows hissed all around us, and then Steinar took one to the shoulder, and another slashed through his leg. Nevertheless, he kept moving forward. When we arrived in a partial clearing, Steinar took a blow to the head, landing him to the ground. I've never seen the fierceness or power of the wolf."

Magnar nodded in understanding. "An angry wolf will disregard all pain in his pursuit of the enemy."

Declan pinched the bridge of his nose. "'Tis then I saw him. The man's laughter was cold and victorious as he held Ragna's limp body in his arms."

"His name!" snapped Magnar, doing his best to quell his fury.

Declan raised his head. "*Jorund* ordered me to deliver a message to you and Rorik."

Magnar fisted his hand. "Ecklund," he spat out in disdain.

The druid eyed him skeptically. "I have heard he weaves hatred amongst the people in the north. Many of the earls refuse to offer him hospitality."

"What is his message?" insisted Magnar.

"To start mourning the death of your Seer for the actions of her traitorous kin. He plans to kill her at the ruins on Rorik's land." He shifted his stance, and hatred flashed through his eyes. "Then another man took a fist to my jaw, and 'tis the last I heard or saw anything. Even now, I fear she might already be dead."

Magnar snarled. “Foolish man! Ragna has brought him nae harm, so I cannot fathom his reasons for taking her. He should fear the wrath of Rorik’s wolf. He cannot grasp the fury of what will happen when Rorik finds out. Clearly, the man does not realize Ragna is Rorik’s woman.”

Declan scratched at his bruised jaw. “Since you have mentioned his name, I do understand his hatred toward Ragna.”

He stiffened, eager to hear more. “Clarify.”

“When Ragna’s mother was the elder Seer, she spoke against Jorund at a council gathered on *Hamnavoe*. His abuse of women had been known throughout the isles. Many of the men—those without daughters—blamed his actions on his youth. However, the women went to meet with the Seers and pleaded for the Elder Inga, Ragna’s mother, to consult the runes.”

Declan huffed out a breath. “On a stormy day, Inga approached the council and went directly to Jorund. She threw the runes at the man. When they landed, each marking on the rune stones faced the ground. The sign clear for all to witness. The Gods and Goddesses had cast out the man.”

“Were you there?” Magnar asked quietly.

The druid nodded solemnly. “The council members banished Jorund, though he had a choice of either Scotland or Norway. Within a week, I had left for Scotland. Tension drummed along the isles, even within my own kin, so I did not ken when he departed.”

Magnar laughed bitterly. “And now he plagues us.”

“When does Rorik return?”

Gazing outward, Magnar sighed heavily. “Unsure. I shall gather men to begin the search for Ragna. As soon as Steinar shifts back from the wolf into the man, I will follow. If I ken Rorik, he will arrive earlier than he spouted before he departed." In a more somber tone, he added, "And when I tell him what has occurred, there will be nae stopping the vengeance his wolf shall pursue for the death of his beloved."

"How can we stop Rorik from this bloodshed?" whispered Declan, glancing at Steinar's rigid form on the bed.

"We cannot."

****

Agonizing pain throbbed throughout Ragna's body as she woke. Its angry fingers crawled over her skin like sharp blades. To fight against the waves of burning torment merely increased the agony. When she attempted to open her eyes, blackness greeted her. Fear cloaked her as surely as the hood over her head—the stench coating the back of her throat. She bit her lip to staunch the bile threatening to heave within her prison. When she attempted to shift on the horse, a firm arm around her waist yanked her back.

With each jarring movement of the horse, Ragna clenched her jaw. Pain hammered inside her skull with each stomp of the animal's trot. She forced her mind to stay focused—to will the pain away. Her mind flashed to what happened, including her shock at seeing Jorund. Why did he seize her? And where were they going?

What of Steinar? Were he and Declan searching for her? Ragna gasped. What if harm had befallen them?

Soft whimpering echoed behind her. Another woman? A child? Her hatred for Jorund increased.

Thank the Goddess you fled, Hallgerd. Your brother's wrath has descended on me.

Her body veered to the right, and Ragna grasped the pommel. The man holding her grunted a curse, slamming her back against him. As the rope bit tightly into her wrists, she attempted to straighten. She swallowed the scream and drew in a shaky breath. Fear clawed inside her, scraping her nerves into a twisted knot. Darkness and pain fought for dominion within her jumbled thoughts. Ragna's head slumped forward, yielding into sleep's dark bosom.

Do not be weak! Use the land to aid you. Remember all that I have taught you, Daughter!

Ragna snapped her head up. "Mother?" Wincing from the pain of the sharp movement, she listened with intent. Her sharpness returned.

Even though her body and mind were weak, Ragna drew strength from the animal beneath her.

From the brisk breeze caressing her fingers.

From the faint scent of the land beyond her hooded prison.

From the training her mother had shown her.

She drew them all to her—absorbing their power and healing.

The tension eased, and the pain lessened to a dull ache within her limbs. Sweat beaded on her brow with the effort, but she gave no care. She prayed her condition in this wretched state would not last long.

She focused her hearing beyond the other horses' steady gallop, seeking out the one she hoped to assist her. Ragna kept a steady rhythm with the horse, waiting, hoping for what she required.

When the breeze quieted, she smiled fully. *Oda, Oda! Fetch the wolf, Magnar!* Raw determination filled her plea and quest.

The path dipped, and Ragna pitched forward. Her muscles burned from the abrupt movement. Again, she resumed her plea. *Find the wolf, Magnar.*

Gruff voices traveled back to her. She stiffened. How many were with her? Tilting her head, she waited until the flap of wings left her hearing. She exhaled with relief. Support would assuredly come soon.

Ragna's horse came to a sudden halt, and the man released his hold on her. The sound of others dismounting from their horses surrounded her. Without warning, strong hands gripped her around the waist. Her feet slammed onto the ground, and she swayed.

"Do not move," ordered her male captor.

Where would I flee? She yearned to spit out the words to the vile man.

Another approached by her side. "I am sorry, Ragna."

She turned toward the voice. "Hallgerd?"

The woman gently touched her fingers. "Aye," she whispered.

"But you left for the coast with David," hissed out Ragna.

"He had received an urgent message from his brother. David made sure I was secured on the ship, along with some of his trusted men to see me safely home. We spoke kind words to each other, and he bid me a good life on *Hamnavoe*. After he left, I was confronted by one of my brother's guards—Vidar. He gave me two choices. I could return with him to Jorund or die with the others. The man had followed us to the coast."

"How did Vidar get you off the ship? Where were your guards?"

Hallgerd replied bitterly, "It was an easy decision for the brute. Vidar slit their throats. There was no one to challenge him, unless you consider an aging man tending to his wares of dried fish nearby on the harbor."

"And *none* to challenge me, Sister."

Ragna's hood was yanked off her head. She blinked to focus her attention on the evil standing in front of her. "Jorund," she spat out in disgust. "What gives you the right—"

The slap came without warning, and she recoiled from the blow. Blood trickled from her lip and down her chin as she stared into the eyes of hatred.

"Stop!" Hallgerd pleaded, reaching out to him.

"Do not touch me!" he screamed, shoving her to the ground. Jorund pointed a finger at his sister. "You are as traitorous as this woman."

Hallgerd buried her head into her hands and wept silently.

Jorund's lip curled as he returned his attention to Ragna. "All will be explained soon." He waved his hand outward. "Welcome to the MacNeil keep—lands which should have been mine. I have decided I nae longer wish to seize back what was stolen from my father, but to take vengeance for the actions against me and my father *here*."

When the man approached near Ragna, she fought the urge to take a step back. His foul breath slithered over her skin, and she clenched her jaw.

His gaze swept over hers. "Vidar has informed me the MacNeil has taken you as his. Pity he won't be here to witness your death. But then, he will soon join you."

"Take them to the dungeon," bellowed Jorund, storming away from her.

The vision! Rorik's death. Oh, Goddess, nae!

Ragna had lost track of the hours. How long had she been on the horse? Had they journeyed through the night? She prayed she had one more day before Rorik returned to Steinn so Oda could deliver her message to Magnar in time. The thought of Rorik dying wove a thread of fear inside her bones, but she instantly banished the terror.

Determined to save the man she loved, Ragna would do all in her power to stop the wrath spewing from the loathsome Jorund.

Chapter Twenty-Two

"You did well, my friend." Rorik patted Bran's thick black mane while sweeping his gaze outward. "Snowfall is light, aye?"

The horse tossed his head and gave out a loud snort. Puffs of air billowed in the icy breezes.

Rorik chuckled. "Can you not see the north tower, Bran? We are almost home. The shelter of warmth, food, and drink."

Again, the horse snorted.

"Aye, *aye*, I ken I rode you hard and with only one day of rest. Yet my news is important. Did you want me to leave you at Vargr?"

Bran remained silent.

Rorik leaned near his ear. "You would have been miserable without me, and I ken you favor Ragna. I shall tend to you myself when we return to Steinn. Fresh food, even apples from the garden."

The horse gave a soft whinny.

On a deep sigh, Rorik raised his head. Joy filled him, and he grew eager to share his good news with Ragna. Resting his hand on his pouch where the precious document from the king lay, his mouth curved into a smile.

His love for Ragna spurred him forward in his requests to the king. And the man agreed with Rorik. Plans were made and discussed at length. A new beginning for Rorik and his duties for the king—one he was sure Ragna would be pleased to learn.

The Dark Seducer had been stripped of his title.

Ragna, my kærr. Rorik let the request drift outward, searching for his beloved. When nothing welcomed him in return, he resumed his attempt to contact her. *Can you not hear me, kærr? Where are you?*

Rorik waited for several more heartbeats and then frowned. Had she learned to block out his thoughts so soon? "Did I not warn you *not* to thwart my attempts, beloved?"

He whistled softly while planning a form of pleasurable punishment for disregarding him. Reaching for the reins, he nudged his horse across the land toward Steinn.

As the gates of the castle loomed mightily before him, he slowed his approach. The guards had already raised the portcullis, and he continued over the bridge and into the bailey—searching for Ragna. However, silence ensued all around him. Not one person filled the place, and no one came to offer their greetings.

Swiftly dismounting from his horse, Rorik led the animal to the stables.

Alan darted out from the building. The lad glanced around him as if expecting another with Rorik. "You have returned."

"Aye," he acknowledged. Rorik peered over his shoulder. "Are you looking for someone?"

The lad ignored his question and hesitantly reached for Bran's reins. "I shall tend to your horse," he mumbled.

Rorik's mind reeled with confusion. Gone was the

bold stable lad who spoke his thoughts often. In his place, stood a timid and fearful lad. “Where is everyone, Alan?”

“Hiding, I guess,” he blurted out while pulling the horse into the stables.

The joy Rorik held within now turned sour as stale mead. Turmoil knotted within him, and he took off running across the bailey. He thought it strange the doors to the castle were open, but he stormed inside and went into the great hall. He found the place lacking in people and warmth.

Ragna! Again, he called out to her within their joined minds. Fear seized like sharp talons, and he called out with more force, “Ragna!”

As Rorik started for the winding stairway, he halted his progress. Magnar stood in the doorway of one of the chambers they used for visitors.

“We need to speak, Rorik.”

With each step he took, his dread grew. “Where is Ragna?”

Magnar turned and went inside the chamber.

When Rorik entered, he froze. His gaze settled on Steinar lying on the bed. “What happened?” he demanded in a hoarse whisper.

“Can you close the door, Rorik? All will be explained.”

Ignoring the order, he tilted his head to the side, regarding his leader with curiosity. The man appeared to be wary, even fearful of Rorik.

Magnar took another step back.

The blood hammered within Rorik’s veins. His wolf rose on a growl. “Ragna!” he bellowed, slamming his fist into the door and splintering the wood.

"You must first temper the anger," ordered Magnar with steely calm.

Clenching his hands, Rorik snarled and stalked toward the man. "Give me the account."

Magnar went and stood between him and Steinar. "Ragna requested to visit Declan. Steinar accompanied her. In her quest to get a message sent here from Oda, Ragna was taken by Jorund. There is more, but I am asking you to temper the wolf."

Rorik's steps faltered, and he staggered back. A piercing howl filled his head. "Where?"

"Taken to your lands."

Rorik's anger became a scalding fury. "*Why*?"

"He craves vengeance for her mother's deeds. The man's mind is surely muddled." Magnar motioned to Steinar. "The wolf fought bravely and took several arrows and a beating in his attempt to save Ragna. He has been in the deep healing sleep and shifted back to the man this morn."

Rorik struggled to keep the wolf contained. "Vengeance, as in *death*?" His voice grated harshly—his rage mounting.

When silence reigned between them, the tempest of his wolf's strength swirled around him. In one swift blow, Rorik's heart shattered. His grief so raw, he roared out his agony within the chamber. His wolf clawed and lunged against him, howling to be set free. Rorik gasped and ripped his tunic from his body.

"Nae!" shouted Magnar. "Do not let your wolf control you!'

But Rorik had already surrendered, allowing himself to become the blood thrall of the wolf. In a shimmer of gray and black, he let loose the beast. The wolf gnashed his teeth and stomped the floor with his paw. A warning to the man in front of him. If any attempted to thwart his path, death would be swift.

With one final cry of anguish, the wolf stormed out of the chamber and through the open castle doors. Blind rage took control, and the beast set his path on the swiftest route. He tore through the landscape in a blur of speed to reach the main pass to his lands.

His cold stare was focused. His blood burned with a thirst for one.

Jorund.

****

Ragna squinted within the darkness of their prison. A small shaft of light seeped through the cracks of stone and wood, and her shoulders slumped with relief. The night had turned into day. She shifted on the cold ground to ease the ache in her back and legs. Her bound wrists were raw and bleeding from her bindings, and her head throbbed from the blows she had taken.

During those long, dreary hours, she thought she heard Rorik call out her name. Hope had filled her, and she yearned to reach out to him. But to do so would bring him to death's door. Therefore, she shuttered her thoughts from the man who held her heart. Her love so great, Ragna would willingly give her life for him. She rubbed her eyes with the palms of her hands.

Hallgerd nudged her in the arm. "'Tis another rat that has scurried past."

"How many do you reckon?" asked Ragna with interest.

The woman snorted. "Twenty-two."

"They are curious of the new tenants of these wretched ruins."

"Especially since we were not welcomed into their home," added Hallgerd.

When Jorund's men had dumped Ragna and Hallgerd into their prison, the woman instantly composed herself. It was all an act for her brother to believe her to be fearful and weak. Ragna warmed to her strength. Sleep came to neither of them, so they shared stories about their lives, which only added more to Ragna's fury at Jorund's cruelty toward his sister.

Hallgerd stretched her arms forward and yawned. "If only I had a blade."

"What would you do?" Ragna hugged her knees to her chest.

"Kill Vidar," she replied quietly.

"Why him first? I thought you hated Jorund more."

"The man wishes to despoil me. He has wanted to bed me since I was a young girl."

Ragna rested her chin on her bent knees. "Does your brother ken his evil ways?"

"Nae. He'd wait until Jorund was not around to witness his vile words or looks." She smacked the ground with her fists. "I have wished for his death many times in my pleas to the Goddess."

"Why does Jorund consider me to be a traitor?" asked Ragna.

A shadow of annoyance crossed the woman's face. "Since your mother is dead, my brother seeks to take out his wrath on you. After Vidar captured me, my brother shared his fury with me on our travels to these ruins."

"Because my mother banished him," added Ragna softly.

"Justice was served on that day. Inwardly, I

rejoiced when Jorund left for Scotland." She stared at Ragna. "Did you ken he wanted me to bring you here? Yet I refused."

Curious, Ragna pressed further. "What do you think your brother has planned for you? Will he not send you back to *Hamnavoe*?"

Hallgerd twisted her hands within the folds of her cloak. "My brother has nae honor. In his quest to punish me, he may give me to his guards for their pleasures. Jorund has threatened me on several instances of what he would do if I ever failed him. This latest action to flee Scotland and disregard his demand shall cost me dearly. For years I have portrayed a weak manner in front of him. I learned long ago that to show strength or chide him would simply result in a lashing. My mother was nae better. 'Tis better to let the enemy ken you are feeble."

"Death should come without warning to him," expressed Ragna bitterly.

The woman laughed. "I like you, Seer."

Ragna grinned and leaned her head back against the rough wood. "And I you, Hallgerd. One day, you must show your true self, even to your enemies."

Silence lodged between them. Another rat scampered along their enclosure, bringing the total to twenty-three vermin sharing their prison.

"Do you fear death?" asked the woman in a hushed voice.

Until she found love, Ragna's answer would have been no. Yet the fear of never having a life with Rorik filled her—to never grow old and gray with her warrior wolf. The agony pressed against her chest.

Lifting her head, Ragna chose to answer in another

way. "I am not ready to die. As long as I have breath in me, I shall fight to live."

The woman grasped her hands. "Good. Because I see a way of escape and I have nae desire to die today. Or any day soon."

"Where?" asked a stunned Ragna.

"I have been listening with intent to the direction of those rats. They slip in over there to the left where the light is coming through. If you recall, the door is to the right. Our captors are not aware this dungeon is *above* ground. These men think we are weak women, which we shall use to our defense. I do not ken what is on the other side, but I grow weary waiting for them to decide our fate."

Ragna squeezed the woman's hand. "And I have sent my sparrowhawk for help. Let us flee this dreadful place and find shelter until Magnar and his men arrive."

Both women crept across the damp ground to the wall. Hallgerd tested the wall for weak areas while Ragna kept her hearing trained on anyone approaching.

"There is a weak spot on these boards," whispered Hallgerd. She pointed to a section alongside the women. "The wood has rotted from the rain and snow."

Standing, Ragna tried to slip her fingers between the two boards. "Push on the one to the left."

The woman braced her body and arm against the board.

When her hand managed to ease partially through, Ragna ordered, "Keep forcing your strength there."

"My feet are slipping in the soft dirt," protested Hallgerd.

"Then dig in harder." Ragna managed to grip a section of the board and started to tug.

Voices startled them both, but each woman remained in their positions. When they finally grew faint, Ragna resumed her task. She yanked and pulled, hoping the board would snap. Her fear of being found increased. A loud crunch shattered around them. Ragna glanced down at Hallgerd. The woman managed to break the board she had been leaning against and fell sideways into the opening.

Hallgerd hissed out, “I am stuck.”

“For the love of Freyja,” mumbled Ragna, pushing with all her strength against the board. Beads of sweat trickled down her back. She kicked at the bottom of the board, surprised to see it shift. Quickly crouching down, she clawed at the soft dirt with her fingers. Victory obtained when the rotten portion gave way and snapped.

After brushing most of the dirt and mud from her hands on her cloak, Ragna worked on bending the board back while Hallgerd crawled forward to freedom. The woman switched places with her and bent the board back for Ragna to wriggle out from their prison.

“We are in another part of the castle,” groaned Hallgerd.

Sweeping her gaze all around, Ragna smiled. Snow fell in gentle flakes within the open chamber. She leaned near the woman and pointed. “We came in at the east entrance. Our escape path leads west, and the sky is open for us. I am fairly certain the others have taken shelter where the roof is still standing.”

“Aye.” Hallgerd shuddered. “I would rather face an animal out in the forest than my brother or his men.”

Drawing the hood of her cloak over her head, Ragna proceeded forward.

Their steps led them out through a narrow, crumbling passageway. When they emerged, the forest beckoned them to leave the horrible ruins. Ragna almost gave a shout for joy and offered another silent plea to the Gods and Goddesses for protection.

The steep descent and their bound hands hampered their progress. Once, Hallgerd slipped on a patch of ice, but Ragna was there to prevent her fall with outstretched arms. Every so often, Ragna darted a glance behind her, half-expecting one of the men to be following them. Eventually, their disappearance would be noticed. They needed to make a hasty retreat far into the trees.

The sounds of the forest welcomed them the moment they ducked through branches hanging heavy with snow.

Hallgerd leaned against one of the trees, sighing heavily. “I think I held my breath the entire time.”

Wiping a hand over her nose, Ragna walked around the woman and lifted her head. She observed their surroundings to determine a path. With no sign of Oda, Ragna relied on her inner wisdom to guide them safely. *I pray you have found Magnar and delivered my message.*

“Shall we continue west?” inquired Hallgerd, coming to her side.

Pursing her lips, she gave a curt nod and started forward.

Snow continued to drift down in a steady flow, and another problem presented itself. They were leaving a trail with each step they took. If the snow increased, it would cover the path they were taking. If not, they were doomed. And with heavy snowfall, they would require shelter when the night drew near.

Ragna shoved aside the unrest and kept moving forward through areas of the forest that were not so heavily covered in snow. Snow crunched under her feet, followed by the occasionally snap from a tree branch. Animals scurried out from the warmth of their homes, peering at the women in passing. Each noise adding more to their fragile condition and the strain of their journey.

Too soon, Hallgerd began to breathe heavily. "Can we rest for a moment?"

"Aye," murmured Ragna.

She leaned against a tree for support. "If I sit, I fear I shall not be able to rise again."

Scooping up a handful of snow, Ragna went to the woman. "You need water. Here."

She gaped at her. "How can water help?"

"When was the last time you had drink and a meal?"

Grimacing, Hallgerd confessed, "An evening meal before we departed for the coast."

Ragna arched a brow in challenge. "You did not break your fast yesterday morn?"

"I hate traveling the seas. 'Tis best when I do not eat."

"You require water if we are to continue on our journey," demanded Ragna, reaching for her hand.

"Aye, *aye*," she mumbled, taking the clump of snow.

Ragna bent and retrieved a fresh patch for herself. The brittle sting of the water soothed her parched lips and trickled down her throat. She reached for another and stilled. Sounds muted and sharp at the same time floated along the breeze. Ragna dropped the clump of snow.

Hallgerd's hand went limp by her side, and her eyes grew wide with fear. "They have found us."

Yanking the woman's arm, Ragna urged her forward. "Run!"

Fear drove them both, moving quickly through the dense forest. When Ragna tripped, she slammed into a tree. Dazed, she pushed aside the pain and stumbled onward. Their breathing now coming out in short gasps as the voices from the enemy sounded closer. She dared not look behind her.

Hallgerd tripped over a tree root and sprawled forward.

When Ragna went to reach for the woman, searing pain exploded along her back and neck, landing her on the ground. Blinking several times, she tried to shake off the dizziness. Rough arms wrenched her to standing as she tried to focus. Several men now surrounded her and Hallgerd.

Jorund stalked toward Ragna. He retrieved his shield from the ground and held it outward. "Strong oak, aye?"

Hallgerd stood and spat on the ground near her brother. "Does it take *five* men to capture two women?"

A swift blow knocked the woman back, but no sound passed from her lips.

"You are nae longer my problem." Jorund motioned to the man at Hallgerd's side. "I give her to you as your thrall. Though you might want to cut out her tongue, Vidar, if she continues to spout foul words."

Terror flashed briefly over Hallgerd's features, and Ragna let out a sigh when the woman refrained from issuing another response.

Jorund shoved Ragna forward, and she stumbled through the trees. With each step drawing her back to the ruins of Rorik's land, her hope lessened. Even the swell of pain in her back was beyond tears.

A bird chirped in passing, and a lone hare scampered out of her path. She ignored their distraction until another thought wove its way into her when they began to make their ascent.

Ragna stole a glance at the other men. "'Tis reckless and unwise to bring harm to a *Seer*," she proclaimed in a stern tone.

A frown creased one of the men's brow. His steps slowed.

"Be quiet! These men do not care what you say." Jorund's voice grated harshly in their peaceful surroundings.

"I have heard a Seer can curse you with one word," protested one of the men.

Jorund stormed to the man. In one slash, his blade sliced across the man's neck.

Ragna looked away from the horror. Ignoring the warning from the Jorund, she continued with more fortitude, "The Goddess, Freyja will curse you, along with my own words. And Odin shall deliver the worst—you shall not be welcomed in the Hall of Valhalla."

Two of the men grunted their displeasure and moved away from her.

"Silence! Or your tongue will be removed!" threatened Jorund, thrusting his blade mere inches in front of her face.

She glared at him as he shoved her forward.

When the ruins appeared before them, Ragna turned on the vile man. "If you strike me down, not only will the Gods and Goddesses demand their justice, but also the Wolves of Clan Sutherland." Ragna stared with intent at each of the men, daring them to challenge her.

A great howling thundered across the land. Instantly, one of the men fled back into the forest.

Ragna searched the area. *Magnar has found us!* But it was the sharp cry of one wolf that made her heart pound fiercely. Rorik was here as well.

Her body trembled, and she gripped her hands tightly. *If death takes my warrior wolf, take my life along with his, Goddess.*

Chaos erupted into shouts, and looks of terror dotted the faces of the few men who were left.

"Our men are armed. You have witnessed how a wolf can be slain. Let us remove this threat from the land!" shouted Jorund, shoving his sword high.

But the men refused to be swayed with his words and took off into the trees, leaving only Vidar.

Jorund screamed out his frustration and lunged at her. Grabbing her braid, he dragged Ragna along the path. Her steps stumbled while she tried to keep up with his forceful pace.

As they approached the entrance of the abandoned keep, one wolf snarled and gnashed his teeth with menacing fury atop a large stone block. Drenched in the blood of the torn and lifeless bodies strewn across the ground, the wolf roared out his anger.

"Rorik!" screamed Ragna, unable to hold back the tide of feelings coursing through her.

The wolf jumped off the stone and began to stalk

toward them. Vidar released his hold from Hallgerd and fled. The woman quickly darted to the protection of the other side.

"Do not come any closer!" shouted Jorund, slamming Ragna against his chest.

She felt the bite of cold steel pressing against her throat. When she swallowed, the tip of the blade dug deep into her skin.

Quietly, Magnar's wolf crept forward, along with Declan and the other men from Steinn.

"Do you not care for this woman?" shrieked Jorund, spittle landing on Ragna's cheek.

Rorik's wolf paused. In a mist-filled shimmer, the wolf became the man. His eyes remained those of the wolf, and his nostrils flared with rage. "Release my woman, and I will allow you to fight with honor to the death—man to man."

"Nae others will interfere if I take your life?" argued Jorund.

"I pledge my word." Rorik's voice hardened ruthlessly as he held up his fist. "Do you ken my words, Magnar? Nae others."

The leader of the wolves transformed into the man. "Aye!" Magnar went and retrieved an axe from one of his men, along with a tunic.

Declan removed his tunic and tossed it outward to Rorik.

Ragna watched in stunned silence as her beloved quickly put on the tunic and accepted the weapon from his leader.

Rorik glowered at the man. "Release her now!"

Jorund hesitated and then shoved her aside. With a loud battle cry, he lunged at Rorik.

Magnar was instantly at her side, pulling her away from the onslaught of the battle. The man cut through her bindings. Ragna clutched her hands against her chest, holding her breath, fearing death would stake its claim on Rorik. She could do nothing but watch in horror her vision unfolding.

"You reek of death!" bellowed Rorik.

"'Tis another man's blood."

Rorik snarled. "The stench of evil cloaks you. Soon, *Nidhogg* shall feast on your bones."

Ragna swallowed the scream within her throat.

A gentle hand rested on her shoulder. "Do not worry. Rorik is biding his time to make the kill."

Ragna tried to find comfort in Magnar's words. She kept her focus on the man she loved. When it appeared Rorik was stalking his prey, she whispered, "He is using the wolf's power?"

Magnar dropped his hand. "Aye. He gave his enemy honor by fighting man to man, but nae blade will Jorund hold upon his death when he departs this world to the next. 'Tis more than what I would have offered. I would have let my wolf rip his heart from his chest."

As Jorund insisted on taunting Rorik, his blade strikes became weaker. And in a final overhead swing, Rorik buried his axe into the man's chest. Before Jorund slumped to the ground, Rorik removed the sword from the man's grip.

Rorik flung the blade outward. "As a warrior, you are not worthy to hold your sword. Let Odin's hounds feast on your body!"

Blood gushed forth through Jorund's mouth as he crawled in an attempt to reclaim his weapon. Yet death took him before he reached his blade.

When Ragna's warrior turned around, all traces of his beast had retreated within his eyes, and the stunning emerald orbs she loved stared back at her. He dropped his axe onto the ground. She watched in a haze as his powerful strides bridged the distance between them.

A cry of relief broke from her lips. "Rorik." Burning tears rolled down her cheeks, and great sobs shook her as she ran into his open arms.

Rorik crushed her against him. "*Ragna*," he breathed the word against her neck.

She melted into his strong embrace. His lips were hard and searching. And when his mouth found hers, his kiss healed the pain and anguish of almost losing him.

Chapter Twenty-Three

Rorik growled, trailing his fingers over the bruises on his beloved's back. Shifting onto his side, he tried to temper the rage from the abuse Ragna had suffered. Even the man's death by his hand had not quelled the fury. In the blood haze of the battle, Rorik had never known the power he held over life and death. He almost allowed the wolf to slay any in his quest for Ragna and vengeance.

His love for Ragna left him without breath at times, and the mere thought of her death sent him on a bloodthirsty path.

Rorik drew in a shuddering breath and let it out slowly. He almost thought the wolf controlled him. Nae. It was the beauty in his arms. Her love a power like no other. Even their lovemaking had been intense on their first night back at Steinn.

"Why are you *growling* again," murmured Ragna on a yawn.

"The man dared to cause you pain," he grumbled, placing gentle kisses along the marred skin. Each kiss a prayer to the Goddess to spare his beloved any more pain.

Ragna scooted away and turned to face him. She sighed. "Must I endure another blistering torrent of words? On the first and second day, I can understand your anger. But this is the *third* day."

"Death almost came for you," he argued, the pain still raw within him.

Her features softened. "As it almost did for you. I reckon my heart stopped beating several times during these past several weeks. Shall I confess to you once again how painful it was when I first saw you on the hill through Oda's eyes?" Ragna's lip trembled, adding, "My heart shattered at the thought of losing you without saying what was in my heart."

"Forgive me. I forgot you had your own pain as well," he uttered softly while reaching for her hand and drawing her back to his side.

"Nae, *nae*, my warrior wolf. 'Tis nothing to forgive." She trembled beneath his touch. "I am choosing to close the door on those memories. To heal. As you must."

"Give me your word you shall never seal off your thoughts from me again," he commanded.

"Aye, my wolf, I give you my vow," she grumbled. "Yet I feared your death if I had opened my mind to you."

Sighing heavily, he argued gently, "But I thought *you* dead and became a thrall to the wolf's blood power."

Ragna placed her hand gently over his heart. Her voice soothing as she urged, "Let us banish this conversation. The man is dead. Bruises fade. And we both endured. Let us forge a new beginning."

He brushed the back of his hand over her rosy cheeks, doing his best to ignore the bluish tinge of a bruise along her jaw. "You are correct, *my kærr*. I shall do my utmost to refrain from growling."

"Or uttering curses," she added, wrapping her arms

around his neck. She grazed her teeth along his chin. "You have yet to fully give me your account of what happened between you and King William."

He chucked low, gently circling the pert bud on her breast with his finger. "If I am not allowed to growl—except in pleasure—then you are not to ask questions about the king of Scotland in our bed."

Ragna pouted while rubbing her lush body against him. "This is not our bed. Nor our home. We have not discussed where we shall live. We have not made plans for our marriage. Would you rather speak in the great hall around Magnar, Elspeth, Steinar, *and* all the other wolves who have now descended at Steinn?"

"Did you hear Bjorn and Ivar singing below our window last evening?" asked Rorik, smiling. "Much drink was probably consumed before they dared to venture into a song."

"Goodness! I thought it was Elspeth's goat, Una," teased Ragna.

Rorik grimaced in good humor. "When you are in my arms, I forget about the others. In truth, they are expecting an account."

"We have not left this chamber in three days. I'm amazed nae one has announced themselves at the door," stated Ragna.

He slid his hand over the curve of her hip. "Except when a kind woman set trenchers of food and drink outside our chamber."

She grinned. "Most likely, Elspeth."

"Soon Magnar shall be pounding on the door, demanding my presence," he protested while tucking a stray lock of hair behind her ear.

"The leader of the wolves can learn patience,"

declared Ragna.

He smirked. "*Never.*"

Rorik kissed her nose. Rising from the bed, he went to the table and retrieved the sealed parchment hidden within the folds of his cloak. Hastily returning to the bed, he sat on the edge. He held their future outward to his beloved.

Excitement gazed back at him, and Ragna settled into a sitting position. "The king approved of your plan?"

Smiling broadly, he acknowledged, "And more. I want you to break the seal."

With a shaky hand, she took the parchment. After breaking the seal, she slowly unfurled the document. Ragna laughed nervously. "'Tis good I can read the Latin."

Rorik remained silent while she read the king's proposal. He'd only pray she would be in agreement. He would not proceed without her.

She gasped once and then continued reading. When she finished, Ragna handed him the document. "He has granted you more lands in exchange for your father's?" Her voice barely a whisper.

Tossing the document onto the furs, Rorik nodded and stood. "I never wanted the lands. And after what happened there, I've sworn never to return." Crossing to the hearth, he dumped more wood into the dwindling fire and braced his hand against the stone hearth.

Her footsteps sounded behind him. Wrapping her arms around his waist, Ragna rested her head against his back. "Nae matter the blessings from a druid *or* seer, there would always remain the stain of blood and a battle on the land. Ghosts would haunt us there."

"When I met with the king," began Rorik, covering her hands with his. "I intended to state my new role in the brotherhood and present him with the MacNeil lands—*lands* which I truly did not want. King William is on this quest to reclaim lands seized from him while in prison under the English king, Henry II. Therefore, I judged it wise to give him my lands."

"Yet he presented you with a gift of greater lands," she asserted. "Where is Glencannon?"

Rorik separated her hands from around his waist and turned around. He cupped her face, staring into her eyes he loved so well. "They are south of Vargr and Steinn. A day's ride from either castle. I have traveled through the lands, once. 'Tis a beauty, Ragna. There is even a grand waterfall tucked within the mountains. We can build a home of your choosing nearby."

When she frowned, Rorik fought to rub his fingers over her skin to banish the worry. "Speak to me, beloved."

"And your duties?" she lamented.

Dropping his hands, he responded, "To traverse through the Highlands in search of those working with King John…as a wolf. I can track and listen without being known. Think of me as a shadow bordering the landscape."

Ragna's brow furrowed suspiciously.

Without giving her time to consider another question, Rorik lifted her into his arms and settled them both down on the large chair by the window. When she started to protest, he placed a finger against her warm lips.

"I have not forgotten you have duties on the isles," he admitted in a rush. "What I propose to you, *Seer*, is to spend part of the year in Scotland and the other half on *Orkneyjar*. We have many moons to discuss and plan. If you so desire, we can journey back and forth between the two countries when the need arises. Furthermore, we can profess our vows to one another here *and* on the isles."

Rorik held his breath, fearing her reply.

Her smile came slowly. "You have thought of everything, *wolf*. Except for one."

"And that would be?"

Ragna leaned near his ear. "We both hate crossing the seas."

He roared with laughter. "Easily solved if you are in my arms during the crossing."

She groaned and leaned her forehead against his shoulder.

He tipped her chin up with his finger. "Then you will not consider my plan?" In a softer tone, added, "The Dark Seducer died when I fell in love with you, *kærr*."

Her tongue slipped out along her upper lip, teasing him. "Since you have wisely thought of including me and the people of *Orkneyjar* in your plans, how can I say nae? I love you, Rorik. I endured the North Sea to save you. The next time we venture across the sea, we shall be together." She gestured outward. "I have grown to love Scotland with all it has to offer. And you have tempted me with a waterfall near a home that will not be as large as this one. I prefer the longhouses which dwell on our isles."

Rorik's heart soared with her declaration.

"How long do you reckon we have until the wolves storm into our chamber?" she mused, raking her fingers across his chest.

"One more day," he growled, nudging her thighs apart with his hand.

Her scent filled him, and when she moaned, Rorik covered her mouth in a burning hunger for more of his beloved.

****

Late November 1206

Leaning against the oak tree by the river, Rorik tried to concentrate on the conversation between his friends. Each wolf arguing over who could make the best mead. Gunnar confessed that speaking with the bees gave him the advantage, and the honey tasted sweeter. Steinar dismissed him, stating the bees' wings were tipped with salt from the sea breezes, adding more to their honey, and his mead was foremost. Yet Bjorn and Ivar agreed that the waters from the *Orkneyjar* made for a heady mead, since Freyja had blessed the streams and rivers.

Magnar refrained from entering the heated debate. He appeared content to skip stones across the river.

"What do you say?" asked Steinar, pointing a finger at Rorik.

"Any cup of mead will make me happy," he confessed dryly.

Steinar waved him off dismissively.

"His mind is on the marriage bed," boasted Ivar.

Bjorn snorted and then coughed into his fist. "A deed which they have already done."

"They have yet to profess their vows," argued Gunnar, sliding a glance to Rorik.

Rorik searched beyond the trees for Ragna. *Where*

are you, my kærr?

Patience, my warrior wolf.

To steer the current topic to another, Rorik asked, "Any wolf want to take on the mantle of the Dark Seducer—to procure secrets for king and country?"

A grumbling of protests ensued around him.

"I prefer my women quiet in the bed chamber," declared Bjorn, scratching the side of his face.

Ivar scoffed. "Or mine moaning deeply."

"Once a woman is in my arms, they would not want to discuss anything but my pleasuring," declared Steinar, lifting his horn of mead toward Rorik.

Pushing away from the tree, Rorik nodded to Gunnar. "Surely you would welcome obtaining secrets in the bed chamber than stealing."

The man sputtered on his mead. He wiped his mouth with the back of his hand. "Nae, nae!"

"Ah. Have you become a monk?"

Gunnar threw Rorik a dark glance. "I am *nae* monk. I suggest we abandon the Dark Seducer to the pits of Hell."

Rorik folded his arms over his chest. "Is this a grisly place?"

"Scorching fires that will flay the skin from your bones," he responded curtly, taking a long draw of his mead.

Nodding in understanding, Rorik responded, "Sounds like the great dragon, *Nidhogg*."

"Aye," echoed Ivar, Steinar, and Bjorn in unison.

"'Tis settled," announced Magnar, abandoning the rest of his stones and striding forth. "The Dark Seducer is finished." He placed an arm around Rorik's shoulders. "What new name shall we present you with?"

"None at the moment," returned Rorik, dryly.

While the other men resumed their conversation on mead, Magnar steered Rorik away from them. "I received a message from David. Jorund's men who fled before the skirmish have been captured and are now in the dungeons at Vargr."

"Death should follow swiftly," snapped Rorik.

Magnar continued, "In addition, Hallgerd is welcome to stay with him and Jon at Thurso. She did not want to travel home to the isles unless one of them could make the journey with her."

Rorik shifted his stance. "One cannot blame her for all that has happened to the woman. Ragna mentioned to me the woman's strength during their brutal ordeal."

"'Tis a shame Ragna's brothers could not be here to witness your marriage," remarked Magnar.

Wincing, he replied, "Most likely Jon did not take the news well. However, Ragna received a message and package from David. He explained they will make the journey to visit to us on the isles early next spring."

"They are good men," conceded his friend.

Rorik nodded slowly, recalling his conversation with David. *It will take a lifetime to undo my actions to you, Ragna.*

The past is done, she soothed within his mind.

Rorik bent and reached for his horn of mead against the trunk of the oak tree. He took a sip. Curious, he asked, "Who will escort Hallgerd to Thurso?"

"Steinar leaves for the coast tomorrow and will guide her safely to her brothers."

"He has a task for the king?" asked Rorik.

"Is there not always a task for William?" Magnar

commented as if the answer were obvious.

A scent of wildflowers and herbs drifted by Rorik. He inhaled sharply and lifted his gaze.

As Ragna emerged forth from the trees, he dropped the horn. The vision that greeted him stole the breath from his lungs, and he pressed a fist against his chest.

"Breathe," encouraged Magnar, leaning near him. "How many days did the women keep you two apart?"

"Four *long* bloody days," he spat out in irritation.

"Loki's balls," muttered Magnar. "Nae wonder your mood was so foul at the evening meal and in the morn. Why didn't you use the secret passage to get into her chamber?"

He snorted in disgust. "Your *wife* insisted on giving her another chamber near yours. Something about a gown and mending."

Magnar let out a great roar of laughter. Smacking Rorik firmly on the back, he stated, "I would have stormed every chamber."

"Exactly what I said," admitted Rorik. "But your wife can be very convincing in her reasonings. And she did remind me of how we have only rebuilt sections of Steinn after the fire, including the repair of certain chamber doors. Then there was the example I had to set for the young chieftain."

"My wife is a wise woman. Speaking of Erik, here he comes," announced Magnar.

The lad bounded toward him. Giving no care for the others, he wrapped his arms around Rorik's waist. "I shall miss you when you leave."

"Aye, *aye*," soothed Rorik.

Erik straightened and took a step back. He wiped a hand over his nose.

Rorik crouched down beside the lad. Placing a firm hand on his shoulder, he said, “Your duties will keep you busy until our return.”

“True,” reflected Erik.

“I hear your lessons with Gunnar are going well. You are overseeing a new pen for Una, and the stables are being expanded. In addition, you are discovering, with Magnar’s assistance, to hear the problems of your people and their needs. All that is required of a new and good chieftain.”

Rorik ruffled the lad’s hair and lowered his voice. “Moreover, do not forget to take time out to forage through the forest for injured animals and birds, climb many trees, and swim in the river.” He grabbed a fist-full of dirt and dead leaves, bouncing it lightly within his palm. “There is much you can learn from the land. I welcome your account on my return.”

Erik tapped his hand against the small dirk secured within his belt at his waist. “Do not forget about my training in the lists.”

“Aye.” Rorik tossed the dirt mixture outward. “When I return, I shall expect you to show me a new defensive move.”

The lad beamed and hugged him tight again. “Do not be gone so long.”

“I will miss you, as well,” whispered Rorik, choking back the emotion. Breaking free, he stood and motioned Erik to join the other wolves.

After ridding the bits of dirt from his hand, Rorik straightened his tunic and then gazed outward to his beauty. Ragna strolled as a woman in love toward him. Her bruises had faded, and in their place were rosy cheeks and full red lips. She swept him a glance, while

Declan, Elspeth, and Hallgerd kept pace with her.

Woman and Seer—you are both mine.

Though she wore an ivory cloak pinned with a simple broach, Rorik admired the deep blue gown swaying with his beloved's steps. The gown hugged every curve of her luscious body—one he craved to feast upon soon. When she laughed at something his uncle said, Rorik smiled fully. It took all his control not to cross the distance and scoop her into his arms.

After placing a kiss on Declan's cheek, she turned and made her way toward Rorik.

Rorik grasped her hand and brought her close, inhaling once again her heady scent. He kissed the vein along her wrist.

Ragna chuckled low and throaty. "*Wolf.*"

"*Seer.*" Rorik winked.

Gazing outward, Rorik uttered in a strong voice, "'Tis an honor you have joined us here today. Though I have already claimed Ragna as my wife, and she has taken me as her husband, we are sharing our pledge and blessing with those gathered—from friends to kin."

Rorik's arm encircled her waist as he returned his attention to her. Tugging on a long silken strand of hair, he murmured, "You kept it unbound."

Her eyes shone with love for him when she spoke, "For you, my warrior wolf. *Always* for you."

Rorik swallowed. "*My kærr*, never did I believe in marriage or love. My heart remained frozen. My mind determined never to find happiness. I deemed myself unworthy."

He trailed the back of his fingers over her cheeks, adding in a voice raw with feelings, "Yet it was your love that filled a void, hardened by years of torment. It was as if the sun shined for the first time when you were brave enough to love *me*—to show me a power greater than the wolf who roams within me. Though the depth of my love for you frightens me at times, I intend to never turn away from its joy, nor you. When storms rage around us, you have my body and shield for protection. Until my last breath, *Ragna*, I will forever love you."

Placing her palm over his heart, Ragna sighed. "Love touched my heart many moons ago in a darkened alcove amid a celebration. The love so powerful, I shoved it aside, unprepared for what it meant. I ken our love frightened us both."

She smiled at him while a lone tear slid down her cheek. "My love for you is as deep as the caverns that fill Odin's home on *Āsgarthr*. Never shall we be parted. Not only do I honor you, *Rorik*, from the great House of *Aodh O'Neil*, but also your wolf. I cannot love one without acknowledging my love for the beast who dwells within you. *Forever* I shall love you, even when the stars fade and the lands are nae more."

His lips slowly descended to meet hers. "*I love you*," he murmured before taking possession of her lips in a fiery kiss.

She moaned, and Rorik deepened the kiss until the crowd broke out into boisterous laughter and shouts of approval.

Rorik drew back from her moist lips. Showering kisses along her cheek and jaw, his mouth grazed her earlobe. "You do ken the feasting will last three days?"

Coaxing his lips back to hers, she whispered, "Feasting in the great hall *or* our chamber?"

He teased along her bottom lip with his tongue. "I

shall meet you in our chamber in one hour. Everyone should be deep into their cups by then."

Ragna's moan surrounded him. Before he had a chance to claim another kiss from his beloved, someone pounded him on the back.

With a scowl, Rorik glanced at the man.

"There is plenty of time for the bedding. Now, we drink to your wedding!" belted out Declan, thrusting a horn of mead into Rorik's hand.

"My thanks, Uncle." Rorik accepted the offering with a smile.

Hallgerd approached and presented Ragna with a horn of mead, as well. "May the Gods and Goddesses favor this union and bear you many children."

Ragna bowed her head slightly at the woman.

A rousing cheer erupted again as the crowd began to make their way back to the castle.

Rorik blocked his beloved's path. "Let us give them some distance."

She laughed and took a sip of her mead. Licking her lips, she declared, "Hmm, 'tis so sweet."

After draining the entire contents of his horn, Rorik tossed it aside. Cupping her warm chin, he bent and licked the droplets she had missed from her lips. "Much sweeter when mixed with your scent."

Ragna quivered under his touch.

Dropping her horn onto the ground, she wrapped her arms around his neck. "I love you. Kiss me again, *wolf*."

"Gladly—" Rorik's last words were smothered against her lips.

Epilogue

Late March 1207 ~ Scotland

"'Tis a warm spring day," murmured Ragna, resting her head against his leg.

"Aye," he conceded quietly.

While Rorik kept his focus on the soothing flow of the waterfall, he continued stroking his fingers in a lazy path over the dip and swell of her hip. Mists of spray reached him under the shelter of a giant yew tree, and moss-covered stones hugged the mountain that cradled the roar of the waters.

He marveled at the gift of land from the king.

Grateful for a mild winter, Rorik at once went to work drawing up plans for their new home. He secured the wolves and other men from Steinn to assist in building a house to suit his beloved's certain needs. It was a simple dwelling like Ragna had desired. Many an argument had been tossed around. Should the hearth face north or east? Where would the kitchen gardens start and end? As they plowed the land, his beloved suggested moving the house closer to the waterfall, which fed the nearby river. Then there was the main chamber. Determined to have the large chamber facing the rising sun—a sign of new life, Ragna spent many days directing the men.

Smiling inwardly, he recalled many a curse flung

out after his wife would cluck her tongue in disapproval over an entrance, beam, or type of wood they were using.

When everything had been agreed upon, the men proceeded forward. After they were finished, Declan blessed the land and home.

Peace and contentment filled him. A life Rorik never dreamed he'd possess—too far beyond his reach. He swept his gaze to the beauty beside him. At times, his heart thundered as loud as the roar of the waterfall in front of him whenever she stepped into his vision.

A lifetime to cherish and love you.

"Are you eager to return to *Orkneyjar*?" he asked softly. Rorik had one task to complete for the king before they departed to the isles for the summer months.

"Aye and nae." She shifted slightly and patted the soft grasses. "I have grown to love this land, but then again there is the summer gathering of seers and druids in *Kirkjuvágr*, and my home—" Ragna paused and rested her hand on his leg. "*Our* home in *Kirkjuvágr*," she amended.

His hand stilled. "Late spring and summer shall be spent on the isles."

"Will you be restless with nothing to do?"

Snorting, he resumed his pleasurable stroking along her skin. "Nae. I have meetings with Berulf and plans on mending the roof on *our* dwelling. Then there is an important task Magnar has requested of me."

Turning onto her back, Ragna presented him with a feast of her body, tempting him again to plunder her sweet nectar. "Can you share this task with me?"

Scrubbing a hand over a day's growth of beard, he

replied, "Find Thorfinn and deliver a message to him."

Her eyes widened. "And if you find him?"

"Urge him to come into the brotherhood, *again*. Magnar thinks another wolf might be able to convince his brother that he belongs with other wolves. Magnar fears if he is left alone his brother will journey a darker path with his wolf."

She smiled up at him. "'Tis good Magnar is attempting to contact his brother. One day, Thorfinn's travels will lead him back to Magnar."

"A vision, Seer?"

Ragna wrinkled her nose in disgust. "Nae, *nae*. Although I have learned that more than one vision can present itself within another one. With Declan's assistance, I am learning more about my gift of sight. His wisdom is great."

"My uncle is returning to the isles with us. A way of making peace with his past," mentioned Rorik.

"Aye," she whispered, closing her eyes.

Ragna stretched out her legs, and Rorik's cock swelled at the invitation.

Plucking a wildflower, he trailed its petals over the swell of her breasts. "You tease me, *wife*."

"How? You are the one teasing me, *husband*." Her silky voice held a challenge.

He chuckled low. "I find I can never get my fill of your beauty—not only your body, but within. Your soul shines like nae other. There are moments I do not feel worthy of your affection. I'd endure a thousand deaths to earn your love."

Rising from her position, she placed her soft palm against his cheek. "Oh, my *warrior wolf*, how wrong you are. You are noble, honorable, *and* worthy of love.

Journeys are meant to seek truth, wisdom, and *love*." She graced him with a beaming smile. "We simply traveled a longer path to reach each other. And we are both stubborn."

Rorik took her hand into his. "We were not ready all those moons ago."

Nodding her head, she reflected, "The Fates decreed we walk a path of loss and pain before we were able to accept what we already knew within our hearts."

Kissing her fingertips, he remarked, "Your skin tastes like spiced apples and plums."

She giggled. "Because I have been eating most of what Elspeth gave to us. I imagine I have a lot of the sticky fruit covering parts of my skin."

He glanced to his left and plucked another delectable piece of the fruit from a small vessel. "Would you like more?"

Ragna parted her lips in response.

Gently, he placed the fruit past lips already swollen from all his kisses and into her mouth. She closed her eyes on a sigh.

Rorik's mouth went dry as desire slammed into him, and he let out a low growl.

"You are growling."

"A growl of pleasure," he corrected.

When she opened them, her eyes shone like the stars, and he swooped down to capture her mouth in a passionate kiss.

She drew back slightly, tracing a finger along his lower lip. "Come bathe with me in the water?"

"'Tis warmer here," he suggested, nipping lightly on her finger with his teeth.

"But I am sticky," she pouted and scooted away

from him. Quickly standing, she darted across the grasses to the river.

This time he growled in frustration and stood. Rorik breathed in the late spring air and relished the power of the land beneath his bare feet. When his beloved entered the water, her laughter rippled all around him, and Rorik smiled fully. He placed a fist over his heart, treasuring the beauty before him.

Slowly, he stalked toward her. “I have other plans than bathing!”

I love you, Wolf!

Rorik roared with delight. *I love you, Seer!*

Note from the Author

Rorik MacNeil's charm swept me away when he stepped forth in the first book, ***MAGNAR, The Wolves of Clan Sutherland***. He emerged as a tall, dark, and sinfully *sexy* alpha male. I swooned each time the man entered a scene. A character who was definitely a wolfish rake. And whenever Ragna entered the scene, the angst between them sizzled up the pages. Two characters whose feelings of hatred to each other were merely a façade for their true inner desires and wants.

So, how do I write this persona of a hero? With the Dark Seducer, I contemplated how to redeem Rorik. In truth, did he need redemption? *Aye*! His tortured soul demanded rescue, and I found myself peeling back the layers in a quest for the truth about the man.

Once again, I have woven King William *The Lion of Scotland* into this story. I've always been fascinated with this king, and he will continue to be a central part in the series. In my research, I became drawn to his attempts to gain back certain lands and castles in England after they were stripped away under the reign of Henry II. The negotiations for their return with Kings Richard I and John met with no success.

As a side note in history on Rorik's surname, The *Uí Néill* Clan were the foremost political dynasty in Ireland between the 7th and 10th centuries. Their famous ancestor is Niall of the Nine Hostages, a legendary 4th century King of Ireland.

I hope you've enjoyed Rorik and Ragna's love story. It was truly a labor of love to reunite these two individuals. I believe you might have guessed the next story. This wolf is known for his exceptional battles fought at sea. In his search to seek the ultimate treasure for Scotland—a prize valued by both Norse Gods and Kings—Steinar MacDougall must surrender what he treasures the most.

Until then, may your dreams be filled with Irish charm, Highland mists, and the Wolves of Clan Sutherland!

Other Books by Mary Morgan ~

Order of the Dragon Knights ~
Dragon Knight's Sword, Book 1
Dragon Knight's Medallion, Book 2
Dragon Knight's Axe, Book 3
Dragon Knight's Shield, Book 4
Dragon Knight's Ring, Book 5
~*~

Legends of the Fenian Warriors ~
Quest of a Warrior, Book 1
Oath of a Warrior, Book 2
Trial of a Warrior, Book 3
Destiny of a Warrior, Book 4
~*~

Holiday Romances ~
A Magical Highland Solstice
A Highland Moon Enchantment
To Weave A Highland Tapestry
~*~

The Wolves of Clan Sutherland ~
Magnar, Book 1

A word about the author…

Award-winning Celtic paranormal and fantasy romance author, Mary Morgan, resides in Northern California, with her own knight in shining armor. However, during her travels to Scotland, England, and Ireland, she left a part of her soul in one of these countries and vows to return.

Mary's passion for books started at an early age along with an overactive imagination. Inspired by her love for history and ancient Celtic mythology, her tales are filled with powerful warriors, brave women, magic, and romance. It wasn't until the closure of Borders Books where Mary worked that she found her true calling by writing romance. Now, the worlds she created in her mind are coming to life within her stories.

If you enjoy history, tortured heroes, and a wee bit of magic, then time-travel within the pages of her books.

Visit Mary's website where you'll find links to all of her books, blog, and pictures of her travels.

http://www.marymorganauthor.com

Thank you for purchasing
this publication of The Wild Rose Press, Inc.

For questions or more information
contact us at
info@thewildrosepress.com.

The Wild Rose Press, Inc.
www.thewildrosepress.com

Printed in the USA
CPSIA information can be obtained
at www.ICGtesting.com
LVHW012324271223
767606LV00049B/1685

9 781509 237432